FORMERLY FINGERMAN

JOE NELMS

TYRUS
BOOKS

Published by
TYRUS BOOKS
an imprint of F+W Media, Inc.
10151 Carver Road, Suite 200
Blue Ash, OH 45242. U.S.A.
www.tyrusbooks.com

ISBN 10: 1-4405-8170-3
ISBN 13: 978-1-4405-8170-0
eISBN 10: 1-4405-8171-1
eISBN 13: 978-1-4405-8171-7

Printed in the United States of America.

10 9 8 7 6 5 4 3 2 1

Library of Congress Cataloging-in-Publication Data

Nelms, Joe.
  Formerly fingerman / Joe Nelms.
    pages cm
  ISBN 978-1-4405-8170-0 (hc) -- ISBN 1-4405-8170-3 (hc) -- ISBN 978-1-4405-8171-7
(ebook) -- ISBN 1-4405-8171-1 (ebook)
  I. Title.
  PS3614.E4443F67 2015
  813'.6--dc23
                              2014026148

Cover design by Sylvia McArdle.
Cover illustration by Claudia Wolf.

This book is available at quantity discounts for bulk purchases.
For information, please call 1-800-289-0963.

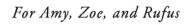

For Amy, Zoe, and Rufus

The commonest thing is delightful if only one hides it.

—Oscar Wilde

Brad

It had to be a hundred and five degrees in the chicken suit. Everyone else was enjoying an unseasonably pleasant fall day, but Brad was sweating balls.

"Half-price Chicken Lickens today, ma'am."

His feathered arm stabbed out into the air, and the flier it held flapped impotently at a passing pedestrian. She continued without breaking stride or making eye contact, a decisive dismissal lacking even remote consideration. That was the general policy of Manhattan women. Despite the implied legitimacy of corporate backing his costume would seem to provide, Brad couldn't offer up an honest-to-goodness deal on chicken fingers without having them think it was some sick come-on. Chances were there was a guy across town dressed exactly like him and employing a similar approach, but not affiliated with a restaurant of any kind. So Brad was largely ignored.

A Cornell graduate handing out fliers in a chicken costume wasn't such an impressive career trajectory that his former professors would ask him to come back and talk to the seniors about it, but it did put some walking-around money in Brad's pocket and gave him somewhere to go every morning when he pretended to leave for a real job. Also, the anonymity the enormous chicken head gave him ensured that he wouldn't be discovered accidentally by his wife or her friends, three of whom had passed by already today. This was a temporary job, after all.

"Like to try a white-meat wrap, sir?"

"Shove it, asswipe."

He had found an unlikely ally in the chicken suit next to him, manned by a fellow named Owen. Like Brad, Owen's status as a hands-on marketing representative for the Chicken Shack was intended to be short term only. Owen had big plans. He just hadn't gotten the break he needed yet.

Owen had failed his NYPD cadet evaluation. He hadn't quite passed his fireman's test. There had been no word on the results of his nurse's aide exam, but it had been two years so he was assuming the worst. His newest plan was to become a bailiff, ripe with potential since it was a position of authority and the uniforms looked sort of cop-ish.

Owen had earned his degree in criminal justice from an accredited online university, studied his thrift store criminology textbooks every night, and watched plenty of *Judge Judy* to supplement his book knowledge with what he considered higher theory and practical psychological application. Surprisingly, it was going better than his previous endeavors.

He had passed the physical exam and, to Brad's secret, cheek-biting surprise, the intelligence exam. Now, the only thing between Owen and a promising career within the city's courtrooms was a psychological evaluation. Thanks to the privacy his own chicken mask provided, Owen was able to spend several hours a day practicing what he considered to be meaningful and significant courtroom-appropriate facial expressions in preparation for this final hurdle. Most passersby didn't even realize they were being used as rehearsal partners.

"Chicken Toes, three for a dollar, today at lunch."

"You're blocking the sidewalk."

"Please be seated."

"Fuck you."

Owen claimed the curses didn't bother him. He would have to get used to that type of behavior if he was going to work in the criminal justice system. He looked at the hostility as good training. Sort of a blessing.

Brad and Owen spent a good deal of their shifts critiquing and fine-tuning Owen's performance. It was a helpful process for Owen. And it kept Brad from falling asleep.

"How was that?"

"Did he sit down?"

"No."

Somewhere in the recesses of his chicken torso, Brad's phone rang. From the Miley Cyrus ringtone he knew it was his wife and not a recruiter. He had no exciting news for her. He had not landed a big job interview. He was not considering any offers he needed to sit down and discuss with her as a couple. He let the ringtone run its course, blaring through the overly ambitious phone speakers, providing an incongruous, temporary soundtrack to his flier distribution activities. Mercifully, the call finally went to voice mail.

As usual, Brad would call Gracie back when he took his bathroom break (urinating was a fifteen-minute affair involving partial to full disrobing, and therefore limited to predetermined intervals). That was a good half hour away, which would give him plenty of time to make up a story about whatever meeting he would pretend to have been in. Perhaps a brainstorming session for a new client. Or a briefing for a pitch. Either one was the opposite of the truth.

The phone's message alert chimed about ten seconds after the phone stopped ringing, so the message was probably something short in the family of universal husband/wife check-ins. *Hi, it's me. Call me when you can. Love you, bye.* Her usual mix of efficient and arguably sweet. Poor thing. She had no idea.

"Did you tell Gracie you got laid off from Overthink yet?"

"Of course not. I told her I got promoted to senior art director."

Owen considered the lie for a brief moment before nodding inside his mask.

"Smart."

Actually, it was. If Brad's plan worked out.

He lacked the courage to tell his wife on the day his humiliating downsizing had occurred. Reeling from the suddenness of the blow, he had decided perhaps he would wait until he found the perfect time—over a glass of wine or maybe after he won the lottery——to gently break the news of his underemployment, followed quickly by a lengthy and/or charming explanation of why it was actually a good thing. A door-closing, window-opening, Japanese-word-for-disaster-*and*-opportunity sort of thing.

Certainly there are those who would have classified his reticence as cowardice. And they would have been right to an extent, but it could also have been argued that Brad recognized in his life a tendency for things to work themselves out. Not in the world-changing Oh-Dr.-Fleming-would-you-mind-cleaning-up-these-petri-dishes-Hey-look-you-discovered-penicillin kind of way. More in the Oh-no-I-got-a-flat-tire-Hey-look-I'm-right-in-front-of-a-tire-store   manner.   Lukewarm luck.

When Brad broke his leg in high school, he spent his recovery period working on the oil paintings he had always talked about but had never done. The experience ended up rounding out his résumé enough to qualify him for acceptance to Cornell. A few years later, when he lost his apartment because it turned out sub-sub-subleases usually end that way, he crashed on a buddy's couch. A month later that buddy jumped off a bridge, which meant as long as Brad kept his mouth shut and paid the super cheap rent on time, his buddy's centrally located one bedroom was Brad's. One time, when he forgot his wallet, it happened to be the day that management bought the whole office lunch. Things just always seemed to work out.

In recent years, awareness of this pattern had bubbled up to the top of Brad's consciousness. Not so much that he would count on low-octane good luck prevailing in every situation, but enough that he felt he could afford some ennui-fueled gambling, vaguely understanding that chances were, while he might not win big, he probably wouldn't lose his shirt.

Whatever the crisis was, there was usually a vine waiting for him when he finished swinging through it. And like a lazy, mildly bored Tarzan he would grab it and swing away to his next adventure, usually in an upwardly mobile and generally happier direction. It was an unpredictable methodology but with the track record laid down so far, it was hard to argue with.

So when he got shitcanned, he decided to wait and see what happened before taking any drastic measures. The morning after, he showered up and hit the road the same as usual.

After a few hours on his laptop in a coffee shop polishing up the old curriculum vitae, tightening his portfolio site, scouring employment postings, and submitting himself to every agency within the tri-state area, he spent the day meandering, wandering the city streets, eventually ending up tired and hungry outside the Chicken Shack. A large chicken on the sidewalk in front handed him a coupon and then informed everyone in the vicinity that the honorable Judgey McToughGuy would be presiding over today's proceedings. Brad took it as a sign and went in.

The break from his aimless walk gave Brad some time to reflect on his predicament without having to worry about avoiding slow-going fatso tourists and sketchy homeless guys. And to wallow. Free time was horrible like that. Rife with the potential of self-doubt.

What now? What if this time nothing happened? What if there was only a certain amount of luck one was allotted in life and Brad had already pissed his away on primo parking spots and avoiding DUI checkpoints? He stopped short of anything as trite as *Why me?* but he was definitely in the neighborhood. He had been unemployed for nineteen hours already, after all.

"Brad?"

Brad didn't have to see who was calling out to him to immediately understand that he was in a bit of a pickle as he sat there in the back booth of the empty Chicken Shack, wiping guacamole off of his lower lip. Someone recognized him. Now what? Brad would have to explain why he was sitting alone in a dumpy fast food restaurant when he should have been hard at work, or at least in an office, across town. Truth be told, who would give a shit where Brad Fingerman ate lunch? But this was not the mindset he was in. At the moment, his worldview was thoroughly tainted by shame.

Brad turned to find the chicken from outside standing next to his booth, now headless to reveal the sweaty face of Owen. He hadn't recognized Owen when he heard him outside, but that was probably because they hadn't seen each other for years and Owen was using one of his court voices. Most likely "Rusty."

Brad knew Owen from his earliest days in the city when he had dabbled in hipsterism. Owen had worked the counter of a store in Williamsburg that sold some "hilarious" T-shirts, a line of 1970s sitcom-themed lunchboxes, and a few old school straw fedoras, but mostly irony. Owen didn't really understand the attitude. He genuinely thought the T-shirts were funny.

Brad quickly outgrew the trend, ditching the pornstache and the fixed-gear bike in favor of a look that was more upwardly mobile. He did not ditch Owen, however. Their relationship had begun as a satirical endeavor on Brad's part, but had blossomed into a genuine acquaintanceship. And while they hadn't physically seen each other in a dog's age, Brad would non-ironically "Like" the occasional Facebook post from Owen. So technically, they were still friends.

"Owen? How are you? I thought you worked in Brooklyn?"

"They closed. The owner said the shop was getting too commercial."

"Ah."

The chances of Brad and Owen having overlapping social circles could be measured in the millionths of percentage points. In fact, Brad may have lucked into the one person in the city he could be completely honest with. He could lay the whole story out for Owen and not worry an iota about him accidentally spilling the beans to anyone Brad knew these days.

"Sit down, Owen."

"Oh, I can't. My boss says a chicken eating chicken makes the customers uncomfortable."

Brad picked up what was left of his quesadilla and joined Owen in the break room to catch up and unload. Half an hour later, Owen had to go back to work and Brad had decided to join him.

It was perfect. Brad couldn't spend his days walking around the city like a vonce. Someone who knew him would see him and mention it to Gracie or tweet it or something, and he would be caught off guard when he was inevitably (and most likely innocently) asked about it. If that were a one-time only risk, he could probably talk his way out of whatever suspicion it brought. But his term of unemployment would be an unpredictable length, and he could only tell so many stories before the walls crumbled.

But this. Standing around wearing a costume that no one could possibly recognize him in for what would surely be the short while it took for him to be picked up again professionally. This was just right.

This was the vine.

It was three weeks before Brad got a response to his many job applications. Apparently, there was one single agency in town that was both hiring an associate creative director and hadn't heard the story of Brad's imposed hiatus from the business. Red Light District Advertising.

He was perfect for the Red Light job. Now he just had to get hired before someone over there talked to someone who talked to someone who talked to someone back at Overthink—which, considering how small the world of New York advertising agencies was, would probably be by about four thirty the following afternoon.

But his interview was the next morning. If he nailed that, he had a fighting chance. And fight Brad would. Red Light was a much better agency than Overthink, and the new position would include a paycheck that was a schload bigger than his old one.

In the meantime, Owen tried his best to keep Brad's spirits up.

"Hey man, you've got to see the bright side of the situation. You're a smart guy with a hot wife. You have an interview at your dream job tomorrow. And your hamburger commercial is going to run on *America's Biggest Hair* tonight."

"Pizza commercial."

"Even better! Brad, you've got to make the best of it. Look at me. I have my last test next week. And you've got your interview tomorrow. You never know what could happen. We'll both be moving on to bigger and better things before you know it."

"Fingerson!"

A squat, stubby man wearing a short sleeve shirt and a nametag that read "Chuck—Ass. Manager" stood in the entrance of the restaurant scowling at the giant, schlumpy chickens in front of him.

"It's Fingerman."

"You and Owen clock out early. It's too slow today. I'm losing money on you."

"But what about our dinner?"

"You don't work a full shift, I don't feed you. You know the rules."

Brad could see Owen deflate inside his chicken suit.

"Oh, man. I was counting on the money and the meal."

"Clock out."

Brad and Gracie

Before the axe dropped at Overthink, Brad was pulling in a hundred and fifty grand a year. Not amazing by New York standards, but pretty good considering the effort he put in. Plus, he had a couple of marginally funny frozen pizza spots currently on the air.

Aside from that, there had been a series of minor victories in his career—a few impressive print ads, some strong web stuff, and a couple of spec commercials made with a friend's camera and a crew he paid with take-out Chinese, beer, and cigarettes. He had arrived at Overthink four years ago as an art director, and managed only to languish in relative obscurity. Brad presented plenty of good work to his boss, but, like ninety percent of the conceptual work in the industry, it never got produced for some reason or another—the account team changed the strategy, the storyboards didn't test well, the client thought the background color was poopy, whatever. There was always something keeping him from scratching the itch that only produced work created solely by him could reach. But really, that's why he was in this business in the first place.

Advertising tends to be the refuge of cowardly artists—the almost-were screenwriters, painters, photographers, sculptors, glassblowers, novelists, and playwrights—who didn't have the derring-do to try their craft without a comprehensive health plan and company-matching 401(k). Pussies.

Brad's chosen medium of unexploited talent was painting. He had always doodled, drawn, and even photographed, but his real love was painting. The thing that made him profoundly happy was capturing his unique vision on canvas. He just didn't ever do it.

Not anymore anyway. Once upon a time Brad spent late nights in the studio, alone with his brushes and paints and single-minded vision. He even had a few shows back in his hometown of San Antonio. Oh, big stuff.

All it took was one overly practical college mentor to point out that most painters died broke and usually with syphilis. It was suggested that Brad find a major that used his talent in a more pragmatic way. *How can you turn that wonderful vision of yours into a job? Advertising! Ah ha! Why make pretty pictures for free (if we're being honest here) when you can make them for big corporations that pay you a lot of money? Then you can paint on your own time. It really is the safe way.*

And with that, Brad and his irrevocably cracked artistic foundation were ushered out of that sage advisor's office to make way for a girl who was torn between a career in nursing or maybe helping out at her mother's flower shop.

Since then, Brad had spent almost a decade pumping out his share of close-enough-to-creatively-satisfying advertising ideas. They had served to sate his ambition the way a Kate Hudson movie makes you *feel* like you were entertained even though you know you weren't. The effect is masturbatory, but short of taking an actual risk, there is little else.

And then there was the vodka job. As far as onanistic art went, that was a game changer. A sort of make-good for the indignity of spending his twenties void of creative integrity. Maybe the best and worst thing that ever happened to Brad.

The vodka job ended in disaster, of course, the proportions of which threatened to make a verb out of Brad's name industry-wide. But it also gave him a taste of the possible. He wanted back in. And he wanted back in at Red Light.

The position at Red Light would be a dream. The accounts were high-rolling, super visible, and inevitably award-winning. And it paid two twenty, which would be enough of a jump to quickly pay back all that he had borrowed from his savings to cover his lie to Gracie.

Not that she would care. Or notice. Brad's wife's job as a divorce attorney paid very well. She had started specializing in gay divorces about ten years ago. Her bosses at Hunter & Partners thought she was crazy, but she carved out a niche and kept making them money. Eventually, she started making the firm so much money that they couldn't pay her enough to stick around. Gracie pulled stakes and walked out to start her own firm. Gay divorce became all the rage and Gracie was in the pole position to take advantage of it.

Gay couples in Manhattan tend to land in a juicy financial demographic, often with the high net worth associated with ambitious professionals who don't have kids. Closets full of Jimmy Choos. Duplexes with views of the park. Vacation homes in the Hamptons. Money.

Legally married or not, these disentanglements always involved plenty to sort out, and by the time the rest of New York's tony law firms had figured it out, Gracie had firmly established herself as the lawyer of choice among the homoccenti. Now she set her own hours, worked from home a good deal of the time, and was making a boatload of money doing it.

Not that Gracie was driven by money. She wasn't. What she craved was success. Which meant the net effect of her gay divorce domination was that she wasn't exactly a stickler for financial details in her own life. She was too busy working to care. She could tell you precisely what the cheating cocksucker her client was suing had spent on Polish hookers and Cialis in the month of October two years ago, but ask her what her own cable bill was and she'd have to hazard a guess that it was somewhere between three and four hundred dollars. It was one fifty.

In her mind, if there was cash in the account, there was cash to spend. And there was always cash in the account. As far as she was concerned, Brad's salary was a cute addition to their bank statement. Hat money.

But still. As a point of pride, Brad wanted to contribute. Actually, he wanted to be the breadwinner, but that would mean doing something big. That would take nothing short of creating and selling a groundbreaking campaign comparable to the "No Means Yes" campaign for Brass Balls energy drink that recently swept the Cannes award show and had become overnight, to the dismay of N.O.W., the national let's-do-a-shot catchphrase of backward-hat-wearing meatheads. It was, incidentally, a campaign that was done at Red Light.

So maybe he was close.

Gracie, Champ, and the Vodka Job

Brad's walk home had taken him a good fifteen blocks out of his way. He wished it were more. These days there always seemed to be an excuse to stop by the grocery store or pick up the dry cleaning or sit by the river on the bench between the Latino fishermen and the crazy homeless guy and not talk about his day for forty-five minutes. Once he got home he would put on his Happy Brad™ face and dodge and parry and worry that he was a painfully transparent lout. But not yet. Just a few more seconds, please.

He certainly wasn't going to jump into the river, but it felt so good to sit and stare and pretend he was going to. He would hit the water and sink peacefully into the silt at the bottom without worrying that all the toxic waste and spent needles were ruining his Scotch & Soda blazer. Impossible on all levels, but satisfying to imagine.

One day he and Gracie would laugh about the whole Brad-got-fired-and-lied-about-it thing. At some point, years from now, Brad would have a hell of a dinner party story to tell as he and his fellow titans of industry sat amidst some perfect New York City elite social circle tableau. Probably on the Upper West Side. Brad would close his eyes and shake his head with an aw-shucks smile as he took a sip of his cabernet while his wife told him to go ahead and tell everyone. Gracie would laugh and maybe wink at him knowingly, although he honestly couldn't remember her ever winking before and would she really pick up a habit like that at this point in her life? Maybe. Maybe she would wink at him, now that things were all better. It helped to think that these things were possible.

In a few months, the benches would be too cold for anyone but the filthy gentleman sitting ten feet downwind. Then what? Brad would kill time walking the streets in the bitter cold? Camping out at a coffee shop? Oy. Running an errand in the late afternoon could be explained away with relative ease. But sitting blankly in front of an untouched latte on the tail end of a work day? Risky business. Something had to change before then.

Gracie stood at the stove in the kitchen cooking dinner. She was a strict vegan, so the safe bet was that it was some form of tofu. Tofu-shaped chicken cutlets. Tofu cut to look like steak. Tofu flavored to smell like barbecue. But probably tofu. That was the thing about vegans. They're happy to wax poetic about how good the lifestyle is for you and deliver smug lectures about the wide variety of food options you can have when you're a vegan. Usually though, things boiled down to one question: What shape would you like your tofu?

Gracie being a militant vegan made Brad a vegan. Sort of. He was vegan when Gracie was around. Mainly because she did all the cooking, ordered all the food from Fresh Direct, and spent her Saturday mornings at the Union Square farmers' market. Outside of the apartment and left to his own devices, though, Brad was perfectly fine with a slice or a cheese steak or a stick of mystery meat from the guys with the carts who called him *my friend*. Didn't matter. We're all going to die soon enough.

At restaurants with Gracie, Brad stuck with the rice dishes. It was easier than listening to a mini-lecture on exactly how the steak he was savoring was killed and hung by a hook through its ribs in a meat locker until it could be served as a rotting corpse. Gracie always claimed she could smell the rage of the dead cow seeping through his pores for days afterward. It wasn't worth it and he liked risotto.

So really, he wasn't a vegan. More of a vague-an. A very strict diet of organic, pesticide-free, sustainable, biodynamic, hormone-free, non-GMO, locally grown, free-trade products. Unless he was eating a bacon cheeseburger at the deli next to his office. Somehow Gracie never smelled any rage from the stuff she didn't actually see him eat.

Her attitude toward consuming meat was another reason to keep the whole Chicken Shack thing on the DL. As if wearing the chicken costume/sweat box weren't enough. Handing out coupons for rotting corpses of rage would definitely set her off. Being underemployed was complicated.

Brad remained in the doorway of the kitchen. He wanted a beer badly, but not quite badly enough to disturb the serenity of Gracie not noticing him. She was beautiful. And successful. And focused. He should have stayed out longer. Pretended he was working late.

Did she suspect? She was so smart, so sharp, it was hard for him to imagine that she hadn't noticed anything out of the ordinary. Some of the subconscious tells he must be showing. A disturbance in his psyche. The whimpering nightmares that started out of nowhere. Something. Or was her shrewd lawyer mind willfully overlooking what must be at least a tiny bit apparent to her? Did she love him that much? If that was the case, Brad had no choice but to consider himself a lucky man. His wife cared enough about him to let him act like a jackass. No judgments. Just unmolested jackassery. Would he do that for her? He would now. Brad decided then and there that if she ever got herself into a situation like this, he would totally overlook any crazy machinations and bad acting she might employ. But he really, really hoped it would never happen to Gracie.

Finally she looked over.

"Dude, you smell like shit."

Gracie was never one to mince words. It was something Brad had come to accept. He wasn't sure if her cut-to-the-chase word choices were a result of her chosen profession or if that was the way she was wired and accordingly had become successful as a no bullshit attorney. *Dude* was what she called him when she was happy to see him. *You smell like shit* was what she said when he didn't smell good.

"I went to the gym."

Change the subject, you idiot. Make up some work gossip.

"Hey, looks like they might go with my taste test campaign. If Garbarini doesn't screw it up. Did I tell you he's cheating on his boyfriend?"

"Does he need a lawyer? Have him call me."

"Oh, uhh . . . I . . ."

Dammit. Should have thought that one out more.

Brad bent over to look a little deeper in the fridge.

"Grace, didn't I have some—"

"Hey, pisspants, you're out of beer!"

The voice came from the living room, but it wasn't hard to hear. It belonged to a person to whom talking loud enough to take over whatever space he was in came naturally. There was no mistaking its owner. Brad stood up and took a moment to let the situation sink in. He turned to find a somewhat apologetic Gracie, and then stated the obvious.

"Your dad is here."

"For dinner."

"And you forgot to tell me."

"Oops."

Brad nodded, accepting that his life sucked a lot right at that moment. He begged himself to think of the glorious potential that tomorrow held, but it couldn't quite outweigh the sheer gloom of what lay ahead in the next few hours. An evening with Champ Bailey.

Champ wasn't a big man, but his overabundance of alpha-male charisma made him seem ten feet tall. Loud, opinionated, and loaded with plenty of F.U. money. Champ had retired at the ripe age of fifty-two, thanks to the lung-out case.

Throughout his career, Champ had been a workaholic pit bull of a lawyer working as a plaintiff's attorney who shied away from no fight. He thrilled at competition. Champ lived to win, and the courtroom was the perfect arena for him. He had a reputation as a man who would sue his own mother if he found out she had mixed his formula with a little too much water when he was a baby. He worked long hours and took on way too many cases. It was exhausting, but it honed his skills to a razor-sharp edge. So when the lung-out case came along, he was, to say the least, ready.

The call came on a rainy Saturday afternoon. Champ was in his office reviewing files and planning to stay well into the night when his phone rang.

"Champ Bailey."

"Do you handle lung-out cases?"

"Excuse me?"

"Do you handle lung-out cases?"

"You're calling a law firm, sir. Do you realize that?"

"Yes. I need help with a lung-out case."

"What the hell is a lung-out case?"

A lung-out case is a case in which an elderly, church-going, law abiding, African-American grandfather takes a particular brand of asthma medicine. He takes it as prescribed by a doctor like they tell you on the soothing commercials with the woman catching butterflies in a big field. The asthma medicine keeps his asthma in check and he lives a happy life. Until he starts wheezing. Then he goes to the doctor who sends him to a specialist who sends him to a renowned pulmonologist who sends him to the University of Pennsylvania pulmonary clinic because his right lung is failing and no one can figure out why. And then a bunch of people with the exact same wheezing all happen to be using the same asthma medicine. And they all have to have a lung removed. Lung out.

Champ dropped everything to represent this group of one-lunged victims, knowing immediately that this would be his Mona Lisa. He sunk his pit bull teeth into the lung-out case like it was a bacon-flavored memory foam pillow and didn't let go. He played the press like a cheap fiddle. He coached his clients like Bear Bryant. He wouldn't bargain. He wouldn't negotiate a settlement. He wouldn't entertain any offers to pay his clients off. Champ Bailey knew he had this category-dominating global corporation by the short hairs, and he kept yanking and yanking until a panel of sympathetic jurors found the Pulmax pharmaceutical company very, very guilty and informed them that they were on the hook for close to two billion dollars. Naturally, a good chunk of that check went to Champ. And then he retired. Seems you can compete at golf, too.

When he finally realized he was standing in front of an open refrigerator that held zero beers, Brad snapped himself back to the real world and closed the door. Might as well dive on in to the deep end and see what happens. He called into the living room.

"Hey, Champ. How's the hockey game?"

"These fairies couldn't outskate a peg leg."

That sounded about right. Brad now had a small, albeit brief, reprieve. Yes, dinner and the inevitably overbearing conversation that accompanied it would blow, but at least for the next twelve minutes Brad had something to do. A concrete task in which he could take pride and know that, when complete, he had accomplished something meaningful. Something real.

"I'll go get more beer."

Dinner was as painful as Brad had anticipated. Gracie talked and Brad prayed the conversation wouldn't turn his way. But Champ smelled weakness and zeroed in on him.

"So, Brad. How's the ballet?"

"I work at an advertising agency."

"Oh, right. Sorry. I always get women's jobs confused."

"It's fine. We're doing great work. Good stuff."

"Son, why don't you get a real job? Maybe go see my friend Jerry down at his dealership. He could put you to work tomorrow. Everybody loves Camaros."

"Yeah. I know. But I'm not really good with cars."

"You're better with flower arranging?"

"I'm not a florist. I'm an art director."

Brad began to sweat the tiniest bit. If only they were eating something spicy he could blame it on. They weren't. He thought about baseball to calm himself down. If only he knew anything about baseball.

Gracie squeezed his forearm and smiled.

"Senior art director."

Champ grunted. "What's the difference?"

"It's just that it takes time to climb the corporate ladder, Daddy. Brad, tell him about the interview."

Ah, well. That he could do. Brad paused briefly to both enjoy the moment and re-acclimate himself to the idea of telling the truth.

"Well, Champ, I have a job interview tomorrow."

"To be what? A midwife?"

He winked at Grace, proud of that one.

"No, it's for an associate creative director position in a better agency downtown."

Champ rolled his eyes. "Why the hell would you go from one Mary job to another one just like it?"

Champ was not the kind of guy you could explain a situation of Brad's type to. Not the vodka job, anyway.

You see, Brad was the breed of cagey art director who bucked the strategy handed out by the Overthink Advertising account team. Their thinking had been to create campaigns for the big Molotov Vodka pitch with the theme *Made from Russia's finest potatoes*. Research had shown that their target market of men aged 29–46, income over one hundred thousand, who considered themselves metrosexual but not gay, would respond to this notion. Research had proven it. And the client was expecting it. But Brad zigged when they zagged. Ho ho! They never saw this rogue thinker coming.

Okay, maybe Brad wasn't actually rogue. Or cagey. A better term would be lazy, or perhaps petulant. Attention deficit disorder could certainly be invoked if push came to shove, but honestly, if you looked close enough, it was clear to see that Brad had simply forgotten that the vodka ideas were due on the fifteenth. Until Phil Brenner's assistant had called on that very day and asked if Brad wouldn't mind sharing his ideas with Phil. At the time Brad and his copywriter partner Matt had been lounging in their shared office heatedly debating Madden cheat codes. Matt had forgotten as well.

They panicked briefly and then did what any responsible creative team would do after dicking away two weeks of company time under the guise of making advertising. They made advertising.

Any experienced creative worth the sack God gave him knows there are a few go-to formulas you use in a pinch. Tried and true chestnuts to get you through a famine of ideas: The frantic customer meets the super-confident sales guy, a phony competitor complaining that the product you're advertising is putting him out of business (*This vacuum cleaner is just too good!*), a celebrity spokesperson, animals acting like humans, the hapless husband/savvy wife combo (also see dumb neighbor/smart neighbor), a cross-country road trip involving some contrived use of the product, the slo-mo montage over a chest-beating musical anthem, the old "We're giving to charity with every purchase." There were a million of them. If all else fails, throw a puppy in somewhere. You see these hackneyed, polished-up turds interrupting your sitcoms every day. They come from guys like Brad and Matt.

In under half an hour they cobbled together a campaign featuring a series of images stolen off Flickr involving people who'd had too much to drink along with the tag line "Maybe too good"—a variation of the complaining competitor scenario. On the way to present the idea to Phil, they spitballed an intro that included words like "gritty" and "organic" and "visceral" to rationalize the low rent art direction that held the ideas together. Naturally, the ordained strategy was nowhere to be found in the lot. They had forgotten that as well.

Phil had been a tough read since his divorce, but like most creative directors under the gun to find the one shining gold nugget in a field of dung piles, he was willing to overlook laziness and shitty attitudes if the work was good enough. Plus he loved dick jokes.

Brad and Matt sold the campaign like their lives depended on it.

"You see this girl is holding her friend's hair back while she vomits."

"And the copy reads, 'Regret is for the weak. Molotov Vodka. Maybe too good.'"

"Mmm hmmm. Go on."

"In this one, it's a guy with his arms around two different hot girls. See, the blonde is passed out with her head in his lap."

"And the copy reads, 'What, you think threesomes just make themselves? Molotov Vodka. Maybe too good.'"

"Mmmm hmm."

"This one has a guy right about to vomit on his sister's wedding cake."

"The copy reads, 'At the very least, years from now you'll have the best stories in the entire rehab. Molotov Vodka. Maybe too good.'"

Silence.

"I like it. Tell Krevolin to have his team retrofit the brief to cover this strategic direction."

The key to advertising is knowing your audience. And in this case, the audience wasn't really the pretentious J.O.s referred to by the creative brief as the *target audience*. It was Phil, the overgrown frat boy of a creative director who was still staring at the threesome ad. In this case, the divorce might have tipped things for Brad and Matt. Phil had been on a bit of a tear. The threesome ad was particularly intriguing to him. He pointed to the blonde.

"She looks like she might be open to that kind of thing."

Sold.

Of course these exact ideas would never run in *GQ* or the *New York Times*, but they were perfect for guerrilla postings, and the line "Maybe too good" would translate to all sorts of cleaner FCC-friendly and network-approvable incarnations. Brad and Matt were invited to present their ideas to the client. Quite an honor, indeed.

But none of this would even register as the English language to Champ, who was convinced that Brad's job was nothing more than coloring with crayons and adding the words "20% off" to soap packaging.

Champ's bloodcurdling peals of laughter and hernia-inducing guffaws would wait patiently through Brad's explanation of the Molotov Vodka pitch meeting. The magnificent presentation Brad made. The hilarious jokes and anecdotes he told throughout the meeting. The way the clients looked at him almost maternally as he guided them through his genius campaign for their product, and how it worked as a seamless three-sixty program—*Just look at that Facebook initiative!* Phil sat overwhelmed with pride as Brad finished presenting his brilliance. He had hit a home run. Stuck the landing. Killed it. But that's when Champ would be silent.

Champ had pegged Brad for a loser early on. Brad didn't hunt, couldn't golf, and had wet his pants at his own bachelor party thanks to the dozen or so boilermakers Champ and his uninvited hunting and golfing buddies had forced on him. So even if Brad were to tell the story of his spectacular performance, Champ would somehow know there was an epilogue where Brad blew it. Which there was.

Needless to say, after winning a plum account like Molotov, Brad was the cock of the walk. And he knew it. Everyone knew it. He became an instant star in the agency. And unlike Matt, who understood that when you got down to it, they were just pushing fermented potato juice on the American public and lucky to have their jobs, Brad ate it up. The week after the win, he promenaded down the hall like he was going to his own movie premiere, accepting the attendant attention as a matter of course.

"Bradley, well done!"

"What up, Mr. Molotov!"

"Hey Brad, maybe you and Matt can help us cast that bra commercial. We could use your eye."

Oh, life was good. Brad and Matt went to work bringing the vodka campaign to life and taking their pick of the other choice assignments at the agency. Goodbye frozen pizzas and hot flash treatments. Hello lingerie and video game accounts. In fact, hello new agencies.

Brad called his headhunters. He and his partner had single-handedly landed a monster liquor account—the advertising world equivalent of having your dick spontaneously grow nine inches. Time to move on to the next level. Time to get paid.

Brad told his headhunters he made one hundred and seventy-five thousand. They in turn told the agencies that Brad was making two ten, but would make a lateral move if the accounts were right. Because he loved making advertising that much.

Every day when Gracie called to check in, Brad had fresh and exciting news about the interviews his headhunters were piling up. She was invariably happy for him, and half the thrill of landing the interview was savoring the bragging rights he exercised with his wife. Modern man's version of a caveman bringing home an elk he slayed with his bare hands to feed his family.

The interviews were with the best agencies in town. ChangBaby, Seaton/Dara, Dogfight. Everyone wanted a little bit of that Brad magic. Phil was no fool. He preemptively called Brad into his office and handed him new business cards.

"Congratulations. Mr. Senior Art Director."

Brad took the cards and couldn't help but smile. His plan was to play it like he was not that impressed and couldn't be won over by a token gesture. But he failed. Brad Fingerman, senior art director. That really had a nice ring to it, and he hadn't even had to take a single meeting.

"Wow, thanks Phil. What a surprise. But, I was going to talk to you anyway about a—"

"Of course, that comes with a big raise."

"Ahh. Right. Well, then.

"And Schott's old office."

"What happened to Schott?"

"Didn't work out. Which reminds me, I want you to talk to Osbourne about some work we need on the Massive account."

Sports drink work. Sexy. Well played, Phil.

"Great. I'll do that."

Brad got up to leave.

"Thanks, Phil."

"Thank you, Mr. Molotov."

Phil's ploy worked. Brad decided he might just have a bright future at Overthink and turned down the offers to meet with other agencies. Some of the biggest stars in advertising had done it that way. Company men all the way to agency partner. Overthink/Fingerman. Nice. Hmmm, maybe Brad was a company man after all.

A few weeks later, Brad, Matt, and Phil had gone over to the Molotov headquarters to show them the latest incarnations of the *Maybe too good* campaign, including the microsite/app that let visitors play online strip poker with live, sexy Russian female potato farmers. Phil was already making room on the awards shelf.

After once again dazzling both his new client and his boss in this presentation, Brad led them all to the bar next door for a celebratory martini. One martini easily turned into to two and then three, and the third one led to joke after joke in which the punch line was "Maybe too good." The idea of a fourth martini was floated, but Brad had a different thought.

"Let me handle this."

He called a waitress over and ordered with confidence.

When she returned bearing a full tray, Brad commandeered the floor and informed his audience that it was time to *really* celebrate and made a short, tasteful toast to the new relationship between client and agency. And then he noticed that no one was joining him. Or smiling. They just kept looking at the tequila shots that had been placed in front of them. Finally, a junior member of the client team broke the silence.

"Molotov doesn't make tequila. This is our competitor."

If it is possible for silence to grow, then that is what happened next. It seemed like three hours, but it was probably more like two seconds before Phil spoke.

"Well, it's getting late."

And that was the end of that. The party broke up instantly with a few hurried goodbyes and Phil making sure to insert himself in between the clients and Brad's attempt to apologize and explain himself. Matt avoided making eye contact with anyone in the hope that they would all forget he was there and especially that he was Brad's partner.

Phil walked the clients out with a few hushed assurances Brad couldn't quite make out and even got a laugh out of them before they cleared the door. Once he was sure they were safely tucked in their cabs, Phil came back into the bar to stare at Brad. Stunned. Flabbergasted. And then finally he said three words as if they were the most obvious things in the world.

"You're. So. Fired."

Word spread quickly. Brad attempted damage control with his headhunters, but they weren't much help. As in, they didn't take his call or call him back. He no longer had a job because he had acted like an ass around a major client. That was a tough sell. Not responding was their unmistakable way of saying, *Sorry, Brad. Give us a call the next time you sell a gigundo campaign and* don't *screw it up.*

So there he was, unemployed and unemployable after blowing the chance of an advertising lifetime.

That would be the part Champ would laugh at.

Actually, he would smile slowly at first, savoring the rich texture of predictable flameout. Rolling it back and forth across his tongue like a rare Pinot. Mmm. The luscious taste of *I told you so* with top notes of *What do you see in this guy?*

Champ would smile until he was absolutely sure it was the worst possible outcome. Then he would really let loose with the laughter. Like a hurricane. A torrential downfall of laughter that would soak Brad to the bone. And the bitch of it was, Champ had one of those really infectious laughs. Once he started, everyone would start laughing. At Brad. Champ. Gracie. Maybe even Brad himself. And especially the people Champ retold the story to. Which would be everyone. Everyone. Including Jerry down at the Camaro dealership.

"I'm interviewing because it's a better job, Champ. Better accounts, bigger salary, more opportunity."

Technically, that was still the truth. He had just left out the colossal failure part. Brad was always good with selling concepts.

Champ stared blankly.

"Hmmph."

Brad was getting lightheaded. He pretended to wipe some food off his mouth so he could at least take care of the upper lip sweat that, in his mind, was making a big cartoon water mustache on his face.

Champ eyed him with the deep and precise stare of a courtroom shark. He knew something was bullshit here, but couldn't put his finger on it.

"Well, just make sure your dress is ironed."

Frank "Fancypants" Fortunato

"You call that guy about the thing?"

"I saw him on the street."

"He get the thing?"

"He got the thing, but he can't get it to the place."

"Why not?"

"He's got to talk to a guy."

"What about the other thing?"

"That he can get, but not when he told us."

"Is it still in the place?"

"It's still in the place, but we need the other other thing."

"So tell him to get another one."

"He can't. The guy with the other other thing is away."

"So what are we supposed to do if we don't have it?"

Sal shrugged.

Frank Fortunato simmered as his eyes drifted to the hockey game playing quietly on the TV hanging in the back room of the grimy office they worked out of. The Rangers were down by three in the second. Star goalie Glenn Bozlinski was doing his best impression of a sieve. Like he had been told to do. Good. Frank would make a killing on that game. At least something good would come of Glenn's raging gambling addiction.

But still, the guy with the other other thing was away.

Sal's shrug was not the answer Frank was hoping for. He was looking for a nod. Or a wink. Some definitively positive movement or grunt that indicated the affirmative. Some tic or hand motion that meant "Don't worry about it. I'll go to Plan B." Instead he got the shrug. To an outsider, that might mean "Gee, Boss, I don't know what to do. What do you think?" But to Frank and Sal and anyone else affiliated with This Thing of Theirs, it meant someone was about to get some bad news. News whose headline would probably read something like *You're dead*. There was no other way around these things. If the guy with the thing had come through, then maybe something could have been worked out. At the place. By the guy with the other other thing. Frank had given very specific instructions that the thing had to be at the place. And it wasn't.

"You want me to take care of it, Frank?"

"No, I'll do it myself."

Sal gulped. Frank could see his associate's simple mind spinning. This was big. Frank Fortunato hadn't lifted a finger in the last twenty years unless it was to pick a piece of stray lint off his brand-new suit. He had people for the real dirty work.

Of course, Frank had put his time in early on. He didn't get to the top of the Maraschino crime family by being lazy. Legs had been broken. Judges had been bribed. Piles and piles of money had been stolen. A couple of dirtbags had been sent to a better place, but that was part of the game. Frank knew very well that he could have been one of those dirtbags had he made one misstep. But he hadn't. He was too smart. He quickly rose to the top of the heap and never looked back. There was no longer any mention of his former self, the working thug. No, Frank Fortunato had reinvented himself to become more than simply the phony head of the Corona Sanitation Transportation Corporation. He was the head of one of the most powerful crime families in New York.

One of the most powerful. That distinction never sat well with him.

With so many layers of secrecy among the Mafiosi, it was difficult to quantify for the purpose of rank exactly which was the most powerful crime family in New York City. It was pretty reasonable to presume there were five very powerful crime families along with assorted minor wannabes. So after much debate and feather-ruffling it was decided among the top five bosses that they, along with the reporters they paid off, would refer to themselves individually as "one of the most powerful." The hope was that this way maybe they wouldn't feel the need to shoot each other over a matter of pride. What they also agreed on (at least four out of the five) was that Frank could not change the name of his crime family.

It had been Maraschino for almost a hundred years and the general consensus had been that to change the name would be not only an undignified breach of Mafia etiquette but possibly confusing to lower-tier mobsters and mainstream media, perhaps even leading some people to believe that an entirely new gang had become One of the Most Powerful Crime Families and encouraging the idea that there was potential for competition. There wasn't. So why make trouble?

After grudgingly accepting their decision, Frank came up with a new plan. He set out to make his own name bigger than the family name. He would become larger than life. Dominate the tabloids. If he couldn't claim to be the most powerful and didn't have the juice to change the name of his own gang, then he would secure the title of best-known and most-liked alleged crime boss.

And so the makeover began. He had his hair cut by Mr. Jon (the same guy who cuts Hugh Jackman's hair when he's in town). He lost twenty pounds. He bought designer suits. He spray tanned. And then he paraded around the hippest, hottest restaurants and clubs with his new look and a series of models, each thinner and nip-slip-ier than the last. The tabloids took notice. Soon Frank Fortunato had become the character he had dreamed of being, landing on the front pages several times a month. The public ate it up. He was bigger than the Mafia. The one flaw in his plan was born from a seemingly minor character trait.

He was cheap. Frank was cheaper than a backup dancer's weaves. He loved to look the part, but he couldn't stomach paying for it. So he traded Mr. Jon a set of stolen rims for his haircut, had the finished product photographed from every possible angle, and then went to Vinnie DiMassio in the old neighborhood for all subsequent shearings. He made a big to-do about buying a seven thousand dollar Brioni suit, and then had it quietly returned after it was knocked off by a backroom tailor on the Lower East Side. Certainly he could have worn some of the expensive suits that so often ended up in his meat locker after falling off a truck, but that would have been cash out of his pocket. Those suits were to be sold. For money. Even his spray tan was straight from a bottle picked up at Duane Reade by an underling who knew better than to open his yap about it.

Frank Fortunato was a chiseling bastard.

And finally the tabloids that weren't paid off by the Mafia noticed that too. The *Daily News* was first on the case. An ambitious (read naïve) reporter spotted a knockoff designer tie around Frank's neck. *Hermes* was spelled *Hemres*.

It made the front page. The headline read, "Cheapfella!"

Naturally, the reporter was never heard from again. But it was too late. The damage had been done. After elevating himself to celebrity status, Frank Fortunato had been turned into a gigantic human target thanks to his New England-esque frugality. The rest of the tabloids picked up on the angle and the *New York Post* dubbed him Frank "Fancypants" Fortunato. It was not the nickname Frank had in mind. In fact, it was crazy-making for him. He denied wearing knockoffs, but to no avail. All his hard work to remake himself. And for what? To become a joke? Not likely.

The timing of the story was serendipitous. It came the same day Frank found out he had made almost no progress in his fight against stage four prostate cancer.

The beam therapy had failed. Chemo failed. The seeds had given him bowels irritable in Russell Crowe proportions—he was terrified to fart for fear of unexpectedly dropping a load in the middle of a sit down. That would not exactly jibe with the elegant mob boss persona he had put so much effort into developing.

And he didn't care how advanced certain medical practices were and how much they claimed to have lowered the risk of impotence. Any risk in that department was too much risk.

Which meant, according to the best doctors in the Northeast, Frank's options were now exhausted. And there was a ticking time bomb up his ass.

The whole business put him in a foul mood. But it did help him focus on what was really important. They wanted to make fun of Francis Albert Fortunato? Fine. He would reinvent himself again. Only this time, he wouldn't be a target. This time he would make sure the legacy he left was not "one of" but *the* most powerful crime boss in the city. Undisputed.

Aside from frequent trips to the bathroom—just in case—any actions Frank took now were not based on any short-term plans. It was all long-term thinking from here on. He was going for broke because he wanted to go out on top. Like the firemen who work as much overtime as they can in their final year so they can retire with a salary based on whatever hours they pile up during their swan song, Frank was trying to accumulate as much power, fear, and reputation as possible before he bit it. This was his legacy. He wasn't going to risk the mausoleum he bought in Flushing having an engraving that read, *Here rests Frank Fortunato, devoted father, beloved community member, arguably powerful gangster.* He wanted all questions answered before he was laid to rest.

And that process would start with the guy who hadn't come through with the other other thing.

"Frank, you sure about this? I mean, I could talk to Tony Stutters."

Frank slowly turned and stared off in the distance, imagining the ripple effect this first step of his journey would cause.

"No. I said I'll handle it. It's personal."

Brittany and Anfernee

"We got him."

Brittany Marinakos clicked the Pause button on her computer's video player. The playback on the monitor next to her froze on a black-and-white shot of Frank Fortunato staring angrily at the camera that had been so carefully placed behind the speaker screen of his TV. Perfect. Just like she had rehearsed it.

And how fortunate that he chose to punctuate his murder plans with a slow-burn look toward the camera that was oh so powerful. Not in a soap-opera way, but in a real Jimmy Caan, let's-settle-this-mano-a-mano kind of way. The kind of look you always assume precedes some sort of dastardly deed. Or a dance off.

She took a millisecond to remind herself that she was about to put her five years on the job at risk by proposing a mission that could make her a shining star in the FBI. Or ruin her. Then she turned dramatically (presentation is everything, Columbo), making sure to keep her carefully constructed "confident" face on as she waited for Anfernee's reaction.

"You 'got' him? For what? Going to see 'a guy' about 'a thing'? What are you going to charge him with, 'a crime'?"

"Did you see the same footage I saw? He's going to see Carmine. To kill him."

"But they never said that. I can't go to Justice with this."

"Sal *shrugged*."

". . . And?"

And in Mafia talk that was as good as Sal sending Frank a BFF text message describing in detail their plans to slit an associate's throat. It was hard to remember that some people hadn't been as immersed in the Cosa Nostra culture as deeply as she had. It had been twenty-six months now.

Brittany had joined the FBI to please her father. He was a legend in the Bureau. Not for what he did. For what he didn't do. Man, that guy could keep his mouth shut. He saw all sorts of rule breaking and didn't do a goddamned thing about it. His nickname among those who could be trusted was "The Zipper." Because his lips were zipped. Always. Oliver "The Zipper" Marinakos. He worked his cases, stayed right in the middle of the political road, and retired the day after he clocked thirty years.

Since she was a girl, Brittany had tried everything to please her father. She was captain of her high school debate team. Homecoming queen. Twice. She played hockey, for Christ's sake. Nothing ever resonated. It might have been the lifelong depression her dad suffered from, or perhaps he was just a terrible father, but nothing Brittany did ever got more than a "Well, isn't that nice" reaction. Straight As. *Uh-huh.* Scholarship to State. *Super.* League playoffs. *Sounds great.* The playoffs! Nothing. So she quit law school and became an FBI agent, just like him. Seemed like a foolproof plan and the bennies were solid. It was her first accomplishment that he seemed proud of.

Brittany was vaguely aware of her desperate subconscious need to please her father, but she was fine with that. It was fairly non-self-destructive and actually a pretty good motivator, so why mess with it?

And then her dad was hit and killed by a school bus on his way out for a morning jog. Things sort of started to unravel after that as Brittany began questioning every aspect of her life.

What am I doing spending my weekends chasing down kidnappers? Is saving innocent people and making the world a better place all there is to life? I wonder if I should try out for American Idol*? What if I make it to the Hollywood round and have to perform a Motown song with someone who can't dance and they screw it up for me? Why didn't I use my flexible spending account to get Lasik?*

It was about that time that her grandmother started becoming a burden.

The loss of her son was too much of an opportunity for Lola Marinakos to pass up. Life had always revolved around Lola, even when it involved other people's tragedies. *Well, they say your attitude is the most important thing when you're fighting the cancer. By the way, if you're not going to be using your ski house this winter* . . . She wasn't mean, rather, in her mind, realistic.

The phone calls began on the way home from the wake and were soon lighting up Brittany's cell phone five times a day, maybe more. It wasn't long before most of them went to voice mail, but Brittany's sense of family wouldn't let them go unreturned. So every day, she dialed up Lola and listened to her complain about how depressed and lonely she was in between the details of fabu shopping sprees and catty gossip about her bridge friends. Occasionally, Lola would ask how the whole father-loss thing was going with Brittany, but that mainly served as a transition to some other Lola-related subject of conversation.

Had Lola maintained her usual all-about-me behavior instead of ratcheting it up to Defcon 1 levels, Brittany might have never started therapy to deal with her guilt over hating her grandmother, hating her like she was Bernie Madoff talking behind her in a movie theater. And she would have never told her analyst about her relationship with her father. And she would have never faced up to how unhealthy it was to live her life to impress someone who wasn't even around anymore and who didn't care when he was here. And the good doctor would have never asked her the questions that made her wonder what she was doing with her life. And she would have never considered leaving her job.

But she did. That was three years ago. Since then it had been thirty-six months of writing various *GOOD DAY, SIR. ISAIDGOODDAY!* versions of her resignation letter in her head as she pounded away on the elliptical machine. When she'd finally had enough, she acted. Only rather than impulsively tendering a tear-laden, emotionally charged, take-this-job-and-shove-it speech, she made the decision to do something sensible. She called in sick, opened a tub of cake icing, and watched Wendy Williams. And that's when it hit her.

Being famous would be awesome.

Ah, but how? That was the issue. Why would anyone care about her? If nothing else, Brittany was practical, even within her flights of fancy. What did she have to offer the Perez Hiltons of the world? Why would *Entertainment Tonight* want to find out her secrets to staying in shape? What assets did she have that were marketable to the American public?

She made a list. She wasn't bad looking. At twenty-seven, still young-ish. Kind of funny. Decent voice when she remembered to breathe from her diaphragm and act like Angelina Jolie in *Salt*. She had a cool job.

Ooh. That was it. Her job.

Americans love cops. Yes, perfect. What if she could become some sort of law enforcement consultant to CNN or MSNBC or Lifetime? What if she had an interviewer position at a network or a series in syndication? What if she hosted a talk show from the point of view of an experienced FBI agent?

Wait. That's it. She had cracked it. Tyra with a badge.

Now she needed some reason for Hollywood to notice her. How had other talk show hosts done it? Some spent years as reporters, slogging away on local newscasts, covering water skiing squirrels and painfully obvious tips for beating the heat. Nope. Working her way through the ranks of production in the hopes that some producer might notice how cute yet intelligent she looked schlepping cables across the stage and make her a star? Not happening. Getting an agent and audition-ing along with every vapid former cheerleader in Los Angeles? Maybe.

But what she really wanted was the *Scarface* promotion. Straight to the top by way of gutsy moves and unbridled moxie. And to do that, she needed a ginormous case to solve.

Nothing makes a good, nationally devoured, movie-optionable story like a mobster case. That's the kind of thing you can milk for decades and maybe even get Jamie Foxx to star in. So that's what she looked for. A big commercially viable mob case.

She passed on long-term drug stuff. Boring. She claimed to be too busy to join in on the war on illegal downloading. Yawn. She waited and waited until there was some Mafia action on the table. And then she jumped.

It wasn't much at the start. A small construction company shake-down investigation with hints of labor union embezzlement. Probably nothing prosecutable as usual, but Brittany begged to be assigned to the case and locked her jaws onto it until she found something. Noth-ing big, but something. The company had a few silent investors and one disgruntled partner who talked a little too much when he was in his cups. There was definitely some money being laundered there.

Rather than moving in for that small kill, Brittany convinced her superiors that there was more to the case and asked for more time and resources. The truth was she had no idea if there was more to it, but this was a Mafia case and she was going to squeeze that bastard until she was sure there wasn't a drop of juice left inside. So she squeezed.

There was, in fact, more juice in the form of a link to the Maraschino crime family. It was precisely what she had hoped for and exactly what she needed to implement her plan to become a household name.

Two years of slogging through paperwork and bureaucracy and ass kissing later, Brittany was about to get her shot at running her own mob sting operation. And then she heard Frank telling Sal about the guy and the thing. Cha-Ching! This was more than she could have ever hoped for. No longer a simple money-laundering affair or a city hall bribe, but an actual murder plot. Real Jamie-Foxx-on-line-two kind of stuff. And now, she faced one last hurdle. Her direct superior, Anfernee Fine.

Anfernee Fine was not a stupid man. He was a company man. Long ago he had figured out that succeeding in the world of government employment had very little to do with how smart you were, how clever your ideas to improve workflow were, or even how well you did your job. No, it was Anfernee's conclusion that the yardstick of success in the FBI was one that measured a murky mix of seniority, lack of offense, and an easy-to-recite summary of press-friendly cases with clever names in which you played some role. Not necessarily the top cop hero role. But *a* role.

So that's what Anfernee did. Not that he was lazy. Certainly he could have proven his intelligence, improved workplace efficiency, and performed far and above what his job description called for. But that would have gone unnoticed. Working hard in a government job, even the FBI, is like trying to perfect the balance of spices in a McNugget. Nobody cares.

Instead, he played by the rules and avoided making waves of any kind. As flawed and weighed down with red tape as it was, the FBI wasn't going to change anytime soon, so he decided to roll with it. Why beat your head against the wall when all it's going to do is give you a headache? It made more sense to attach his name to projects that, if successful, he could claim some degree of participation in and, if failures, he could walk away from virtually untouched. Frank Fortunato and Brittany Marinakos were not the only ones with self-serving PR plans.

Part of Anfernee's own internal approval process had to do with names of projects. He needed a quick and easy-to-remember nickname that associated him with the case. Nothing he would use on a day-to-day basis, but something that he could drop into conversations as extra support to his granite-like foundation of mediocrity. *Oh, that construction company extortion racket sting? I was the foreman of Operation Demolition. The White Slavery bust? Of course I know about it. You're looking at the John Wilkes Booth of Operation Abe Lincoln.* They didn't always make sense. But they were memorable and would associate Anfernee with these high-profile cases in the minds of his coworkers and superiors enough that he could count on job security for years to come.

It was this philosophy that had taken Anfernee straight to the middle. Number one hundred thirty-eight with a bullet. No longer the grunt, but not really the boss. He was one of the guys the never-in-the-field bosses looked to for approval of their milquetoast proposals, asked to write memos and reports, and relied on to "look into" things. All tasks he could farm out to underlings while taking credit for their hard work himself. He would probably never make chief this way, but chances were even better that he would never get canned no matter how bad the economy got. And he was fine with that.

Anfernee's burning ambition was to continue employment until he no longer needed to work. Another eight years and he would be riding his pension straight to Henry's Fork for an equivalent period of fly fishing.

In other words, he was no Brittany. So, it was unlikely that he would show too much excitement this early in the process. There were so many details to hear before he gave his approval. What was Brittany's plan, exactly? How would she justify the warrants they would need? Would the name of her plan play on the front page of the paper? Was it amenable to memorable ancillary nicknames that could be applied to him? Critical stuff. Stuff that everyone else in the department was already thinking about.

Not surprisingly, when Frank Fortunato made his big play to become the celebrity mobster, the FBI took notice. If there's one thing the American public likes more than a big flamboyant bad boy, it's a big flamboyant target. And Frank was playing right into the inevitable cycle of celebrity. He had started to believe his own hype. It was simply a matter of time before he was ripe. The fact that he was now planning a murder really worked out well for everyone involved. Except for the guy with the other other thing.

The decision on how to bring the Maraschino family down was a much-debated one within the department. Some factions felt strongly that they should stay the course of undercover work that would lead to the arrest of lower-level gangsters who would then be coerced to flip on their bosses, the bosses then coerced to flip on their bosses, and so on. They referred to it as *The Domino Theory*. Another camp championed focusing solely on income-tax evasion. Their plan was to determine the inner workings of the Maraschino crime family and calculate its total cash intake before swooping in and arresting the grand poobah for income tax evasion. *Operation Tax Cut*. Yet another camp favored good old-fashioned catch and punish. Chase down the guys who were doing the crimes and put them in jail. *Project Clamp Down*. Behind closed doors, this was referred to as *Project Old School* as it was considered to be a pretty outdated and pointless plan.

None of the names were particularly savory in Anfernee's mind. They lacked pizzazz. Why was it so hard for these people to come up with something clever? How was he supposed to attach himself to *The Domino Theory*? It didn't exactly scream nickname-friendly. The Ace of *The Domino Theory*? No. The Big Daddy of *The Domino Theory*. Sorry. The Dominator of the . . . oh why bother?

Eventually, in the tried-and-true manner of an oversized bureaucracy, it was decided by the higher ups that the Mafia-catching budget would be split equally among the various factions. Essentially giving the green light to any and all agents who came up with an idea. All they had to do was convince their supervisors.

Brittany didn't have a catchy name for her plan. It was the one omission of her pitch. Not that she hadn't tried to come up with something clever—*Operation I Spy Wise Guy, The Badfellas Commission, The Godfather IV:*

Uncle Sam's Revenge. Nothing sounded right. She knew it was important to Anfernee and was hoping to overcome this obvious shortcoming by adding plenty of drama to her presentation, perhaps crying if necessary.

"Anfernee, Carmine Mastramouro is 'the guy.' Frank's going to kill him."

"You think?"

"Trust me. I've been watching Fortunato. I've got audio of his meetings. I've got pictures of his associates. I've established motives. All I need now is permission to pull the trigger and I'll destroy this guy."

Anfernee considered her for a second.

"Do you have a name for this mission?"

Brittany had chosen her bulky sweater today for just such an emergency. Who needed flop sweat staining their pits as their brain thumbed through possible name files, grasping for anything that would pull this one out of the burner—puns, movie titles, names of old boyfriends and pets, anything. And suddenly, like a TMZ reporter on deadline, it just appeared in front of her eyes.

"*Project Fancypants.*"

It was so easy she had overlooked it for the last two weeks. And now it came out of her mouth as if she had been sitting on it forever, just waiting for the right time to drop this brilliant bomb.

Anfernee silently considered the name. *Project Fancypants.* It was bold enough that the brass would be impressed with his team's brazen determination, but vague enough that he could claim it was a simple surveillance mission that went out of control in the hands of a renegade agent who was definitely not him. And he already had the perfect nickname in the case of success—"The Tailor of *Project Fancypants.*" Bingo.

Anfernee nodded. Just a nod. Not a notarized approval letter. Later, Anfernee could plausibly be able to say he had merely stretched or yawned and had been misinterpreted. Unless she actually caught Frank Fortunato. Then his nod would take on an entirely different meaning.

Brittany quickly scooped up her presentation materials and headed out to start work as Anfernee sat silent and still, wary of giving any further indications of his thoughts.

"Thank you, Anfernee! You won't regret this."

The Interview

"And then you were at Overthink for three years. Nice company."

The heat in Geoff Pedretti's sunlit corner office was on the verge of aggressively uncomfortable. Geoff had apologized for the temperature earlier, but a suspicious person might wonder if it weren't some sort of bizarre test to weed out the weaker candidates. Of course, compared to doing time in a synthetic chicken suit on a city street in a globally warmed September, it was practically cool. Brad waited patiently as the CEO and chief creative officer of Red Light District Advertising perused his résumé again, as if there were some secret code hidden within the meticulously designed piece.

Sitting in this office, Brad felt like he had been granted a temporary visa back to his New York. The New York he knew and loved and missed so desperately. Mmmmm, New York advertising. The walk through Red Light to Geoff's office had been a luxurious indulgence. The supporting staff there were different from the ones at Overthink, and yet so very much the same.

Hello skinny-jeans-chunky-glasses-web-designer-guy. Hi super-casual-account-exec-who-still-looks-like-an-uptight-suit-in-his-jeans-guy. What up, secretly-ambitious-asexual-intern. Oh, we've never met, but I know you all too well. And I already love you.

True to their archetypes, no one had said a word or cracked a smile as Brad passed by. Fine with him. It felt good just to be back in the hive. He'd win the other bees over later.

Geoff looked up and smiled.

"Great people at Overthink. Shame about the lawsuit."

"Yeah."

"They still have that little blonde receptionist?"

"Actually, she was the one that sued."

"Boy, she was a real piece of ass."

"Well . . . yeah."

Geoff continued to smile at Brad the way retirees stare at grandchildren before offering some freshly baked cookies or admitting they don't recognize them.

He was taking Brad in. Twenty-five years of interviewing people had made Geoff believe that he was a pretty good judge of character. He wasn't. He had passed on several of the brightest candidates to come through his office for reasons as simple as a stray collar (not organized), a makeup covered zit (what *else* is she hiding?), and a Boston accent (you can't trust foreigners). Many of these candidates had gone on to great success at Geoff's competitors, but he was enough of an egomaniac to ignore this trend. He believed in his gut. Forget Golden Pencil awards, recommendations from friends, amazing portfolios. He looked into a person's eyes.

He was, after all, the mind behind the *Actually, that* is *a banana in my pocket* Moxoto mobile phone campaign. He knew what it took to be great.

Geoff found Brad's eyes to be particularly revealing. He sensed what he thought at first was a deep and profound desperation. A lost soul in need of approval. A man who was giving life one last chance before visiting a bridge and telling some passing stranger "It's not worth it anymore."

The only thing was, Brad wasn't sweating. Not a drop. Not like a desperate man should be. Geoff always turned the heat up for interviews. He thought it was a swell way to see how candidates handled pressure. An imposed anxiety. It was a great means of scaring up the highly resonant fumes of loser. But this Brad fellow was having none of it. Geoff started to question his initial judgment. Perhaps that wasn't desperation in Brad's eyes. He looked again and revised his original assessment. *Well, well, well. This kid is a cold-blooded killer. Ice in his veins.* Exactly who Geoff was looking for. After all, that's what marketing was all about. The testicular fortitude of a veteran lion tamer. The oversized cashews of Seal Team 6. Stuttering John–caliber cajones. Someone who could look a client in the face and tell them, "You're wrong and I'll prove it to you." It was maybe the worst way to handle an account, but Geoff had been rewatching the entire run of *Mad Men* and was considering a change in the way his company did business.

Brad had prepared for every possible question Geoff could have asked. The one thing he didn't prepare for was silence. Thank God he had remembered to put his cell phone on vibrate. A call going off in this vacuum would sound more obnoxious than farting while having your pants tailored. He could not have been more uncomfortable as Geoff continued staring/smiling at him. Was this a challenge? Was Geoff looking for some other response? An offer to set him up with the litigious receptionist, perhaps?

Finally, Geoff shook himself out of his trance and affected a look that said *I care.*

"Tell me about yourself, Brad."

That was all Brad needed. He launched into the pitch he had been over so many times in the bathroom mirror. He opened with a joke about how much he loved work—"Maybe a little too much, ha ha"— followed quickly by a serious but concise review of his experience, awards and accomplishments, and finished with a fascinating anecdote about a project he worked on that required a certain creative acumen that only a clever chap like Brad would possess.

"Well, that is very impressive. Let me talk to my people and bounce your portfolio across a few department-head desks. I think we might be able to work something out."

"Really?"

"Absolutely. Brad, it was great meeting you. And sorry about the heat. That was my little test."

Brad took the wink that followed to mean that he should kind of pretend to understand what that disclosure meant. He stood and shook Geoff's meaty hand while looking confidently into that Stepford smiling face one more time. And then it was over.

Project Fancypants

A man in a dark suit and sunglasses stood in the hallway on the fourteenth floor of 1635 Broadway trying very hard to look as if he were supposed to be there when his earpiece crackled with Brittany's voice.

"Number five, how are we?"

The man in the suit raised his cuff to his mouth and spoke quietly into the hidden microphone.

"We're all clear. Over."

"Tom, are you still wearing your sunglasses?"

The man in the dark suit paused for a second to review his situation and then, realizing his surveillance faux pas, whipped his sunglasses off and jammed them into his jacket pocket.

"No."

There was a heavy sigh over the earphone wedged inside his left ear.

"You know we have cameras and mics all over this building, right?"

"Pshh, yeah." Duh.

"Just make sure no one gets by you, okay?"

"Affirmative."

The man in the dark suit without sunglasses gave the hallway another once-over. All clear. But Jesus, did he have to pee. Probably just his prostate pushing his bladder around. It happened to Tom more and more often these days, especially when he spent a lot of time on his feet. He knew he should have it checked out, but he also knew what getting it checked out involved. It would wait.

An elevator dinged its arrival on the fourteenth floor, and Tom arranged himself in front of the opening door to make sure no one got off the elevator. An elderly couple on their way to a doctor's appointment started to exit when they saw Tom's stern face. Tom shook his head and told them, "Wrong floor."

Tom appeared to be quite serious. The unrelenting pressure of having to urinate lent a certain gravitas to his statement. The couple froze for a beat before looking at the lit floor number inside the elevator. It was the right floor, but who wanted to argue with this visibly upset man?

"Sorry. Our mistake."

Tom nodded and the old couple then backed into the elevator, letting the doors close in front of them.

Inside the surveillance vehicle disguised as a plumber's van parked outside 1635 Broadway, Brittany sat with two underling agents watching a bank of monitors set up to observe the route Carmine would presumably take this morning.

Brittany's research had been exhausting. She had called in every favor she had with undercover agents, informants, and reporters around the city. She left no rock unturned. There could be no mistaking what was going down today at 1635 Broadway.

Frank Fortunato's plan was to meet Carmine Mastramouro in the lobby and shoot him dead. Frank's bloated ego had convinced him that he could buy off or kill any civilian witnesses foolish enough to testify against him. And he probably was right. Which is why Brittany had brought her own witnesses.

Her plan was to catch him in the act, gun in hand, just before he fired. It was very theatrical and would make a compelling front page. And her case would be bulletproof. Captured on video from start to finish. FBI agents planted in the elevator banks to not only stop the crime and catch Frank, but to serve as impeccable eyewitnesses. The tabloids would refer to her as the new Eliot Ness. Her name would become synonymous with law enforcement. Hello, Oprah.

Her cell phone rang. It was the call she had been waiting for her whole career.

"Marinakos, go."

"Target is two blocks away from 1635 headed south on Broadway."

"Stay on him. Let me know."

She hung up and hit the walkie button to talk to all the agents working for her.

"We're T minus two minutes from go time. Tom, can you check that north stairwell one more time?"

"Check."

"Yes, check them. You know, make sure they're clear."

"I meant affirmative."

"Just do it."

Tom had not been Brittany's first choice, but her department was shorthanded and she needed men. He wasn't the best agent she had ever met, but Brittany knew Tom could at least be counted on to follow some very simple instructions. Carmine would exit his therapist's office at eleven o'clock exactly. Same as every Wednesday morning. He would take the elevator down on his way to meet his boyfriend for coffee across the street. Like clockwork.

Tom's instructions had been to make sure the fourteenth floor was clear of any interference, basically busy work to keep his head in the game. Brittany knew Tom could be a little unfocused at times, so she had warned him there was a good chance that Frank would send backup *soldati*, *picciotti*, *sgarrista*. Basically everything but pirates. Tom assured her he would be on his toes with his eyes wide open. Once he had cleared the area, he was to wait for Brittany's signal that Carmine had entered the elevator a few floors above, hit the Down button, and wait to catch a ride down with him to the lobby, ensuring Tom would be there when Frank attacked.

Not that Tom could do anything to stop Frank. There would be other people there for that. Highly trained agents who would quickly subdue Frank and prevent any real injury. Tom's real job was to be the handsome guy with twenty-twenty vision and a squeaky clean record who saw it all. Perfect for the witness stand. But he better not be wearing those goddamned sunglasses.

Up on the fourteenth floor Tom moved quickly to the stairway door, passing the men's room on his way. The stairs were clear. No mobsters, no henchmen, no sneering men in skull-and-crossbones hats and curly mustaches. Yet. Whew.

As he headed back toward his post in front of the elevator, he stopped in front of the men's room. Man, he had to pee like you read about. If he was calculating correctly, they were still T minus about one minute until he had to make his move. Plenty of time. He slipped into the bathroom, fumbling with his zipper as he hustled toward the urinal.

Brad navigated the interior of the Red Light office on his way to the front door, mentally replaying the last ten minutes of his life. He came to the conclusion that his interview could not have gone better. It was the same feeling he had after the presentation he gave the day he got fired, only without the embarrassing ending. He took a moment to savor the feeling of being immersed in an agency once more. While fleeting, it was nevertheless inspiring. Who knew the vapid poseur culture of advertising could work as such a salve for the soul?

Yes, this pasty Tarzan with a hundred dollar haircut had swung from one vine, let go, done a few flips, posed for the cameras, grabbed another vine, and swung away. He was back.

It felt good to swing. Life had its ups and downs, but in Brad's world, the ups were worth the downs since usually neither was life-threatening. Sure he forgot when the vodka assignment was due, but if he hadn't he wouldn't have come up with the brilliant idea that skyrocketed him to interagency fame. So he blew the vodka thing only weeks later. A few weeks of unemployment was an easy trade for a deep notch in the bedpost like Red Light. There was always another vine. Would it be inappropriate to attempt a Tarzan yell? Probably. He settled for growling a quiet *Ungowa!* to himself as he worked his way through the kitschy office.

He exited Red Light's fourteenth floor office to face the elevator in an empty hallway and pressed the Down button. His phone began vibrating. Gracie.

He pulled it out and soaked up the moment. It was time to answer her call. Hitting the green answer button meant he had the go to tell her the good news. The great news. That he had fucking owned it and was back on top. They were back to really being the couple he had been pretending to be.

Oh, but wait. Why do that on the phone? You can't get a congratulatory (ahem) *hug* over the phone. Brad smiled to himself and declined Gracie's call for the last time. He would delay gratification for a few more minutes to share the news in person. God, he was so mature.

As he waited he allowed himself an indulgent thought.

Things are finally turning my way.

It was T minus nothing. Frank was headed into the building lobby. Carmine was headed down in the elevator.

"Showtime."

It was so great when Brittany could say dramatic things that really had two meanings, even if she was the only one who realized it.

Brad almost didn't hear the elevator ding.

Standing in the hallway, he was too lost in his tiny dreams of success, picturing himself striding confidently into the Red Light office wearing the warm glow of self-assurance that radiates from those who know they're The Man. In his mind he had just shared a joke with the guy in the coffee cart outside (staying in touch with the little people), picked up his usual paper from the newspaper vendor (*Morning, Mr. Fingerman. How 'bout them Giants?*), and chuckled good naturedly at the people gathered around the three-card Monte hustler outside 1635 Broadway (Suckers!). Brad's future self made sure to say *hi* to the cute young receptionist who greeted him a little too warmly every morning. Probably a crush, but who could blame her? *Good morning to you too, Christy. But no thanks, I'm happily married.* Which reminded him. Hmmm, perhaps an upgrade to a platinum wedding band. And a well-earned man-cation. Nice.

Inside the waiting elevator Carmine cleared his throat and raised his eyebrows. Coming or not? Brad snapped to and glided on in.

Brittany scanned the monitors and focused herself on the exquisite timing they had all agreed on.

"Perfect, Tom. Just stay cool. Everybody's in position."

The flush broadcasted over Tom's microphone to everyone on the walkie network. He had raised his mic hand to respond to Brittany when the AutoFlush sensed that he had moved away from the urinal. It wasn't his prostate after all. It was the jumbo coffee he poured down his gullet on his way to work, after oversleeping. Which took more than the T minus thirty seconds he had hoped to spend peeing. Damn those late night infomercials.

"Be right there, Brittany."

"Wait, that's not you?"

A cold tingle quickly walked its prickly fingers up the back of Brittany's spine as she stared closer and closer at the feed from the camera in the elevator. There was Carmine standing next to a guy who was not Tom. This was not her plan.

"Who is that? Why is he there? What's he doing? Can we get him out of there?"

Brittany and her fellow van mates watched helplessly as the elevator doors closed.

One team member raised his eyebrows and actually cracked the tiniest smile.

"Not anymore."

There's nothing worse than a smug underling agent.

"Tom, how did he get past you?"

"I'm in position, Brittany."

He sounded as if he were walking briskly.

"No, Tom. You missed him."

"Oh . . . Oops."

Now was the time for Plan B. She needed a Plan B.

"Stop the elevator. We have to get him out of there."

"That would compromise our entire operation, we can't—"

ZZZZZZPPPTTTPPZZZPT.

Every monitor in the van went black as all three agents clasped their hands to their headphones before whipping them off. The squeal of feedback was audible even as the headphones hit the floor.

"What just happened?"

Smoke filled the interior of the truck. Mr. Smug didn't look so smug anymore.

"Uh, sorry."

Tom wasn't the only one who picked up a jumbo coffee on the way to work this morning. But of the two, Tom was the one who didn't spill his barely touched, Trenta Pike Place Roast on the computer that every camera and mic was running through.

"Holy. Shit."

As the video system flamed out and smoke poured through every nook and cranny of the van, passersby could hear the three plumbers within coughing and cursing, and one of them finally screaming, "ALL UNITS GO GO GO! TAKE HIM DOWN! I REPEAT TAKE THE TARGET DOWN!" into their walkie talkies before bursting out of the side door.

All units go. Tom heard the call and jumped to action, jamming his finger into the Down button over and over as quickly as he could. Maybe this was his chance to make up for the bathroom break.

On the street several agents disguised as regular Joes and Janes sprang into action. The coffee guy whipped out his gun. The newspaper vendor hopped over a stack of magazines and ran for the entrance. The three-card Monte dealer left an eager German chump midgame to follow the other two undercover agents into the building.

Brittany and her crack team made it into the lobby only to find it completely empty. Frank was nowhere to be found. Plan B was a bust. The Agent Formerly Known As Smug posed a theory.

"He's gone. Maybe he isn't going through with it."

Fat chance. Besides, Brittany had too much riding on this to take that risk. Plan C. What was Plan C?

"The stairs. He took the stairs. He didn't want to do it in the lobby. We have to check every floor. Let's go."

They hit the north-side stairs running. As they raced up, story by story, agents peeled off to individual floors. Brittany barked orders as she raced ahead of them all.

Brad and Carmine's elevator was quiet. Brad stood next to the doors and did his best to contain himself, but how often does a guy like him have days like this? His restraint didn't last more than two floors. He looked over his shoulder and caught Carmine's eye.

"Just had an interview."

Carmine widened his eyes to affect the smallest possible courtesy reaction. *B. F-ing. D.*

Brad considered singing the chorus of "The Bitch Is Back" but decided that wasn't quite the tone he wanted to set. He really wished he could think of some other relevant, comeback-related song, but he came up empty and decided to just keep it simple.

"Went great. I mean really amazing."

Carmine forced himself to nod. *Whoopee.*

"Think I'll stop by home and tell my wife about it before I go back to work. Give her the good news, if you know what I mean."

Oh, yes. Brad was feeling it. Carmine wasn't.

As Brad smiled and congratulated himself on being a handsome devil with a bright future, he noticed something on his left shoe. A scuff of dirt. The one flaw in his perfect day. He knelt down to wipe it off as the elevator dinged to a stop on the fourth floor. Two black shoes stepped into the open doors.

Brad worked on the scuff mark, secretly grateful that someone else was entering the elevator. Maybe *they* would be interested in Brad's remarkable interview.

Some of the dirt he had scraped off floated up to Brad's nostrils. He let loose a tremendous, soul-shaking, eye-watering sneeze. No one said, "Bless you."

"Yup, I think things are finally looking up for me."

The scuff mark was a stubborn one and not coming off easily, but Brad wasn't about to give up. He had been patient, paid some humiliating dues, and kept his secret shame from his wife long enough for everything to work out perfectly. He would be damned if half a square inch of dirt was going to taint this brilliant canvas of a life he had just put the finishing touches on. He was on his way back to the top of the heap. Back to the official New York of Brad Fingerman. His new job now merely a matter of administrative formality that would trigger positive reactive measures across the rest of his existence. Money. Esteem. Confidence. Potence. He might even tell Champ to go fuck himself. Not really, but it felt good to imagine saying stuff like that.

In fact, if the scuff mark had come off easily, Brad would have stood up, turned around, and seen Carmine's eyes go wide like saucers at what was waiting outside the elevator. Brad would have seen a look of recognition in those saucers. And then he would have seen a wash of realization in them. A look that said something unavoidable and terrible was about to happen. But Brad was busy with his scuff mark, so instead he only heard the last two words of Carmine's life.

". . . Holy crap."

Not understanding the true sentiment behind the statement, Brad naturally assumed it was about his amazing tale of good fortune, that he had cracked his elevator buddy's cold veneer. "I know. It's great, right? It's like my friend Owen told me, if you keep a positive outlook . . ."

FUMP-FUMP-FUMP-FUMP-FUMP. The silenced gun above Brad's head fired five shots directly into Carmine's heart.

". . . sometimes you get lucky."

The black shoes moved away as Brad finally cleared enough dirt off his shoe leather to be deemed acceptable for his victory walk home. He stood up to continue the conversation with his new friend. Instead he found that Carmine looked decidedly worse now than he did for the first ten floors of their ride.

"Hey, are you okay?"

Carmine continued staring ahead as he slid down the back wall of the elevator, streaking blood behind him. Down the hall, footsteps faded away as a stairwell door slammed shut.

". . . Whoa."

The elevator doors began to close when a herd of footsteps swarmed the hallway and a firm hand stopped the elevator.

"FREEZE! FBI!"

Brittany and three other agents stood ready to pounce just outside the elevator, guns drawn. It took about 0.8 seconds for Brittany to understand what had happened.

She had failed.

They were too late. Carmine was dead and Frank was gone. There was no video or audio of the crime. Her father might have referred to her situation as FUBAR.

Brad finally broke the tense silence.

". . . What the fuck?"

It was an innocent enough question and perfectly justifiable considering Brad had not been privy to Plans A, B, or C. But innocent or not, it sparked a reaction in Brittany that even she didn't expect. They hadn't seen Frank on their way up. And she needed to bring someone in, even if it meant thinking up a different name for the mission. Project Innocent Bystander, for example.

She grabbed Brad and slammed him against the elevator wall.

"You're under arrest. You have the right to remain silent. Anything you say can and will be used against you in a court of law . . ."

There was more, but it was all lost on Brad. He was reeling as he watched his luck go from a royal flush to snake eyes in the time it took to clean off his shoe.

Tom had waited for the elevator for only a brief moment before deciding to take matters into his own hands. Brittany had said all units go, after all. They might call him a maverick, but he wasn't waiting for any stinking elevator. He ran to the stairwell on the south side of the hallway and headed down two and three stairs at a time, gun drawn and ready for action.

By the time he got to the second floor he was exhausted and still hadn't quite figured out exactly where all units were supposed to go. He paused to catch his breath. It was then that the yelling from a floor or two above echoed down the cement stairwell. He turned to start back up when a man in a great hurry whipped around the corner and headed down toward him. Tom thought fast.

"Hey Buddy, have you seen a bunch of FBI agents around here?"

"Uh, no, sorry."

As Frank Fortunato tried to push past the charged-up agent, something clicked in Tom's government-trained mind.

"Sayyyy. You're Frank Fortunato."

"I get that a lot. Excuse me."

On a less excitement-filled day, Frank could have probably convinced Tom that he was his own distant cousin and walked away. But this particular time, Tom wasn't having it. Better to play it safe and arrest the wrong man. He'd let the government's attorneys worry about the legal ramifications. That's how they did it on TV.

Tom pointed his gun at Frank.

"I need you to come with me, sir."

Brad Gets Debriefed

It would have been difficult to determine who was more relieved in the lobby two minutes later. Was it Brad finding out that he was no longer a suspect in a front page murder case he had nothing to do with? Or was it Brittany discovering her mission had been snatched from the jaws of bureaucratic death by the buffoonish police work of her least-favorite agent? Suffice it to say that each verged on ruining their underpants only moments before they found out the good news.

Tom dragged a handcuffed Frank out of the south stairwell door at the same time Brittany and her hangdog crew were schlubbing their way out of the north stairwell door. Both sides froze at the sight of each other.

"Tom? Did you catch Frank Fortunato?"

Tom beamed like he had found the afikoman.

"This is him for sure? I knew it!"

Tom fist pumped the air. Yes!

"Wow. Gold star, Tom."

Brittany took a moment to make sure she had all the details of her amazing luck straight. Yes, Carmine had died, but he was a lowlife who was going to meet a similar end regardless of what Brittany did. The press would forgive that uncomfortable detail. But this. A mob boss caught fleeing the scene of the crime by her ace in the hole, Tom. It wasn't an open and closed case, but it was a damn good one.

Especially since she had an eyewitness.

She turned to Brad and snapped at her crew. "Get those cuffs off him. And give him a Kleenex for God's sake."

The agents scrambled to see who could get their keys out first, and then Brad was free.

"Sorry for the misunderstanding, Mr. . . ."

"Fingerman, Brad Fingerman."

"Mr. Fingerman. I hope you understand we were just being careful. Now if you wouldn't mind, we'd like to give you a ride to headquarters and get a statement from you."

It took a second for Brad to readjust his point of view from pre-life-sentence-convict back to free-as-a-bird confused guy. This new perspective snapped into focus right about the time Frank launched a world-class scowl from across the room as Tom escorted him out of the building. Maybe it was directed at Brad. Maybe it was a more general reaction to getting caught. Could have just been that the handcuffs were a little too tight. Either way, it was hard to ignore.

And then he realized what Brittany was asking him.

"But, I didn't see anything."

An hour later, Brittany handed a still-shaking Brad a cold can of soda, one of the few amenities her tiny office could provide witnesses on short notice. It was a Pepsi. Not his regular drink. Brad was more of a Coke man. He held it between his legs. At least it was something to stare at besides his fingernails.

"Can I get you anything else?"

"No. I'm fine. Really. Can I go now?"

"Well, actually we have a few more questions for you."

"Look, I told you everything I know. I got in the elevator. I bent down to clean off my shoe and then pow, this guy is dead."

"You must have seen something, heard something, smelled something. Anything."

"I'm sorry."

Other agents had been building cases against Frank Fortunato for years. Run of the mill stuff for mob bosses—third-hand hearsay and vaguely relevant circumstances. Low-level wannabe gangsters caught with enough weed to turn over the guys they bought it from, guys who had a relationship with the Maraschino family. Drunks who claimed they saw Frank leave through the back entrance of a restaurant the night its owner had all four limbs broken. But the feds' efforts were largely pointless and at best annoying to Frank. They had never come up with anything concrete. Not like what was sitting in Brittany's chair. Not like this FBI goldmine.

"It's okay to be scared, Brad. I'm sure you've seen Frank's picture in the paper. Probably heard the rumors about him killing witnesses."

"Wait, what? He kills witnesses? Holy shi—"

"They're only rumors. Trust me. We can protect you."

"I'm not scared. I didn't see anything."

Brittany sighed. "Look, Brad. What's it going to take? If you testify I can make sure they never find you. I can get you a new name, a new job, a new life. Maybe somewhere nice, like Idaho or Georgia. You pick it. You can start all over."

"What are you talking about?"

"The Witness Protection Program. You're an ideal candidate."

"Can't someone else testify? Don't you have other witnesses? What about the slow guy who arrested Fortunato?"

"Yes, we have Special Agent Lewis. But he wasn't there in the elevator when the murder actually happened. And we have other witnesses, but all they can do is put Frank at the scene of the crime. It's not enough. This could be the biggest case in twenty years. That means lot of media coverage, which means we can't make one mistake. We have to be perfect. We need your testimony so we can put Frank Fortunato away for life."

What was going on here? This wasn't how the vine system was supposed to work. Tarzan's vines always took him where he wanted to go. They didn't take him to maybe somewhere nice like Idaho or Georgia. The logic of the elaborate jungle transit system was such that the vines in question hung at angles that avoided sending the ape man directly into massive tree trunks. That was George of the Jungle territory.

Holy cats. Brad might not be Tarzan. But he couldn't be George, could he? The premise was untenable. Which meant the vine being jammed into his hand was the wrong vine. No way the Witness

Protection Program could lead to anything productive or sexy career-wise. What kind of agencies might they have in Idaho? Definitely not a branch office of Red Light. And that was the point of today, wasn't it? The rebirth of Brad. He just had a killer interview for his dream job. His confidence was back. He felt taller. The Fingerman renaissance was scheduled to begin any second now. Sitting in the offices of the FBI was simply a post-traumatic stress induced courtesy. Not only did he have no interest in helping the feds, but the process would completely derail his comeback tour. No, no, no!

On top of all that, he still hadn't returned Gracie's call. Plus, he'd need to invest in a wardrobe refresh before he started at Red Light. Was his phone ringer on? What if Geoff called right now to tell him to come in tomorrow and pick an office? He had to get ready. Time was a-wasting!

God help him, but clearly Brad's best course of action here was to be honest.

He looked up from his now warm, unopened Pepsi can.

"I wish I could help. But I swear, I didn't see anything."

"All right. Take some time and think about it."

Brittany handed Brad her card. "Seriously, we really need you."

Brad put the unopened Pepsi on the table, took her card and put it in his wallet. But honestly, he was only being polite.

Back to Normal

The subway ride home took forever. Or maybe it took a few minutes. Brad couldn't remember. His head swirled as he relived his drastic change of fortunes and focused on accepting his good luck. He'd had a great interview and beaten a murder rap all in less than three hours. Technically, a great day.

He had revived his plan to pop in and surprise Gracie with his great news (the job, not his release from FBI custody). She was working from home and it had been awhile since she had been impressed with him for anything besides some phony accomplishment he had cooked up for the sake of continuing his façade of employment. Today he had something real for her. Something he could honestly brag about. Perhaps he could add afternoon delight to his banner day before heading back to his minimum wage job handing out fliers in a chicken suit. God, success felt good.

James the doorman gave Brad the same obsequious smile he always gave when residents came through the revolving doors before saying the exact same thing he always said.

"All right."

All right. Not that Brad had asked how everything was going. Or how tricks were. Or how he was feeling. He smiled hello and James, as usual, offered up an "All right." Kind of a utility tool for almost any conversation a doorman might have with a tenant.

Hey, James. My toilet's clogged up again and my buddies are coming for poker night.

All right.

*Oh, James, would you mind keeping my spare keys behind the desk
down here? You know how forgetful I am.*
All right.
*James, I'm having a half pound of rock-star hashish delivered by an
albino midget who's on the run from a band of Ugandan warlords.*
All right.
Didn't make the slightest difference. Although, today James did
seem to hold his suck-up smile a little longer than normal. And what
was with him watching Brad walk the entire length of the lobby? That
guy was just plain unsettling.

Maybe he was on alert because of his creepy doorman. Maybe his
adrenaline-addled senses were heightened to the levels of a meth head
at a fireworks show thanks to his felony arrest and release. Either way,
Brad's ears picked up the pounding by the time he was halfway down
the hall of his floor.

THUMP. THUMP. THUMP. Something was banging against a
wall. It sounded like a fight. With rhythm.

Brad walked up to his front door and listened. It was coming from
his apartment. And it wasn't a fight.

As Brad entered his apartment and saw a tool belt that didn't belong
to him on the floor, he got the distinct feeling that James had lied to
him. Things were definitely not all right.

He had watched enough *Maury* to know damn well what was going
on, but Brad decided to go see the raw and unforgiving truth anyway.
Jesus, this was a weird day. He sighed and trudged down the hall.

And there in the bedroom was Gracie. With the cable guy. And
they were having the kudos sex Brad was planning on having with her.
The awesome, toe curling, gasping for breath, where-have-you-been-
all-my-life sex Brad had felt so confident in anticipating. What could
she possibly be congratulating the cable guy for?

Fortunately, both Gracie and the man she was currently involved
with were facing away from the doorway Brad was standing in, so

there was no need for anyone to say, "Do you mind?" or "Well, this is awkward."

"Oh God. (THUMP) Oh God. (THUMP) Oh God. (THUMP) This is the (THUMP) best sex (THUMP) (THUMP) I've ever had. (THUMP) (THUMP) So much better (THUMP) (THUMP) (THUMP) than my husband. (THUMP) (THUMP) (THUMP) And the plumber. (THUMP) (THUMP) (THUMP) And the neighbor. (THUMP) (THUMP) (THUMP) And my old boyfriend I saw last week. (THUMP) (THUMP) (THUMP)."

To be fair, a lot of this was Brad's interpretation of what Gracie was trying to communicate. Most of the sounds coming from her mouth weren't actual properly enunciated English words, but rather a series of feral grunts, moans, and slurps. But he was pretty sure he got the gist of it.

Brad stood very still, slack jawed, silently stunned. Never saw it coming. And now he could do nothing but let this tsunami of betrayal wash over him.

". . . and the florist (THUMP) (THUMP) (THUMP) who I thought was gay (THUMP) (THUMP) (THUMP) but really wasn't. I mean (THUMP) (THUMP) (THUMP) *reeeeally* wasn't (THUMP) (THUMP) (THUMP)."

Brad's cell phone started to vibrate. By the third ring it synched up with Gracie's thumping. Apparently the whole universe was in on the joke.

His right hand hit the answer button and held it next to his face. After a few moments, he moved his mouth enough to speak, although out of courtesy to his wife and the cable guy, he kept it to a whisper.

". . . Hello? . . . This is he . . . Oh, hi Geoff. What's—oh . . . Already? I thought you were going to bounce my portfolio across a few desks . . . Who did you hear that from?

"(THUMP) (THUMP) (THUMP) (THUMP) OH-GOD-OH-GOD-OH-GODDDD"

". . . It's trending on Twitter? . . . Yes, I know social media is forever. Is there any chance I could . . . ?"

"(THUMP) (THUMP) (THUMP) And the grocery delivery guy. (THUMP) (THUMP) (THUMP) And some bartender I met on Craigslist. (THUMP) (THUMP) (THUMP) Oh my God! (THUMP) (THUMP) (THUMP) This is the (THUMP) (THUMP) (THUMP) best sex I've (THUMP) had in hours."

As reality hammered itself into Brad's consciousness on so many levels, he pulled himself together long enough to whisper to Geoff, "I have to go. I'm a little busy right now. Thanks for calling . . ."

"(THUMP) I'll definitely (THUMP) be thinking about you (THUMP) the next time I force myself (THUMP) to have sex with my husband. (THUMP) (THUMP) (THUMP)."

Brad dropped the phone without hanging up.

"Oh . . . (*THUMP*) God . . . (*THUMP*) My . . . (*THUMP*) Marriage . . . (*THUMP*) Is . . . (*THUMP*) A . . . (*THUMP*) SHAMMMMMM-OHHHH-GODDDD!"

In his office, Geoff listened for a few more moments before nodding to himself, content that he had made the right decision after finding out about the vodka thing. Besides, who doesn't mute their porn when they answer the phone, for Pete's sake? Very unprofessional.

No sir, Fingerman just wasn't up to snuff.

Brad stood in the doorway for a few beats longer, not to enjoy what remained of the final bit of quality time he would ever spend with his wife, but to wrestle his ego into submission. This was it. The universe had given him what he thought was a buffet of opportunities but was in fact a confluence of ultimatums.

Waltzing toward a silver anniversary with Gracie. Out. Working as an advertising superstar or even a midlevel flunky in New York. Dunzo. Trying to live a normal life as Brad Fingerman, the guy who the Mafia probably wants to behead for what he may or may not have seen. Sorry, not happening.

Someone had declared checkmate in a game Brad had no idea he was even playing.

There was only one vine left.

The New Brad

"I saw it all."

Brad had been sitting in Brittany's office for half an hour before she came back from lunch. This dated, beige utilitarian workspace was all he had in the entire universe. His apartment was forever tainted by cable guy sex. Advertising had broken up with him without so much as a sort-of sincere *It's not you, it's me* speech. Chuck the ass manager most likely already had some brand new loser in Brad's chicken outfit. Brad was homeless. Physically and psychologically, simply untethered. So he sat and waited for Brittany, imagining her as his new best friend and tour guide for the world he was about to enter.

The time alone gave him an opportunity to try out a few clichés to help him get his bearings in this freshly minted reality.

I should have seen this coming.

Hmmm. Nope. Looking back there had been no signs of infidelity on Gracie's end. They talked. They laughed. They rarely fought. She leaned on him when times were tough. Their sex life was good. Certainly, if we're comparing individual scores, Brad's wasn't as good as Gracie's. But as a theoretically monogamous couple, there had been nothing terribly obvious to indicate she was looking for more than he could offer. From what he could tell, she adored him. The truth is he should not have seen this coming.

It's for the better.

Another swing and a miss. As devastated and angry as he was, Brad was still in love with Gracie. His opinion of her moral constitution had somewhat diminished, but there was no denying the attraction of soul mates and, even this far into the marriage, he still felt a bit of a tingle when she laughed at his jokes and kissed him before she got out of bed in the morning. Granted, he had grossly misinterpreted her devotion to both him and the institution of matrimony, but love is love, goddammit. It just happened to be buried at the moment by a dung pile of shame and self-pity. And once those faded, he was well aware that he would be left to deal with the raw nerves that had been exposed by infidelity. It was safe to say that a full and completely healthy recovery was a matter of years. Or decades. So, no. This was not for the better.

Whatever doesn't kill me makes me stronger.

Fair enough, but how strong did Brad care to get? He wasn't all too sure he wanted to increase his strength in the first place. And since he didn't have a choice in the matter, now what? So this emotional beat down was going to give him super strength. To do what? Take more beatings?

This is why Brad hated clichés.

"You saw it all?"

Just to be sure, Brittany asked him exactly what it was he was talking about.

"The murder or whatever. I saw it all. And I'll testify."

"What's going on, Brad?"

"I was scared of Frank Fortunato. Remember?" He mimicked Frank's I'm-going-to-get-you scowl. "So I lied. But now I'm ready to testify."

"Just like that?"

Well, no Brittany, not just like that. Let me tell you about the DIY Kama Sutra clinic I witnessed on my brand-new nine-hundred-thread-count sheets this afternoon. Or the sound of a recently flourishing career getting flushed down the toilet once and for all. Or how it feels to have to trust a complete stranger with the rest of your stupid life, because if you stay still too long Zeppo Corleone is going to stick something sharp through the soft spot on the back of your skull. Shaddup, you.

The just-like-that justifications were none of her G.D. business so Brad skipped ahead to the next action item on his agenda.

"Well, there's one thing."

"Uh-huh."

This was it, right? It had to be. If not this, where would he go? What could he hope for? An open marriage with the utility workers who service his apartment? A promotion to Senior Chicken Suit Guy? Do they sell bulletproof wigs? No, thanks.

"Tell me again about the Witness Protection Program."

Stump

"Did somebody call for a plumber?"
"Why yes, I really need some help cleaning my pipes."

The Facial Action Coding System was developed in 1976 by Paul Ekman and Wallace Friesen to taxonomize human facial expressions. The system defines and classifies various contractions or relaxations of one or more muscles of the face. These are called Action Units. There are thirty-two of them, and they can appear and be recognized in many different combinations. Today, the coding system is a standard tool employed by psychologists, detectives, and animators to dissect and understand human behavior, analyze emotions and, in the case of officers of the law, determine when persons of interest are lying.

Based on observations of her frontalis, pars lateralis, zygomaticus minor, and orbicularis oris, it was clear the woman on the monitor, despite her enthusiasm, was not telling the truth. There was no chance she had called for a plumber. For that matter, the plumber unzipping his pants in her doorway was no plumber at all. Look at his buccinator and his levator labii superioris. Ha! Fat chance.

Not that this was a shock. The video Christopher Stumberg had decided to study that night had been plucked from the Classic selection of the website that hosted it. Most of these were works of fiction, performed by terrible actors. But they made for interesting analysis. The site had a huge library of video and to really learn the Facial Action Coding System, you had to watch a lot of faces. The toughest reads were found in the Amateur section. There was almost never a story to them beyond a web cam accidentally left on, or someone

saying, "You're going to erase this afterward, right?" and the partici-
pants were generally happy to be involved, so there wasn't a lot of lying
to be found.

The actors in the classic videos were more of a challenge. They had
the subtleties of Facial Action Units down. Probably a subconscious
residual of a childhood surrounded by hustlers, junkies, and liars. He
was making assumptions here, but it seemed logical. There was a reason they got into porn.

Christopher backed up the footage about thirty seconds. Actually,
on closer inspection, while the lady of the house was lying about making the phone call to the plumber, she did appear to genuinely want
some help with her pipes. Interesting.

A hair over six foot three and roughly two hundred forty pounds,
Christopher Stumberg was a thick, muscular presence who had
become accustomed to answering to, appropriately enough, the name
"Stump."

Stump had played his college ball at Slippery Rock (tight end with
occasional punt-return duties), although the school's initial interest in
him had been for his state champion wrestling prowess. Despite offers
to try out for various teams in the NFL, Stump had decided to put his
honors degree in sociology to good use.

He was now a U.S. marshal inspector with fifteen years on the job
and a reputation for being an oddball with eccentric methods. He
was also considered to be one of the best marshals in the history of
the Witness Protection Program, so his quirky tactics tended to be
overlooked. Stump lived to make witnesses disappear, in a good way.
Mob turncoats, former molls, and ex-hit men could all thank Stump
for their new lives as anonymous accountants, nameless butchers, and
forgettable checkout clerks. He placed them all around the country
through his bizarre secret network of business contacts. And he had
never lost one.

There were records of where Stump's witnesses now lived, but they
were kept in a locked vault in a basement somewhere in Brooklyn. The
files were written in a code known to no more than a dozen people

with top security clearance. But the more efficient and reliable file system was deep in the back of Stump's brain. Off the top of his head he could tell you the new names, locations, and occupations of all one hundred and twenty-four witnesses he had placed during his tenure. He could. But he wouldn't.

Stump loved his job and never stopped trying to improve himself in an insatiable drive to become a better marshal. A student of nine different martial arts since the age of twelve, he balanced his warrior side with a rigorous study of Buddhism, knitting, cooking, and gardening. And, of course, the Facial Action Coding System.

His newest accomplishment was the mastery of Leonardo da Vinci's revolutionary polyphasic sleep routine—twenty minutes of power napping for every four hours awake. Stump slept under two hours a day. It was an amazingly effective and efficient lifestyle, and he now regarded the old saw about getting a good night's sleep as a cop-out for weaklings.

When the call from Brittany came, he was ready. Because Stump was always ready.

Brad, Stump.
Stump, Brad.

Brittany took Brad the long way to the conference room. As she'd hoped, Anfernee was not in his office when she had called to let him know her star witness had decided to cooperate. She left a message with the highlights and promised a full report soon. Rather than call his mobile phone, she opted to continue with Brad's debriefing. Anfernee would find her soon enough. If he didn't get her voice mail immediately, certainly word would spread around the office. Fellow agents were already congratulating and high-fiving her as she paraded Brad through the halls.

Her hope of hopes was to run into Anfernee on the way and casually reinforce her ownership of the case in a more public forum than his office. So much of the behind-the-scenes work of law enforcement was politics and showmanship. Naturally, Anfernee would start putting his fingerprints all over Brad (most likely by referring to himself by some stupid, obvious nickname) but the damage had been done. Everyone in the office that day knew she had landed the big one and Anfernee was nowhere to be found. As if that weren't enough, there was the anticipation of watching the news seep into Anfernee's skin in person. Mmmmm, delish.

"The Witness Protection Program is the premier relocation organization in the world. We've had over eight thousand witnesses in our system with a one hundred percent success rate."

"A hundred percent?"

"As long as you stay in our system and follow our program, nothing can happen to you."

"As long as I stay in your system. Does that mean that some people leave?"

"Yes. Some."

"What happens to them?"

"They usually die."

Brittany and Brad turned a corner to find a very secure door. Brittany waved her ID across a sensor at the side, a beep rang, sounding like the bell signaling the beginning of the next stage of her life, and swept her arm toward the door.

"Shall we?"

Somewhere on the other side of the building, Anfernee finally returned from lunch and checked his voice mail. After the message confirming his five thirty massage, and before the call from his mother wondering if he tried her lemon quinoa recipe, was the call from Brittany—*Project Fancypants* had been a success. This was good. A nice bullet point for the old résumé. Hello Mr. Tailor of *Project Fancypants*.

Anfernee erased the message and pulled the printed version of Brittany's proposal from his bottom left drawer. He signed the blank line marked "Approved" and put last week's date next to it before sliding the paperwork into a manila envelope marked "Confidential." He dropped the envelope in his out box and yelled to his assistant.

"Candice! Why didn't this go out yet?"

Brittany and Brad entered the conference room to find Stump already waiting for them.

"Brad Fingerman, I'd like you to meet your new best friend, U.S. Marshal Inspector Christopher Stumberg. Stump."

Stump was silent. Not because he was shy. He just didn't see the point in idle conversation. This, combined with his natural instinct to constantly observe and be aware of his surroundings, caused him to come across as downright deadpan. He located Brad's corrugator supercilii, orbicularis oculi, and pars palpebralis and waited for him to speak.

"Uh, nice to meet you?"

Brad stuck out his hand. Stump moved to shake it, then grabbed Brad's wrist in a vice-like lock.

"Dude—!" was all Brad could get out before his body snapped to the left to accommodate Stump's expert manipulation. Stump whipped Brad around, placed his foot on the back of Brad's knee, and pushed slightly to crumple him into complete submission.

Brad managed to look up and wheeze at Brittany.

"You're okay with this?"

Actually she was.

"Stump is a little unorthodox. But I trust him with my life. And my back. Do you mind?"

She turned away from the mugging in front of her. Stump released Brad and stepped up to bear hug Brittany.

"You ready?"

She nodded, and Stump lifted up as he squeezed. Brittany's back cracked in a series of muffled pops.

"Ahhh. You are good."

Brad stood and rubbed his elbow as he stared incredulously at Stump.

"This is protecting me? You could have broken my arm."

"But I didn't."

"But . . ."

"In fact, you're not even hurt at all."

"Well . . ."

"I'm pretty sure you got a nice realignment out of that too, didn't you?"

Brad rolled his back. It did feel better.

"'Kay. But what was the point?"

"You need to trust me. So you need to know what I'm capable of. Anyone gets near you, I can do far worse than that."

"All right, but no more chop sockey on me. You made your point. For the record, *I believe you can kill me.* Okay?"

Stump grinned.

"Great."

It was all part of Stump's system. Not everyone got the thrown-down-how-do-you-do handshake. Stump adapted his program to the client. In this case, he sensed the tiniest bit of arrogance in Brad's gait. No point in letting that gain any traction.

Stump had no interest in being Brad's friend. That wasn't his job. His job was to protect a government witness. And to do that, he couldn't have Brad second-guessing him. He had to appear to know more about keeping Brad alive than Brad did. And if that meant instilling in Brad a profound fear that his own bodyguard was capable of killing him, then that's what had to happen. Also it was kind of fun.

With alpha dog now firmly established, Brittany moved forward.

"Let's start the paperwork."

Brittany and Brad sat at the long conference table, while Stump stood watching. Despite the fact that they were in a secure room in FBI offices, Stump was on full alert. Sunglasses on. Knees slightly bent. Breathing regulated. He could stand for hours and God help the man who entered the room without knocking first. Even Brad was careful not to make any furtive movements, sipping his Pepsi nice and easy.

Brittany clicked her pen and got down to brass tacks. "So, here's the story. You're going to disappear. You're leaving your life behind today and starting over completely."

Brad nodded. Fine with him.

"Now it's customary to bring along a wife, girlfriend . . ."

"Both."

That was Stump's favorite joke. Brittany continued.

". . . both if you must. Children or anyone else who might be important to you. Of course they'll have to abide by the same rules you do, and as you might imagine it can be very hard on a marriage to start over as someone else. We do provide counseling to help you through the rocky parts if you need it. Or if you're free and clear, we bring you in alone."

As Brittany spoke, Brad flashed through the events that brought him back to her office this afternoon. He was a Mafia-targeted, chicken costume wearing, fast food restaurant flier distribution technician who had blown a huge interview for the only job in town before walking in on his wife banging the bejeezus out of a complete stranger. Brad realized he was dealing with the anxiety of these memories by twirling the gold band around his left ring finger and eased it off his hand like a tipsy salesman in the middle of a lap dance. He slipped it into his pocket, and felt his finger sans wedding ring. Better.

Brittany wrapped her speech up.

"So, anyone you might want to join you in this new life?"

"Do I have to bring someone?"

"No. But if you don't, you won't be allowed to see them again."

"Ever?"

"Ever."

Brad didn't hesitate.

"Nope. No one. I'm free."

"Great then."

She scribbled a few lines in Brad's file.

"No family to move. That certainly makes things easy. So if you'll sign here, we can get you out of here."

She turned his file around and slid it across the table to him with a pen. Brad raised his eyebrows, unsure of what to make of this paper.

"It's an agreement between you and the government stating that in exchange for a new identity, a lifetime of protection, and a guarantee of safety, you agree to testify in a court of law about what you saw in the elevator with Carmine Mastramouro. We can fill in the details from that day once we get you situated."

"A contract?"

"You could call it that."

"Shouldn't I have a lawyer look at this or something?"

The answer was yes. Any reasonable person would have told Brad to seek the advice of counsel. Except for the fact that there was a ticking clock in the form of Frank Fortunato and his legion of soldiers that may or may not know who and where Brad was at that moment.

"Of course you're welcome to have an attorney look this over, but Brad, you're helping us out. Do you really think we're trying to screw you?"

Truth be told, the contract was little more than a trophy for Brittany to show her superiors. If she could have had a life-size replica of Brad stuffed and mounted on her office wall she would have done that, but most likely that wouldn't fly with FBI office regulations. Instead, there was this piece of paper. There were equal chances it would be filed with the main office or pasted into her scrapbook of work memorabilia. It served mostly as a symbolic gesture between two mutually dependent entities. Like small talk with a hooker. Most Johns don't really care about the recent cold snap; they just want to establish that neither party in the transaction is a psycho while they park their sedan behind the Winn Dixie.

If Brad decided he didn't want to testify after he signed the contract, there was very little they could do. Drop the protection. Walk away. But that was about it. They had no leverage to make him testify. And if he didn't say anything in court, Brad didn't need protection anyway. He was in the driver's seat. And once the trial was done, as far as Brittany was concerned, Brad could spend his life on a beach somewhere pissing away the government's money on rum drinks and foot rubs. As long as she got what she wanted.

Come on and sign, motherfucker.

Brad stared at the blank signature line. There was always counseling, right? Didn't Gracie recommend that to her clients before they divorced? Probably not, but it seemed reasonable. Just to make sure no stone was left unturned. Didn't couples go through stuff like this all the time and survive? Rough patches. Rocky spots. Spats. Didn't he owe her at least that much? They were married, for heaven's sake. On top of that, Brad knew he was a talented guy. The vodka thing would blow over eventually, no? He wasn't always going to be in a chicken suit. Things had to change. They had to. If he just kept his head up and his nose to the grindst . . .

Fuck it. Brad looked up.

"Can I say goodbye to one person?"

Brittany looked to Stump who nodded almost imperceptibly, as if he'd been waiting for the question.

"Okay, but we're going with you."

Brad had no idea where this vine was headed. But even if he ended up faceplanting into a massive sequoia, it had to be better than where he was now.

Brad wrote his signature on the contract and it was done.

Brad Packs Up

Brad called ahead to make sure his wife wasn't still home and there would be no strange workmen servicing his, err, apartment. Gracie was not the one person he was interested in saying goodbye to. But his clothes and PlayStation weren't going to pack themselves.

There was no answer at the apartment, so he called her cell phone. When she picked up, he heard the sounds of the street. It sounded like she was out, so he hung up. She was usually headed to spinning right about now. Or maybe to sleep with the Knicks. She had one of those flexible schedules.

"All right."

This time James didn't give Brad the crazy eye. Just the usual I'm-clocked-in-until-six-whether-you-need-me-or-not greeting, as if everything had been a dream or somehow forgotten. Brad couldn't help but wonder how many Gracie-and-cable-guy type of hookups James was aware of. Must have been dozens. Brad couldn't be the only one getting cuckolded here, right? It's a big city. This was a big building. Twenty-five floors of opportunity. His mind reeled with the possibilities. And who knows what James thought of Brad walking in with a stiff like Brittany and a stallion like Stump. Did Brad now have the stink of adultery by association? Was it just another day at the office for James? Infidelity another delivery to be signed for?

Brad stepped over to ask his doorman who else was getting their cable upgraded on a regular basis, but James cut him off with some rote politeness.

"Yes, sir. Nice weather, isn't it? Can I get you a cab?"

"I just walked in."

"All right."

Brad held his gaze on James for a beat, but the guy kept looking out to the street like a fully realized idiot. Those secrets were going to the grave with him.

"Is my wife still here?"

"Oh, no sir. She left about an hour ago. Looked like she was headed to the gym."

"Uh-huh. Thanks."

Brad headed for the elevator.

"Oh, and congratulations Mr. Fingerman. She said you finally got HBO. She seemed thrilled."

Stump and Brittany waited in the lobby to give Brad the last bit of privacy he would enjoy for a long time. There was virtually no chance Frank could have figured out Brad's address yet, and Brad would be inside on a high floor for a brief amount of time, so this tiny breach could be allowed.

Brad walked into his apartment to find it exactly as he left it this morning. The bed was made. The dishes were done. The view was fabulous. It still smelled a little like sex. So maybe not exactly as he left it this morning.

He went to the bedroom closet, ripped a suitcase from the back of his top shelf and tossed it on the bed. He pulled every piece of clothing he had out of his closet and threw the pile into the open suitcase, hangers and all, like he'd seen in the movies so many times. Then he took them all out and removed the hangers. No way was that ever going to fit.

Surrounded by the pictures and knickknacks that were now essentially memorabilia from his life with Gracie, he couldn't help drifting back into a few fond memories. Their trip to Carmel. Skiing at Big Bear. That one summer they rented the house in the Hamptons and the gardener kept showing up to trim the same hedges every time Brad went for a jog on the beach. Wait. Dammit!

Brad stormed into the bathroom and dumped all of his toiletries into a Dopp kit. He caught a glimpse of himself in the mirror and realized he was crying. He was going to miss this life he and Gracie shared together. Aside from her revolving door of a vagina, it had been pretty nice. They got along pretty good for people who had been married for five years. They laughed at the same jokes, tended to like the same desserts, and both passionately hated Salma Hayek's ridiculous accent. Really, aside from the whole vegan thing and her having relations with a high percentage of TV's most coveted demographic behind his back, there weren't any real problems. Such a shame.

Brad's thoughts were interrupted by the buzz of the doorman's phone. James was calling up. Uh-oh. Was this the heads up that Gracie was on her way back up? Did James have Brad's back? Had Brad misjudged him?

"Hello?"

"Your friend says you got to go."

"Stump?"

"Excuse me?"

"The big guy I came in with."

"That's him. He says you have to go."

"Tell him I'll be right down."

Brad took a moment to compose himself. He should leave a note. Be the bigger person, or at least mitigate the cowardly act of running away with some sort of explanation. That way she wouldn't have to sneak around anymore. If nothing else, Brad was thoughtful.

He grabbed a pen and a few slips of the *Brad and Gracie* stationery her brother always gave them for Christmas. No point in conserving that anymore.

Dear Gracie . . . Nope, too soft.

You filthy whore . . . Mm-mm. Needs to build.

Gracie, I realize I haven't given you what you need to be fulfilled in your life. I'm sorry to say that it's probably best for both of us if we go our separate ways. I am moving on to a new path and only hope you can someday find the happiness you are looking

for. Thanks for the good times, Brad.

He carefully folded the note in half, wrote her name on the front
and tucked a corner of it under the vase of tulips by the door. Then he
pulled it right back, ripped it up, and used one of her most expensive
lipsticks to leave a note on the mirror.

G—

Yes, those white pants make your ass look fat.

—B

Brad left his keys on the dresser, grabbed his suitcase, and walked
out the front door. When the elevator finally came, Brad stood and
stared long enough for it to close without him. Then he hit the Up
button. The same door opened again and he got in. Maybe there was
one last option.

The great thing about the roof deck that Brad's building bragged so
much about in their *Sunday Times* ads was the three-hundred-sixty-
degree view. You could see for miles from up there. There was one
building across the street, but it was about two stories lower than his
so it didn't interfere too much. The other great thing was the access one
had to the edge. A twenty-five-story view straight down. It was beautiful in a way that most people would never see because they would
never stand on the rail like Brad was right then.

His thinking was that maybe there was a clean solution to this,
after all. Brad would simultaneously remove himself from several situations where he clearly wasn't wanted, and he wouldn't be wasting
anyone's time by lying about what he saw in that elevator. On some
level it made sense. It wasn't the East River swallowing him up like
he had envisioned so many times, but the results would be essentially

the same, if a little messier. It felt right. More right than when he pretended from the safety of the bench that he was doing it. The river was for posers. This was the real deal. He might even make the *Post*. Yes, there were definitely pros to this plan. The cons were obvious, but in Brad's current swirling fog of emotion, it was unclear which side outweighed the other. If only there was some way to know for sure.

It would have been so awesome if he had a super-smart dog that ran up and started yanking at his pant leg with his teeth, or a plucky neighbor kid said something cute and/or clever to stop him from jumping, but those were relationships that he had never formed. It was Brad alone standing on the ledge, thinking about what would happen if he took one big step forward. He looked down again. Yup. Still way high. Aside from Stump and Brittany, who would notice he was gone? Frank? He would probably have his men put a few bullets in Brad's flat body anyway, just to make a point. Gracie? It didn't seem like a stretch to assume she would get over it pretty easily. Would anyone really care that this nobody with nothing had jumped?

Something in one of the apartment windows of the slightly shorter building across the street caught Brad's eye. It was a shirtless man waving furiously at him.

Wow. Maybe someone did care.

The man raised his eyebrows as high as he could get them and held up a finger to say *Hold on one second*. Brad looked around to make sure he was the intended recipient of the message. It appeared he was. He nodded his agreement. Did this perfect stranger have some insight into Brad's turmoil and confusion? Perhaps even been in his situation before? Could it be that someone who didn't even know him actually gave a shit?

Window Man smiled and ran off. *Calling the cops? Rushing over to my building to talk me down himself? Checking the Internet to see how to handle this emergency?*

Nope. Not at all.

Window Man came back into his window stripped completely naked. He had a raging hard on and began pleasuring himself like an Amish butter churner working a Shake Weight. Again with the eyebrows, only this time they seemed to be saying, *Now, wasn't this worth the wait? Huh? Right?*

While it wasn't exactly the warm nose of a trusty companion nuzzling his ankles or the adorable voice of a newsboy-capped ragamuffin asking *Hey mister, whatcha doing?*, it did gross Brad out enough to shake him from his suicidal fugue state. He might need to rethink this.

True, the choice to grab the vine that went straight down would be his and his alone, influenced by no one. He would own it. But ultimately, it was tough to justify the control-affirming aspect of it with the end result. Death by homoerotic suicide or the Witness Protection Program? While the latter was intimidating in its potential for a lackluster future, the former would not be treated kindly by the *Post*. Also, Brad would be dead.

Shit.

Brad hopped off the ledge and backed away from the option that wasn't really an option. Window Man was devastated, pleading with the one finger to *wait-wait-wait*. It seemed that something exciting was about to happen, but Brad decided not to stick around for the big finale.

Stump fired up the dark, American-made sedan illegally parked in front of the building and Brittany watched the street as James held the passenger door open.

"James, if you see my wife, tell her I left. And I'm never coming back. And I know there's no such thing as spontaneous herpes."

James considered Brad with the eyes of a man who had seen this too many times before.

"All right."

"Breasts. Two for a dollar."

"In your dreams, sicko."

Owen probably should have seen that one coming. He hadn't meant for today's coupon to sound like a sale inside this passing woman's blouse. Chicken breasts really were the special of the day, and they were being sold in pairs. It was Chuck's idea and it had not struck him that there was anything inappropriate in his marketing strategy. Chuck only knew he had ordered too many chicken breasts and had to unload them pronto.

Stump's government-issue ride pulled up to the curb in front of the fire hydrant and idled. Owen checked his reflection in its tinted windows. Oh yeah, still a very handsome chicken if he didn't mind saying so himself. He went back to work.

"*Chicken* breasts. Two for a dollar."

Stump got out and walked around the car to the sidewalk. Owen held out a flier.

"Wing wangs are on sale today, too."

Stump ignored him and looked around to make sure the coast was clear before signaling to the car.

The back window of the sedan rolled down a crack.

"*Owen!*" came the harsh whisper from the back seat.

Subtleties of speech tend to be lost on people in chicken suits and whispering can be especially tricky. You generally have to be in a position where they can actually see you whisper. Owen looked around and whisper-yelled back.

"*Hello?*"

"*Owen, over here!*"

Again, not much help if your ears are inside a large chicken head and therefore incapable of triangulating voice origins.

Brad rolled the window down a few more inches.

"In the car, Owen!" he half-yelled.

Owen turned his chicken suit around to look at the car.

"Brad?"

Brad leaned into the sunlight for a brief second. The giant chicken did a quick double take.

"Hey man, you're late for work."

Brad motioned him over. Owen walked over and leaned in.

"What are you doing? I told Chuck you were probably just sick, but if he sees you in this car he might not believe me anymore."

"Owen, I'm leaving."

The meeting was not going as Brittany envisioned it. In her perfect world, Brad's friend would not have been dressed like a big, bright junior-college mascot and standing next to their car in the middle of a crowded Manhattan sidewalk. She tried to roll the window up.

"Brad, this wasn't a good idea. We're going to have to cut this short."

"I want to say goodbye. That was part of our deal."

Brittany sighed and hopped out of the car. She caught Stump's eyes and indicated the chicken. Stump looked Chickenman over quickly and decided that he could easily snap his neck through the car window, if necessary. He stood behind Owen. Brittany quickly flashed her badge to the chicken's mouth and opened Brad's door.

"FBI. Get in the car."

"Is this about that website? Because my friend said it was okay to use his password."

"Please get in the car, sir."

There was a bit of cramming, but Owen somehow wedged himself into the back seat. He waited until he was all the way in to take his chicken head off. Brittany and Stump stood guard outside.

It took a few seconds before his eyes adjusted to the light, but when they did Owen brightened visibly.

"Wow! Is this your new job? Your interview must have gone awesome."

"Owen, did you hear that Frank Fortunato got arrested for murder?"

"No."

Brad quickly went over the high and low points of his day, finishing with his plans to testify, but leaving out the minor detail that he, in fact, saw nothing.

"Wow. Congratulations."

"On what?"

"On doing the right thing. Man, that takes guts."

"Yeah. Thanks."

"What about Gracie?"

"Oh, um. She's fine with it. You know, wants me to do the right thing."

Owen let out a long whistle. "Well, good luck."

That summed it up pretty well. Brad looked at Owen and realized that this really was the end of his life as he knew it. No more chicken suits. No more Gracie. No more pretentious ad friends. No more hoping he could fix it all before anyone noticed. It was over. And the best that anyone could do was say, *Well, good luck.*

They shook hands and Owen shoved his chicken head back on. He somehow got back out of the car without breaking character. Instead he looked like an important chicken arriving at the Chicken Shack. That had to be good for business.

Stump and Brittany got back into the car. Brad leaned over and rolled down the window.

"And Owen, good luck on your bailiff test."

The chicken on the sidewalk gave Brad a big thumbs up and then waved goodbye.

The safe house was a modest affair in Jackson Heights. The plan was to stay there under Stump's vigilant watch until arrangements had been made for Brad's new life in AnywhereButHere, U.S.A. Fine with Brad. The newness of everything was still sort of exciting if a little unsettling. This was an adventure. Kind of like hitting Shuffle on your iPod before a run in the park, hoping to God Celine Dion doesn't play, but knowing that if she does you'll deal with it. They pulled into the single car garage and closed the door behind them.

Stump instructed Brad to stay in the car under Brittany's protection while he took a look around this perfectly secure home to placate his compulsive need to protect. Brittany couldn't take the silence.

"Well, this is exciting, isn't it?"

"The Mafia putting a price on my head?"

"Doing something for the American people. Something meaningful. Making a difference."

Brad was not buying what she was selling.

"At least it's probably a high price. That's got to make you feel special."

One of the many things Brad did not like about himself was his name. Brad Fingerman. He had never felt like a Fingerman anyway. It connoted a career spent as a substitute teacher. It was more likely to be the third from the last name in a footnote of a medical journal than topping a movie poster. It was not memorable for any of the reasons one would want a name to be remembered.

One sentence that was never heard in good company was, *Oh, Fingerman? Of the Upper East Side Fingermans?* No, Fingerman was more of a saddle on which bullies, hecklers, and jokesters rode various word-plays amusing to all but the owner of the name. Finger-me. Finger-fuck. Man finger. Oh, it was good times in middle school.

So yes, Brad had always wanted to change his name, but it was never really a viable option, much less a pressing necessity. Until now.

This was his opportunity to do something big. To really cross something off his "Stuff to Change about Myself" list. Part of the Witness Protection Program entry process was the selection of a new name. Brittany had mentioned it when she first offered up the program. When he remembered it on the way to the safe house, the thought quickly nestled itself in the forefront of Brad's mind, and he begin trying various combinations out on an imaginary theater marquee.

Mike Blackstone. Jake Schwartzenstallone. Brock Granite. He would have to walk the fine line between action star and porn actor, but Brad was confident he could pull it off. It was like a whole world opening up to him.

That night, after Brittany had left and Stump had cleared the entire house, yet again, Brad lay in a strange new bed on the verge of sleep, vacillating between thinking thoughts like *Holy God, what have I done?* and dreaming up awesome new names that girls would totally go for.

The wedding ring he had slipped off during his contract negotiation with Brittany sat on the dresser next to his watch. He had pulled it out when he undressed but hadn't quite figured out if he should throw it into the kitchen disposal and be done with it or have it melted down and recast as a keychain. He had decided to figure that out later.

Brad was exhausted.

The Fortunato Thing

"How many times do I have to tell you people, *the low-fat raspberry vinaigrette is mine*. I wrote my name on it and it is the height of inconsiderate behavior to use it without asking. That's called theft. You know in Arabia, they would cut your hands off for that."

As usual, the eyes of Malcolm Middleton's fellow coworkers found something else to look at while he made his indignant speech. Everyone in the break room was by quiet default pleading innocent. Well, that was highly unlikely. Someone must have used the newly opened salad dressing without asking. It didn't crawl out of the bottle on its own. This is exactly why he insisted on locking his door whenever he left his office. Even to go to the bathroom. You couldn't trust anyone around there.

Malcolm shook it off and got ready for another day of the job he loved. Say what you will about his sticky-fingered coworkers and the disrespect they showed for his personal items, Malcolm wasn't going anywhere.

"Middleton, I'm going to give you Fortunato."

"Okay."

"*Okay?* That's it? This is a career-making decision. You're going to be a legend around here after this. And you're just . . . *Okay?*"

"If it's so important, why give it to me?"

"Look, don't turn this into a thing. It's an important case and I want you to act professional. Keep things moving. Okay?"

"Okay, but you didn't answer my question. Why me?"

The room was quiet as Malcolm's boss considered the answer he would give to the one question he had really hoped Malcolm wouldn't ask. He decided to be honest.

"You're the only one who's free."

Malcolm Middleton was a federal judge. In theory, with his experience, he could have taken a high-paying job in a New York City law firm. Except that no one would have hired him. As a lawyer, he simply wasn't aggressive enough. He was smart. He had a deep understanding of and profound respect for the law. But he was a thinker. An über-thinker. He enjoyed the process of thinking. Not the pushy type of questioning found in so many overly thoughtful people, but a pure and deep curiosity about absolutely everything. For Malcolm, examining both sides to the point of exhaustion before saying yay or nay was good sport regardless of whether it was a debate concerning the morality of the death penalty or a question of supersizing his fries. And it generally took him fucking forever to make a decision.

So it was a bit of a relief for both him and Malcolm Middleton Sr.'s entire law firm when his father landed him a job as a federal judge through his network of powerful and influential friends.

Sitting at the front of a courtroom, listening to shark lawyers pick every piece of meat off a legal bone was pure heaven for Malcolm. Their job was to think things over to the point of absurdity. His was to enjoy the process and decide the winner based on the overwrought facts.

For the last twenty-two years, Malcolm had made quite a name for himself as a judge. The judge who would entertain just about every fool motion your overpaid lawyer could dream up. Yes, Malcolm was very popular with that type.

So he had listened to the arguments from both sides of Frank Fortunato's case on whether or not Frank should be allowed to leave jail before the trial. They ranged from logical (*He's a known gangster* versus *He's a devoted family man with ties to the community*) to the outright emotional (*He killed a man in cold blood!* versus *It's his birthday!*). Malcolm considered them all.

While most bail hearings took no more than an hour all in, Frank's took the better part of the day, thanks to Malcolm's unrelenting curiosity. Where did Frank live? Does he have a passport? What kind of ties to the community are we talking about? Is there a party planned? Who's invited?

In the end he decided that the reasons for keeping him in jail (one, he's a suspected murderer with a record longer than one of those pythons they find every two years in a Queens bathroom, and two, there's an eyewitness and surveillance footage) outweighed the reasons for setting a reasonable bail (one, his mother swears he's a good boy, and two, he buys fireworks for the kids in the neighborhood on the Fourth of July). But barely.

The Secret Life of Stump

First came the power nap. As soon as Brad passed out for the night, Stump lay flat on his back in his bed and hauled ass to sleep. Because of his unorthodox sleeping pattern, it never took more than thirty seconds to start the sleep process, followed soon after by REM sleep. As long as he followed his polyphasic routine, he didn't need more than two hours of sleep a day. That was the way da Vinci did it. That was the way Thomas Jefferson did it. That was the way he did it. Which gave him an extra six hours to accomplish all the things normal people complain they don't have time for. He had been at it for three weeks now and so far it was serving him well.

When he woke up twenty minutes later, it was time for yoga. Stretching. Sweating. A little grunting. It usually lasted about a half hour. Then there was another half an hour of jumping rope followed by another hour of pushups, pull-ups, and crunches mixed with a collection of martial arts katas to keep his fighting skills razor sharp. He cooled down with some deep transcendental meditation, showered, shaved, and spent the rest of his free time catching up on his reading, cleaning the house, returning e-mails, and finishing his night/morning with a second twenty-minute power nap well before the rest of America, or in this case, Brad, rubbed the sleep out of their eyes.

Brad finally got up and shuffled to the kitchen to see if coffee was one of the perks of the program. It was. He poured himself a cup and turned to find the door to the room filled with Stump, standing guard in the same position he had been in when Brad retired the night before. New suit, same position.

"Special Agent Marinakos will be here in half an hour."

Brad X

Brittany sat with Brad to fill out some paperwork to submit to the department that fabricated identities. She started with his name.

"Fingerman. What is that, Irish?"

Brad's mother was vaguely Italian and his father was a strain of German, with Fingerman being an Ellis Island clerk's bastardization of a family name a century before. His parents had never thought to ask and all four grandparents were dead, so finding out the original name or its origins was no longer an option.

But, it didn't really matter. If the truth were to be told, the Fingerman line of ancestry could have been classified as Ikea-American. A pressboard background of empty lineage stretching back several generations, his heritage had been rendered meaningless as his family had long ago assimilated into the prefab lifestyle of the United States. His parents weren't Italian-American or German-American. They were American-Americans. No accents. No leftover traditions from the old country. No treasured heritage carefully preserved in rituals and holidays. They forged their life out of materials conceived in conference rooms and refined with target demo research, test results, and focus groups. Certainly they considered themselves individuals, but in fact their lives had been compilations of items selected from a finite pool of products offered to the American public by calculating conglomerates that had determined the lowest common denominator to the fifteenth degree. The Fingermans were generic. Arguably tasteful, but nothing special. Ikea-Americans. And Brad was their son.

"It's German, Italian, English, French. You know, American."

Brittany made a note on a form.

"All right. That gives us plenty of wiggle room. We like to give witnesses names that have some thread of reality to them. Like we're not going to call an Asian guy Chang Baumgartner, that kind of thing."

Jackpot. Maybe with a little quick thinking he could convince Brittany that somewhere along the line in his ancestry there was a Sven Ahssccikerr or an Andre Riflemann. Something that would make sense with a guy like him.

"Smart. You know, I was thinking about names last night and—"

"Brad, don't even think about giving yourself your own butch new handle. It doesn't work that way. We'll assign one to you. And you're going to keep your first name. If we change that it becomes too risky. You might not answer to the new one and people will start to wonder. It's safer to stick with Brad."

Brad's brain rolled its eyes.

"Your last name will be generated randomly by Witness Protection Program software from a database of the most common American names."

"Like Bronson or Damon?"

"Like Jones or Smith. The program will use an algorithm to determine, based on where we locate you, your ethnic background, and the local population, what the least obtrusive name is. It's easier to do it this way so that all legal documents—birth certificate, social security card, driver's license, credit report, et cetera can be generated at one time. Poof! Instant new identity."

Poof! Goodbye Brock Granite. Hello Brad Yawnberg.

They moved on to employment. In most cases, witnesses were kept in holding patterns during the trial and then released into the wild of their new lives once the trial was over. But Brad's was not most cases. It was a humongous case in which many millions of dollars would be spent on lawyers by the defendant to, at the very least, tie the prosecution up with motions and tests and whatever else Frank Fortunato's money could buy. Brittany explained Brad's new situation.

"All right, here's the deal. The trial could take months, if not years, and you probably don't want to be sitting around waiting. So in the meantime we need to get you set up in your new life. What do you do for work right now?"

"I'm in advertising."

Rather than go into the finer points of his current job, Brad walked her through his job history (minus the Chicken Shack and tequila shots) with very little embellishment.

Brittany took copious notes and slid them into Brad's file for Stump to look over.

"Okay. Stump has a lot of friendly relationships with various companies around the country. He'll see what he can dig up for you, take you wherever you need to go, and get you set up. I'll check on you as the trial preparation proceeds."

"Great."

"Now, let's go over exactly what you saw yesterday."

Not great. Brad had been too busy figuring out his new marquee-worthy name to think up a decent story about what he had seen. "A pair of black shoes walked into the fuzzy periphery of my vision, shot Carmine, and then ran off . . . I think" would not have done the job. In fact, it would have probably left him high and dry in Jackson Heights without so much as cab fare. So he lied.

"Can we do it later? I'm really exhausted. You know, psychologically."

Brittany nodded. She understood. The poor guy had been through a lot in the last twenty-four hours. Besides, she had him now. One day wouldn't hurt anything.

"Sure. I'll come back tomorrow morning and we can talk."

As Brittany packed her files up, Brad noticed Stump standing quietly in a doorway watching them. How long had he been standing there and why the hell didn't that guy ever say anything? This is the person he was supposed to trust his life to, and he couldn't tell if Stump was sussing him out as a gutless coward or developing a severe man crush. It was disturbing. The safe bet was on Stump seeing right through his homina-homina-homina bullshit. Brad would have to watch his step around Stump, which would be every waking moment for who knew how long.

Like he didn't have enough to worry about.

Brad spent the day trying to distract himself with History Channel reruns and spent the night pacing in his room while re-creating the murder scene in his mind. Inevitably, every replay ended up looking like some poorly shot assassination film. Every detail crystal clear until the moment of truth when the camera holder forgot their primary responsibility and let the lens drift away to some random scenery that had nothing to do with the action. And no matter how often he rewound the film, the same mistake occurred. But he kept rewinding anyway.

There was the amazing interview. The elevator. Carmine standing there. Carmine ignoring Brad. The scuff mark. That goddamned scuff mark. The sneeze. And then Carmine again. He rewound and tried to focus on a different detail. The song playing in the elevator. The color of the carpet. What frigging floor did we stop on for the murder? He tried to slow down the sneeze and go frame by frame. Nothing helped. Eventually, Brad fell asleep.

His intense mental re-creations had left a sour residue on Brad's psyche and the reenactments bled into his dreams, serving up wall-to-wall nightmares of a very angry Frank Fortunato. Having never paid much attention to the papers and only seeing Frank live in person the one time while they were both in cuffs, Brad didn't have a firm grip on the exact topography of Frank's face. So his brain substituted his junior high school baseball coach's face as a placeholder in the dreams. They were completely different men, but the impression was just as scary. In the morning, Brad stayed in bed for a good ten minutes trying to shake the feeling of impending doom and reminding himself to hit the cut-off man, you pansy.

Brad's shower went a little long since he spent most of it trying to figure out what he was going to say to Brittany. Goddamn, he hated deadlines. The more he struggled to remember some relevant nugget of information, the angrier he got, first at himself for not being more aware of his surroundings, and then gradually his ire shifted toward Brittany. After all, he was the one who went through the traumatizing experience. Not her. Nobody was trying to hunt her down and turn her into a hilarious story told over fettuccini and gravy. She wasn't even there.

She wasn't even there.

Well, hello. It had taken a while, but it had finally occurred to Brad that he was the only person who (in theory) actually knew what had happened in that elevator. He had been so worried about getting it right, he had forgotten that there was no getting it wrong. Everyone already knew the beginning and the ending. All he had to do was fill in the middle.

With anything.

It didn't matter what he told Brittany as long as it was something she could use to put Frank Fortunato behind bars. He couldn't claim there were aliens or showgirls in the elevator, but perhaps some interesting dialogue and a heroic stance on his part wouldn't be out of the question. He just had to lie.

You're in advertising, man! Since when do you tell the truth?

This would be part of his reinvention. His chance to lay the foundation of his future self by creating some macho, confident, in-control character. Someone exactly unlike who he currently was. Perfect. He would give himself a fantastic backstory. Maybe he couldn't choose his own name, but by God this instant mythology would give him a huge step up in his new life.

Like magic, Brad transformed from naked, wet, cowardly informant into naked, wet, and confident storyteller. This is what he *did*. Only instead of cornflakes he was selling murder. *Five shots to the gut! Now with more fiber!* If he could sell tampons and action figures, certainly he could figure out an interesting punch for the setup that was already written for him. All he had to do was finish the script. Couldn't be that hard. He had been carrying his partners for years. Everyone knew the words were the easy part.

Brad turned the steam up and walked through the scenario one more time, only this time acting as his own Jerry Della Femina and Quentin Tarantino wrapped up in one. Quentin Della Femina. He accented it with Jason Statham-esque dialogue, hip, obscure references, and vintage Costner bravery, painting himself in a valiant and pop-culturally relevant light. Yes, this was quite a brand Brad was selling.

And it was easier than he thought. After all, he had seen Frank being escorted out of the building so he knew what the killer was wearing. He had heard Frank cursing the FBI so he had an idea of his accent and speech pattern. And he understood a mainstream audience well enough to pepper the scene with tough but sensitive dialogue that betrayed both a constitution of iron and a heart of gold, shielded by his imaginary forty-two-inch pecs. He debated throwing in a *We can do this the easy way or the hard way, Frank; it's up to you* or *Give me the gun, Frank. I can help you if you let me*, eventually settling on something he heard in a tiny independent Korean film Owen had lent him the week before. And suddenly he had himself a real Aww-shucks/Holy Shit version of the truth. In fact, the more he thought about it, the happier he got. This was exactly what Brad had wanted when he took the FBI up on their generous offer. A complete reinvention. And maybe a screenplay deal. Fuck painting. Screenplays were where the money was.

He was headed to a new city and a new job with a new last name. And now, a new brand of Brad. A Brad with a solid foundation of poise and memorable lines. Like the old Brad, but better. The new and improved Brad. He got a hard-on just thinking about it. Now all he had to do was sell it (the fantasy, not the erection) to Brittany.

Brad Fibs

"You feel better after a little rest?"

"Much. Thanks for the break."

"You got it."

Brittany dropped her stack of Fortunato folders on the dining room table, sat down, and flipped open her notebook.

"Let's get started."

Brad joined her, nervous like she was contagious with some sort of truth-telling cooties.

"So, it's just me, huh? That's a lot of pressure. Isn't there anyone else who can help out?"

"Well, we've got witnesses who are coming forward claiming they heard Frank threaten Carmine and agents who witnessed him on the way there, but as far as murder eyewitnesses, I didn't see anyone else in that elevator. Did you?"

His first test.

"No."

"Of course we had cameras all over the building, the hallways, the elevator."

Uh oh.

They had cameras. Why wouldn't they have had cameras? And why hadn't he thought of this? Suddenly Clint Eastwood Jr. was spinning out of control, his mind reeling as he backpedaled internally. Toss the brilliant script from this morning. The matinee was canceled. Come up with something believable quick, Schpeel-berg.

"Oh. So then you know what happened."

"We all know what happened."

D'oh.

They all knew what happened. They knew Brad was an eyewitness to a stubborn scuff mark and some awkward small talk. They knew he had not tried to stop anything with his rapier wit or *Matrix*-esque physical prowess. They knew he was no Jean-Claude Van Costner.

"Then why am I here?"

"Between you and me, all of our equipment got fried right before Frank got to the elevator. Thank God you were there."

Oh.

Inside, Brad exhaled like a pregnant woman spotting a rest-stop exit on the turnpike.

No video. Nothing. That was just the kind of thing a big fat liar wanted to hear. There was nothing else to contradict his story. No other witnesses, digital or living. Nothing. It was his word against Frank "The Guy Everyone Already Thinks Did It" Fortunato. The show was back on.

So Brad painted Brittany a picture. He wasn't so brazen as to include all of the helicopter kicks and heart-snatching kung fu he fantasized about earlier, but he did throw in a dusting of machismo and a sprinkling of swagger, including the part about how he matched Frank's steely gaze and that he was surprised at how cool he remained when staring down the barrel of Frank's massive symbol of overcompensation. Not quite the blockbuster he had conjured up in the bathroom, but moderate hyperbole nonetheless. It ended up being a concise, easy-to-remember tale of unlikely heroism and awkward dialogue.

Brittany reviewed her notes. Time to double check a few things.

"So he pulls the gun out and says *This is the end, Carmine.*"

"Right."

"And then what?"

"I knew he was going to make his move, so I had to do something."

"Go ahead."

"So I grabbed his hand and we wrestled. I tried to get the gun away, but he managed to get a shot off."

"Five shots."

"Right, five shots."

"Okay."

"Anyway, he breaks free, punches me in the gut and runs away. And then you showed up."

Uh-huh. Brittany paused and gave Brad the kind of easy, thorough stare you lay on a relative right before you loan them the money to start their stupid Internet business. She closed her notebook.

"Great. Let's call it a day."

Nailed It

Brad closed the door behind Brittany and basked in his own minor accomplishment. Sure he had to bob and weave a little bit, but overall he was pleased with how he came across in the story. Not like the enormous coward he was in real life, hiding behind a chicken suit and a web of lies. Nope, just a web of lies this time. As far as Brad was concerned, that was a step up. And he was glad he had made the decision to paint himself in a nonsteroidal heroic light. In retrospect, the action-packed epic would have been too much. Yessir, Brad knew deep down that he had played this one pitch perfect.

Brittany seemed distracted on her way out, but that was to be expected after he dropped that testosterone-saturated chef-d'oeuvre on her. Poor girl. She might have fallen the tiniest bit in love with old Brad just now. He congratulated himself on a performance well delivered.

I. Fucking. Nailed. It.

Bullshit

"What a goddamn liar."

The drivers in the cars next to her couldn't actually see steam coming from Brittany's ears, but it wouldn't be too tough to figure out that she was more frustrated than Madonna at a Dress Barn sample sale. So many things just didn't fit.

Brad had been embellishing his story. A lot. A boyish ploy to impress her? A delusional stance taken to appease her obvious lust for conviction? Was he fucking crazy? And what was with that awful Japanese accent? If that little shit thought he was going to screw up her shot at TV syndication gold, he had another thing coming.

She knew there was a story in there, but not the one he told her. Which meant she had to cool off, let the reality of the situation sink in to Brad's thick skull, and then come back and dig the truth out of his lying liar's memory. And it better be right next time. If Brittany wanted to listen to a load of self-indulgent bullshit, she'd call her grandmother.

Squirrelhead versus Cougar

Malcolm spent the previous evening in quiet contemplation of whether or not the Fortunato thing was a blessing or a curse. He had discussed the issue with Mother, but as usual, after a few hours of listening to Malcolm go back and forth she begged off to go watch her stories. Malcolm was left to his own analytic mental whirlpool. There was a lot to consider. It would be a high-profile case and a clever person might be able to make quite a bit of hay with this. Imagine if the assignment had gone to DiRienz. Now that would be a circus. But it hadn't. It had gone to Malcolm. Was it really because he was the only one free? How long would this take? Would people really be talking about this for the next ten years? Was this the kind of attention he wanted for himself?

It was after midnight when Malcolm finally fell asleep.

"Move it, Squirrelhead."

Malcolm didn't even like coffee, but definitely felt like he needed a little pick-me-up after last night. He was exhausted from lack of sleep. That's probably why it took a few moments, and a couple other choice words grumbled by the Cup 'n Mug customer behind him, for Malcolm to realize that she was referring to his carefully coiffed head. He wondered if perhaps he had gone too light on the mousse this morning.

He turned to find a stunning woman in a leopard dress. Attractive, well put together, and obviously a Pilates enthusiast, she was roughly

Malcolm's age and, by his observation, not wearing a wedding ring. As usual, he did not know what to say. She leaned in and directed him like a parent who's had enough of this shit from her five-year-old.

"Order. Your. Drink."

Stunned by this personification of beauty, Malcolm turned back around to find he was indeed at the head of the line and there was a doe-eyed barista awaiting his order. He did as he was told. Love at first sight is a powerful thing.

"Hot chocolate, please."

Two minutes later, he watched the magnificent Cougar fix her coffee just so and Malcolm fell for her even harder. Skim with two sugars. She was so decisive. So feral. There was no consideration of soy versus regular milk. No reflecting on the potential presence of growth hormone residue in the two percent. No regard for the fat content of the whole milk. She slopped a few ounces from the closest silver thermos pitcher, dumped a pair of sugar packets in at the same time, and stirred. Kapow! Now, this was a woman who knew what she liked.

Maybe it was the sleep deprivation. Maybe the hot chocolate triggered some sort of mortality alarm. But, in the moment that his new dream girl walked by him on the way to the door, Malcolm Middleton acted in a way he had never acted in his entire life—spontaneously.

"I'm not gay."

Whoops. That's not what he expected to come out. His plan was for something a little more Cary Grant-esque. Suave-er. The opposite of what he had just done.

But she stopped and gave him the once-over.

"Well, no shit. Just look at those shoes."

Cheese and crackers! He was in. Malcolm manned up and pounced. Sort of. Actually, he thought about pouncing and then backtracked a little to consider his best option for approach. Was pouncing appropriate? What about some sort of clever line? Or something simple. An introduction. How about a joke? Women liked jokes. Or there was the option of . . .

Too late. She was out the door. Probably to meet some young stud.

Malcolm Middleton was definitely not gay. Despite what most everyone who met him thought. Oh, those knowing looks when he mentioned ice skating. The smug smiles when he pulled out his ornate scrapbook. The pregnant pauses they allowed after mentioning their significant others. It was his belief that suspicion, debate, and mockery regarding his presumed homosexual activities abounded when his back was turned.

To be fair, Malcolm was finicky. He was neat. He knew antiques and dressage. But byproducts do not make the man.

He was heterosexual and understood fully what an anti-pheromone the gay rumors could be, so Malcolm spent a tremendous effort attempting to disprove them to those suspecting snickerers, debaters, and mockers by constantly dropping mentions of curls at the gym, bass fishing, and tequila shooters. None of which he participated in and all of which sounded downright silly coming out of his mouth, but he felt he had to do something.

People did laugh at Malcolm behind his back, but not entirely because he was so femme. There were plenty of other reasons as well. His ugly sweaters, for instance. The fact that he was so uptight about his condiment inventory. His ever-so-slightly-crossed eyes.

And his hair.

Oy, Malcolm's hair. He had a comb-over. *The* comb-over. A terribly obvious affair that was dyed a little too black and manicured like it was Trump's lawn. Not a hair out of place, aside from the tidal wave of locks forcibly marched from the back of his head to the front and then turned abruptly right so as to imply a part. It was just wrong. Especially for a fifty-seven-year-old man. If anything, the tipoff should have been when little kids pointed and laughed. Malcolm assumed it was because they thought he was a closeted queen, but that's not usually the domain of toddlers. Nope, they were laughing at the hair. And sometimes the sweaters.

He had always intended to get married or at least land a serious girlfriend, but so far Malcolm's intense over-consideration of details had led to a lonely life of occasional lukewarm first dates followed up way too late by second date requests that were usually turned down by women who had moved on with their lives, some even to marriage, in

the ridiculous yawn of time in between calls. These rejections naturally had to be analyzed over and over on a granular level, which filled
his free time and might explain why he didn't have room in his schedule to join up with his fantasy lumberjack buddies for a weekend of
drunken four-wheeling. The truth was he was an overly thoughtful
man who took things way too personally, and it prevented him from
becoming too close to anyone for the first fifty-seven years of his life.
So he was alone.

But maybe this vision in coffee was a sign that things were going to
turn around. He decided to think about that for a little while.

Brad X . . . Still

Maybe the most uncomfortable feeling in the world is sitting through your fourth *Naked and Afraid* of the day while a U.S. marshal watches you from slightly outside your line of sight. Stump hadn't moved all morning. Or maybe he had. The guy was so sneaky there was no way of knowing what he was up to unless you were staring right at him. And even then, not so much.

Brad had been to the little boy's room three times already today. Stump had not been once. He had to urinate sometime, right? Or had Stump figured out some way to do it telekinetically? Was he so good at his job that he could teleport this morning's Arnold Palmer into the toilet without budging from his watchful post? But, if so, how would he flush? Again with the mental projection. Of course it was impossible, but a more plausible solution was not presenting itself.

Sometime in the late afternoon, Brad had given up even the awkward head bobs of recognition he had been doling out as he passed Stump on the way to the bathroom. He hadn't gotten a response and figured it was some weird cop thing.

"Mind if I use the phone?"

"Yes."

He already knew the answer. There wasn't even a landline in the house. But the silence between them was so awkward he needed to break it somehow, even if by asking dumbass questions. He sat back down on the couch and tried to bore himself back to sleep until the bureaucratic machinery of the Witness Protection Program cranked out where he would be going.

Stump wasn't playing weird cop games. He was sizing Brad up. Looking deep into his soul, trying to determine how well the specimen would fare in his new life on the run. So far, he was not impressed. Stump's inside coat pocket vibrated a concise alert. He checked his phone, slid it back into his jacket, and considered Brad for a beat longer.

"Let's get a coffee."

Brad jumped at the opportunity to get out of the house. Stump could have said *Let's go light a hobo on fire* and Brad would have offered to drive. Anything to crack the boredom. Stump drove them to a low-rent coffee shop about five minutes away. Cramped. Musty. Littered with two-year-old local garage band music zines. But as far as Brad was concerned, it was the Taj Mahal.

Two entitled baristas stood behind the counter in their skinny jeans and climate-ironic knit caps, waiting to either create delicious coffee concoctions or be crowned the next kings of indie-ville. It was hard to tell which. A few patrons spread out across the tables in front, reading and filling in Sudoku matrices. One of the future kings moseyed on over to the register and addressed Stump, possibly sarcastically.

"May I take your order, sir?"

"Nothing for me."

Stump motioned for Brad to order.

"Can I have a half caf, half decaf, soy latte with agave?"

"Size?"

"Large." Why not? The government was buying.

"One *Gigante* decafcafsoy-te *con* agave. Can I have your name please?"

Brad looked around the shop. He was the only person ordering. The rest of the customers had their coffees. It would be pretty tough to forget that the only coffee being made belonged to the one guy standing in front of the counter. He glanced over to Stump to exchange eye rolls over the ridiculous robotic barista protocol, but Stump was looking out the window, no doubt keeping an eye on any suspicious foot traffic outside the shop.

And then Brad blanked. What had Brittany told him about his name? It was still Brad, right?

"Umm . . . it's, um . . ."

King Jackass clicked his retractable sharpie slowly.

"You want me to take a guess, sir?"

Stump wasn't watching the door closely. He was waiting. He had shepherded too many dopes like Brad through the process to not be able to see this reaction coming. Brad stumbled when asked his name. How predictable. Stump gave a subtle nod to the customer next to the window. The customer whispered something into the cuff of his sleeve.

In an instant, both baristas reached behind their aprons, whipped out large handguns and trained them on Brad's head faster than his eyes could bulge at the sight. Behind him, chairs flew across the room as all three customers jumped out of their seats, drew their own handguns, and pointed them at Brad.

Brad looked quickly to Stump who now faced him, watching, as placid as ever.

BLAM-BLAM-BLAM-BLAM-BLAM-BLAM-BLAM-BLAM-BLAM-BLAM! All five gunmen emptied their clips in Brad's direction as he tried to dodge their fire by dancing around like a CEO on a motivational retreat hot coal walk.

When the smoke cleared and Brad finally stopped screaming, he realized he was not dead. In fact, he was still standing and didn't have a scratch on his body. Stump hadn't moved an iota, although his eyes were no longer focused on Brad's face, but instead on his crotch. Odds were Brad would wet himself. Or worse.

Brad composed himself enough to get a sentence out.

"Holy Christ! Holy shit! Holy fuck! What just happened? Why are you standing there? Kill these guys! Get me out of here. DO SOMETHING!"

Brad tried to position himself behind Stump as the gunmen casually reloaded. Stump shook his head and rendered judgment.

"Fail."

"Fail?! I failed what? Dying?"

Stump nodded to the gunmen. "Thanks."

"No problem, Stump."

"You got it, Stump."

They smiled and slid their guns, now filled with live ammunition, back into their discreet holsters. The "baristas" slid out of their coffee shop aprons and the "customers" put the overturned chairs back in place.

Upon a closer look, Brad noticed the similarities in all three customers. Short hair. Rigid posture. Cheap suits. Company men. Same thing for the baristas. Both took off their imprudent hats and lost their contrived slouches to reveal similar company man characteristics.

"You know these guys?"

Customer number one grinned. "We've done this before."

"What is this, a frat?"

Customer number two righted another chair. "It's part of Stump's relocation candidate training."

"Your . . . this is a thing? A rehearsed thing? You make your witnesses shit their pants on a regular basis?"

Stump raised an eyebrow.

"No. I didn't. But I mean, seriously, what the fuck?"

"We were trying to make a point. Do you know what it was?"

"Don't order the *Gigante*?"

"Be ready. For the rest of your life."

Brad considered the advice. Apparently, he hadn't been giving off enough of a scared-for-his-effing-life vibe in the last few days. It was a valid point but, he was rather busy with his mix of panic, lies, and posturing. Unfortunately, that was not something he could explain to Stump. The good news was that as cruel as his little morality play was, Stump was proving himself to be singularly focused on keeping Brad safe. Whether he believed his story or not, Stump was a true ally. Certainly no one he could befriend or confide in or even be honest with yet, but someone who might be interested in Brad staying alive a little bit longer. It was a start.

As for the fear, well, that was now wide awake and clawing nonstop at the back of his eyeballs. Brad took a deep breath and accepted that the condition was something he would have to get used to. But, really, there was no better way to send that message?

"Uh-huh. Now, that's something you couldn't have let me know in some sort of authoritative tone once we sat down? Maybe told me an anecdote of someone who didn't follow your advice? Written it on a Post-it?"

Stump shrugged.

"You'll remember this."

Brad stared at the television, still steaming about the events of a few hours earlier. And he never even got his goddamned latte. Stump had resumed his position in the doorway and hadn't spoken a word since they got back to the safe house.

"Are you ready for lesson number two?"

Brad turned and scanned the room for any ninjas or zombies Stump might have hired to help him illustrate his next point.

"Is that the one where you light the house on fire to remind me not to leave the iron on?"

"It's about improv. The key to survival in your new life is knowing how to improv in sticky situations."

"Improv? Like I pretend I'm a plumber and whoever is trying to kill me is a cowboy?"

"No, like you think on your feet no matter what the situation is. You im-pro-vise."

"Okay. I improvise some improv. Got it."

"Do you know what the key to improv is?"

"A two drink minimum?"

"Yes, and . . ."

"And . . . a cover charge?"

"As in *Yes, and I would like to add to that thought you just laid out there despite how unsettling it is.* That's how you answer when you don't know where things are going. *Yes, and* buys you time to think. *Yes, and* puts whoever you're talking to at ease. Always *Yes, and*, never deny."

"Yes, and."

"You go along with the premise. Improv until you can extract yourself from danger. Stay in your character. Breaking character is a form of denial. If you break character, someone may notice you. Your goal for the rest of your life is to not be noticed. If someone notices you, they might remember you. If they remember you, they might mention your quirky little character break to someone else. It goes on and on until the wrong person hears and becomes suspicious and you might get killed. Understand?"

"If I don't, are you going to fake shoot me again?"

Stump waited for a real answer.

"Yeah, I get it."

"Let's practice."

"Um, okay."

Stump approached Brad. A little close for Brad's liking. Stump shook his shoulders out, presumably calling up a new character or situation for a round of improv, before settling his laser-focused gaze on Brad.

"You ever see monkey porn?"

"Whoa, I . . . no." Brad stepped back.

"Now see, that's denial. No good. Try again."

Stump cracked his knuckles, sucked a big breath in, and released it. He stepped forward.

"This is important. *Yes, and.*"

Brad sighed heavily.

"Okay."

Stump leaned in as if speaking to a co-conspirator.

"I need some help moving a body. You in?"

"Wha—No. How is this saving my life?" Brad moved back another couple of steps. Stump followed him, suddenly all business again.

"Again, denial. Very dangerous."

"I thought we were going to practice real life situations."

"We are. Try again."

"*All right.* But where are you planning to hide me, a *Law & Order* episode?"

"Again."

Stump rolled his head around his neck a few times, stretched his mouth out, and took a beat to gather himself before speaking.

"Hey, is it cool if I use the 'N' word?"

"I'm not doing this."

Stump pointed his hand, shaped like a gun at Brad, and pulled the trigger.

"Bang. You're dead."

The silence of Brad's incredulity was broken by a Tupac Shakur "I Get Around" ringtone. Stump slid his phone out of his jacket and answered it without ever losing eye contact with Brad.

"Stumberg . . . Yes, we did . . . No, subject did not wet his pants . . . Yes . . . Understood . . . We'll be there tomorrow."

He hung up and slid his phone back into his jacket.

"You got a job."

Tucson

Brad was fine with wearing a disguise. But the one Stump handed him for the trip to Arizona was not one he would have picked out himself. The big, bushy beard and trucker hat were a little too Gyllenhaal-in-between-movies for him. Brad suggested something in a Unibomber look, or maybe a Trenchcoat Mafia vibe, but Stump wouldn't let him leave the house without the beard and hat. The coffee shop was one thing. They had been surrounded by FBI agents hip to the deal. But taking a commercial flight to Tucson was a very different story. Frank Fortunato had a lot of soldiers on the payroll. Who knew who was hanging around the airport? Frank was willing to shoot Carmine in broad daylight. It was hard to imagine him being shy about sending a few thugs with hand cannons to the passenger drop-off area of Terminal B.

Stump whisked them both through security and straight onto the plane before anyone could get a second glance. In his coach window seat, Brad sat avoiding eye contact with the surrounding Middle Americans heading back home on the same flight. Through the airplane window he could see the distant Manhattan skyline.

Looking wistfully at his soon-to-be former home, he thought about his soon-to-be ex-wife. She must be wondering where he was by now. Surely, in one of the many post-coital glows Brad imagined her enjoying since his departure, she had noticed that his side of the bed had been empty for a few days now. At least at night. His absconding made good sense when viewed in its current imminent mob death threat context. But, as far as Gracie knew, her husband had stopped showing up for his marital duties with a cowardly absence of explanation.

Was she calling the hospitals? Checking with the police? Asking around at strip clubs?

Did she care?

That was the big question. Did it really matter that he left? It mattered to him. Deep down, where no one but Brad could see, was a kernel of what he suspected was regret. What a rash decision he had made. What a drastic choice to change his life without so much as a consult with the woman he married.

Of course, Brad understood the possibility that Gracie had an identical twin sister who happened to be in love with the guy servicing Brad's cable was virtually impossible. And the chances of Gracie being involved in some sort of government mind-control experiment were infinitesimally small. An elaborate NSFW staged prank? Stop it. All conceivable options were improbable. But still. It chafed him the tiniest bit that he never gave Gracie the chance to explain herself. And like it or not, he was in love with her and that doesn't just get doused with a bucket of anger and a blanket of harsh judgment.

He wondered and considered and mulled the thing over internally for a moment or two before deciding that there would never be a satisfying answer. And besides, it was too late. The card had been played and, much like a joke that falls flat at a parole hearing, there was nothing to do with that regret kernel but to try to ignore it and move on. At some point, he would have to face Gracie and tell her why he left. He would also have to borrow some money from her to pay for his divorce lawyer. But that day was not today.

The details of who stuck what where, how often, and why would be worked out later, but, at that moment, Brad knew the best thing for him to do was to suck on the bitter pill of cuckoldry and use its lingering aftertaste to remind himself that he needed to do what was best for him. Right now, that was to leave without a word.

The New York City skyline waved goodbye to Brad and wished him well on behalf of all of its residents, and somewhere in one of those buildings Gracie was still the girl whose eyes twinkled when she smiled at him. Back among the one and a half million residents of

Formerly Fingerman

Manhattan, she still had the same laugh when he told his dumb jokes. He would miss her soon, and then what?

God, she made throwing his life away hard.

He squashed his sentimentality into submission, jammed his earbuds in, and turned up his music to drown out his own thoughts. Electronic devices were supposed to be off during takeoff, but if his Daft Punk was powerful enough to bring down the big, bad plane carrying him away from New York City, well, that was life.

Five hours later Brad woke up in Tucson. He had slept most of the plane ride, and the difference in his mood was dramatic. Time to start a new life.

Stump drove their rented Hyundai through nondescript Tucson to a nondescript suburb and into the nondescript driveway of a nondescript home.

They had taken the long way to get there, checking for tails along the side streets as they drove, even going so far as to give the stink eye to an old lady who made the same turns as them three times in a row until she pulled over and let them go on alone. Once he was sure they were clean, Stump made his way to their new home.

Manhattan and Tucson are similar in that they are both situated on planet Earth, populated by carbon-based life forms, and most residents in each city have basic cable. Other than that they are not very much alike.

Manhattan is a rich and vibrant melting pot of race, culture, history, and wannabes. Tucson is a preplanned matrix of chain restaurants strategically positioned to link subdivisions and malls. Brad understood that much by driving to his new home from the airport. He wasn't that anxious to go exploring.

Their new house was a standard issue three-bedroom, two-bath. A cookie-cutter floor plan that could be found at four other addresses on the same street. The rest of the houses in the subdivision were cut from similar cloth, but different enough to give prospective buyers the impression of having a choice. Inside, the rooms were decorated with inoffensive furniture and tepid art work.

Stump cleared the house while Brad surveyed his new kingdom. Clean. Empty. No mob killers. No cheating wife to speak of. So far, an improvement.

"I can live with this."

A stack of brochures on the counter announced that the subdivision's name was "Cactus Bluff" and that it was "The heart of Tucson."

Stump walked in, holstering his gun.

"We're all clear."

"Is this the model home?"

"We needed something quickly. A friend handles sales for the area. His business is slow and this is furnished."

"Uh-huh."

Brad lugged his suitcase into one of the bedrooms to unpack his life in the heart of Tucson.

The next morning the program was good enough to cover a shopping spree for Brad's new non-vegan diet. He had decided to make the jump from superficially committed non-meat-eater to full-blown whatevervore. He only hoped he could maintain the lifestyle.

As they wandered the supermarket, Brad decided to shake Stump down a little about what would happen next. Stump had been pretty tight lipped on the plane ride as a matter of safety, but in the anonymity of Arizona, he opened up a little and explained that Brad would be working for a large packaged goods concern in Tucson. Stump would stay around until the trial and then Brad would be on his own.

"But, I thought I was in the program? Aren't you guys going to protect me afterward?"

"Of course. But if we do our jobs right and you keep a low profile, there's no need for us to be standing next to you all day every day. What's important is that we establish a credible identity for you and then you make sure it sticks. Improv, remember?"

The thought of flying solo hadn't really occurred to Brad. In fact, he really hadn't thought much further than the idea that the program could get him out of the situation he had found himself in a few days ago. Maybe it was time to do a little planning.

As Brad organized his new life in his new room, he thought back on the last time he had moved to a new city and started a new job. He was right out of college, full of potential and ready to rumble. He drove the full twenty-eight hours straight from San Antonio to New York in his excitement. His East Village studio was filthy, riddled with roaches, and, in the winters, colder than a lesbian bartender's stare. But he loved it as soon as he saw it.

As he folded his jeans in his new desert-themed bedroom, he remembered pulling his paints out of their moving box in New York and putting them on the shelf in the closet. Just until he got settled in his job was the plan. Shore up a little security before he released a massive art-by-Brad hurricane on NYC. A few years later he threw them away after promising to buy some higher quality stuff to replace them. Or maybe he left them there. Who remembers. Hmm, with all the downtime running for his life would surely allow him, maybe he would pick up a few tubes of paint and start—

The doorbell rang. Without thinking, Brad threw himself on the ground and quickly wriggled under the bed. Improv. Peeking out from underneath he saw Stump's shoes in his doorway, observing Brad's G.I. Joe action. Stump walked away.

"Don't get up. I'll get it."

On the dining room table, an overnight delivery envelope sat unopened. Stump had assumed his usual position standing stock still in a central location of the house. Watching. Brad walked into the living room and noticed the envelope.

"Is this for me?"

Stump remained silent, but evidently the answer was yes since Brad was not put into any sort of Okinawan headlock when he reached for it.

It was addressed to Stump, but Brad broke the seal on top anyway and poured out the contents—a passport, a social security card, an Arizona driver's license, a birth certificate, an American Express (green card, gee thanks), and a Safeway club card. The new Brad.

He picked up the passport and savored this moment of truth. As soon as he opened it up, his new identity would take hold. A new name. A new beginning. A new life. Like when they fast-forwarded five years ahead on *Desperate Housewives*. Suddenly, anything would be possible.

Brad made a big show of opening it. Presenting himself to the world.

"And the winner is Braaaaaaaaaaaaaaaad . . ."

Holy fucking sweet baby goddamn Jesus H on a Popsicle Christ.

". . . Pitt."

Brad's face dropped. In a split second he had gone from proud owner of a cool new name to a guy hiding from bloodthirsty killers who just found out his new secret identity was one of the most recognizable names on the planet.

"Brad *Pitt*? My name is Brad Pitt? What, Robert DeNiro was taken? I thought the point was to not be noticed."

It was. This was a bit of a problem. The FBI software usually came up with something particularly bland for Stump's clients. And Pitt would have worked just fine if Brad hadn't been named Brad. No one would notice a Larry, Jeff, or Charlie Pitt. They would never think twice about it. But *Brad* Pitt. This was a spot of bother. Especially because Stump knew that the red tape involved with getting a revised name issued was really tough. Like a few months tough. The program was designed to get new names out as fast as possible. But they rarely had to change anyone's name. Asking a government agency to change course midstream was like asking an old person to TiVo *Game of Thrones*. It would take fucking forever and you would end up with a recording of the Spanish version of *Top Chef*. Stump mentally back-fisted himself. Why hadn't he thought to ask them to install a celebrity filter?

"Would you consider 'Bradley'?"

Brittany's Insurance

"Nothing? You can't get anything out of it? Jarvis, come on. It was just a little coffee, right?"

"Actually, it was a lot of coffee."

"And . . . ?"

"And, that's the computer equivalent of kicking a porn star in the nuts. No workee no more."

"So we have nothing."

"We have up to the part where everything cuts out."

"Are you sure you can't get in there and do some technical stuff to recover the file?"

"Well, I can hit the Enhance button a few times. That should do it."

"Really?"

"No, that was a thing in *Blade Runner*. It hasn't been invented yet."

Fucking tech guys. Always with the snark. They sit in their little tech rooms doing tech stuff that no one else understands and make their tech jokes.

Of all the smarmy tech guys, Jarvis was Brittany's best bet of recovering her sting audio and video surveillance. The guy lived to show off his mad skills. But even Jarvis couldn't get the 1s and 0s of her hard drive back in order.

Not that Brittany really cared. She had Brad. Brad was her guy. She would ride him all the way to Moneybag Street in the heart of Emmy-AwardLand. It was just that somewhere in the back of her mind, a shrill, relentless voice that sounded a lot like her grandmother was telling her to play it safe. And to at least *try* speed dating.

She was definitely too career oriented to have a boyfriend right now, but having that video in her back pocket probably was the smart thing. Why not play it safe? Why not push Jarvis to his nerdy limits?

"That's okay. I'll ask Eidelsberg if he can take a look."

Jarvis bristled like Simon Cowell at a Hooters sing-along.

"Come back in two hours."

"Aww, Jarvis. You're the best."

Brad Pitt's New Job

In-house agencies are the bastard children of the advertising world. They have the unenviable task of working exclusively on products their parent company produces. There is no hope of winning new accounts unless the guys in R&D come up with something really socko. The crew in the in-house agency just keeps cranking out work for the same stuff year after year. The excitement of the job tends to be frontloaded into the process of landing employment. And the agency name.

In-house agencies will predictably have those sad and overcompensating names that try a little too hard to be clever, intense, or invoke some sort of energy. *Concept Factory! Turbo! Fifth Gear!* Think of the dopey third-act plot twist of a straight-to-DVD Scott Baio movie. Same idea.

Ask any self-important ad guy (like Brad) and he'll tell you that working in an in-house agency means you're either on your way up and only stopping by for a short period of time before your résumé officially begins or you're on your way down and this is the last stop on a LinkedIn profile that will never be updated again. Or you suck.

More than likely you suck too much to get a job at a hip agency that doesn't answer directly to the vice president of creative services. So instead, you try to scratch your artistic itch by creating brochures for internal distribution, stilted videos on sexual harassment policies, or the in-store product displays derived from the stylebook of the real agency that produced the ads currently running during your favorite show.

On the upside, in-house agencies tend to be fairly low-pressure affairs. They're generally staffed with people who have used hope to fill the massive void left by lack of talent. So they're super upbeat.

Who knows? Maybe today's the day we do something great! Come on, gang! Let's put on a show! But usually, it's the brochure stuff and maybe some trade-show banners for the boys on fifteen. Plus cake. It's always someone's birthday.

Certainly, there are worse places to work. Your daily duties do not include shoveling animal byproducts, scaling high buildings, or breathing toxic chemicals. But for a former *real agency* ad guy, they might as well.

"So what do I do when someone asks me about my past?"

"Lie."

Gee, never tried that before.

"Lie about everything?"

"No. Just the important stuff. Like cities and real names. Change everything just slightly. The closer you stay to the truth the easier it is to remember."

"Seems like a lot of work."

"Oh, sorry."

"Can't I just be vague?"

"You can try."

"I'll do that."

"Good luck."

Stump let the Hyundai glide into a parking space. They could have been in any metropolitan office park in America. The only thing distinguishing the building they were sitting in front of from the two flanking it was the triumphant signage proclaiming it the home of *Assure Worldwide. A family-friendly company.*

"Assure? This is an ad agency?"

Brad knew the answer before he even finished asking the question, but suffered with quiet dignity Stump's explanation of what an in-house agency is.

"Look, I don't mean to be ungrateful, but I thought I was going to a real advertising agency."

"This is a real agency. They make advertising."

"I know, but I mean, with my experience and my portfolio, I really should be—"

"You don't have any experience. Brad Fingerman has experience. You're not Brad Fingerman."

Stump was okay with the silence in which they sat for the next two minutes. Finally, Brad composed himself.

"So what happens now?"

"We're going to meet a man named Alan Silver. He runs the creative department."

"You know him?"

"Oh, sure. Alan and I used to work black ops in Indochina during the mid-nineties."

"Really?"

"Or maybe I met him that time the cops busted in on a Chinatown massage parlor and we both ended up naked in a closet. Man, that was close, *ifyouknowwhatImeanright?*"

"Umm . . ."

"Or is it that I used to play bass for his Marvin Gaye tribute band, Grapevine."

"What are you talking about?"

"I know him."

"Oh. Oh! Is he in the program, too?"

Duh.

"Can we trust him?"

"I can trust him. I put him here."

Alan Silver grew up in that part of Los Angeles that most of us read about in *Parade* magazine or see on reality shows about spoiled sixteen-year-olds. Nannies, private schools, a Malibu address, *They paid how much for that prom dress!?*, that kind of thing.

But a young, short-fused Alan Silver needed more out of life than his ever-rehabbing, former-model mother and power-broker-talent-agent father's money could provide. Adventure. Danger. Excitement. Illicit bong hits and weekend rainbow parties just weren't going to do it for him like they did for his buddies. His bar was higher.

So he went out and found some new buddies. Guys who stole for fun. Guys with nicknames instead of business cards. Guys who could use a boy with a hot temper like Alan's.

Alan was sixteen the first time he got arrested. And the second. By the time he was twenty-one and failed out of several Ivy League schools, he was immersed full time in the fringes of the Los Angeles chapter of the Russian Mafia, running a book and dealing a little coke. Then the bookie business tanked and Alan spiraled into a raging alcoholic with immense debt who owed favors all over town to the wrong people. And that's how he became a contract killer.

Alan generally choked out his victims with his hands. It was easy to do and surgical gloves made it tough to trace. Not that the cops looked too hard. His victims were usually deadbeats and losers who no longer had the option of paying off their debts. Dirtbags no one would miss. And his employers were nice enough to clean up the mess afterward. All Alan had to do was the actual killing. It paid well, the hours were amazing and, as long as you could stomach that kind of thing (Alan just had to find something to get angry about), you would always get work. Unless you got caught.

Alan got caught.

Having been in the business for a few years, Alan knew quite a bit about what was going on. That, in combination with the fact that he really, really didn't want to go to jail, made him an ideal candidate for the Witness Protection Program.

His testimony resulted in the conviction of a small group of Russians who were planning to grab a dignitary's daughter out of a car wash a week after Alan was busted. And all he wanted out of the deal was for the cops to forget about the couple/three lowlifes he had put down. Alan was given a few anger management classes and, under Stump's supervision, moved out to work as a creative director at Assure.

Stump swept his eyes across the horizon out of habit as he ushered Brad into the Assure Worldwide lobby.

"Don't be a wiseass with this guy."

"He's corporate? Uptight?"

"Uh, yeah."

Alan finally let go of Brad's nearly numb hand only milliseconds before it fused to his own, and then smiled even broader.

He was a tall, blond-haired, pale-skinned, barrel-chested, thirty-four-year-old man with maybe the world's largest head resting on shoulders that slumped under its weight. Six four if he was an inch. He looked like a Viking with an MBA and had a subdued vigor about him, as if he really wanted to give you a big headbutt for a hello but had been pulled aside at some point and advised against that sort of behavior. Instead, he squeezed your hand to just short of hairline fractures and leaned in a little too far to smile right in your face when he met you. No way this guy was ever in a Marvin Gaye tribute band.

Brad did not throw up in his mouth when he read the title on the business cards Alan had displayed on his desk, but he felt like, on principle, he should have. *Creative director.* Really? In Dockers? What bizarro world of insanity had Stump brought him to? This was the man who would be judging Brad's work? A Nordic, pumpkin-headed cruise director? The man was wearing a cell phone on his belt! What kind of taste could he possibly have? Oh no, this did not look like a fit at all.

"Welcome to Assure. I hear you're a hell of a copywriter."

"Art director, actually."

"Ooh. Well, that is exciting. Hey, you know what? I think you're going to like it here. We've got some real fun folks and we love doing great work."

There it was. The predictable optimism of the doomed. This is who Brad would be surrounded by as he spent his days selling . . . What was he selling anyway?

"By the way, what does Assure make?"

"Mostly adult diapers. So, how about I show—"

"Excuse me?"

"Adult diapers."

"You mean like for old people?"

Alan's face clouded a little through his smile. Stump's eyes narrowed as he monitored the situation.

"Well, Assure adult diapers are made specifically for individuals suffering with bladder control and incontinence issues regardless of age. Is that a problem?"

"Oh, uh, no. Not at all."

Alan's face exploded into a cloud-free, oversized smile.

"Great! Welcome to Assure!"

Assure Worldwide, Inc. was a company of around two thousand people who made and distributed a variety of products, most of which could be found at your local grocery store or pharmacy. And while their pre-moistened wipes, hand sanitizers, and lip balms sold well, their line of adult diapers was the company's flagship product, and merited its own company-owned advertising agency.

Alan showed Stump and Brad around the first floor, a plastic and nylon tundra of gray office space. Each office was as blah as the next, even factoring in the requisite kitsch supplied by the individual residents. Family pictures, reproductions of vintage ads, last year's holiday party invite, various inside jokes that weren't that funny even to those in the know. A dreary affair overall.

As they made their way from office to office, Brad kept a sharp eye out for Hawaiian shirts—the air-raid alarm of apparel that proclaimed to all that are within earshot that the wearer of said shirt is this close to showing you his latest sunset watercolor painting, explaining the technique behind her new papier-mâché celebrity bust, or playing you that high-larious parody song he's been tinkering around with. Brad assumed the place would be lousy with them, but thankfully, didn't see a one. He did meet everyone in the place, though. And they couldn't have been nicer. How was this an advertising agency without snide looks and bitchy comments? It was unsettling to say the least.

The creative department was populated by thirty-eight people. Whenever they stopped by a new office to introduce the new future employee of the month, everyone stopped what they were doing, leaned back in their chairs, and took their time welcoming Brad to the family. This was the Mayberry of workplaces.

As they made their rounds, Brad internally acknowledged the inevitable, if second tier, roster of advertising archetypes he met. *Hey, über-cerebral-writer-guy. Hi, goth-by-Hot-Topic-interactive-girl. Nice to meet you, big-talking-production-guy. Hello, j-pop-retro-punk-look-art-director-girl. What up, account-executive-who-so-so-so-thinks-he-could-totally-do-that-creative-shit-guy.* No real surprises anywhere. Just the same old almost-artists trying to find their way in a bottom-line-driven world. Only these were the low-rent versions. Not that he saw any of their work. Brad just assumed.

They finished up their tour outside a room that was empty save two opposing desks topped by computers.

"Welcome to your new office."

Brad looked in. Uh-huh.

"Nice."

"Oh, I almost forgot. Your partner."

Alan smiled broadly and Brad began to worry as he realized he was about to be handed a giant anchor and asked to swim. What slack-jawed optimist was Alan assigning as Brad's creative ball and chain? What load of averageness would Brad be expected to lug around? He quietly begged the heavens above for one measly favor. Was it at all possible that some recovering coke head who lost his job at DeMaras/Whittaker in Seattle or DayOne in San Francisco or some other dreamy ad shop had road tripped it as far as his buzz would take him and ended up settling here? Some fellow member of the cognoscenti he could relate to? Or if not, then maybe a hot chick who hated bras?

Brad returned Alan's big smile because he didn't know what else to do. Stump smiled as well, but it looked like he might have a clue what was going on.

Brad raised his eyebrows in anticipation. So did Alan and Stump.

Brad looked back and forth between Alan and Stump. No way.

Brad's eyes widened involuntarily and in direct proportion to Alan's ever-expanding smile.

Stump was going to be Brad's partner. Alan was bursting with excitement like a puppy with his first pig's ear. He clapped Stump on the shoulder.

"Huh? Pretty great, right? I love this guy."

"This is bullshit."

"I don't know. I've worked worse jobs."

Stump had worked way worse jobs. Once he had placed a witness in a mailroom job at a detox center and had to work as the janitor charged with vomit detail. Another time he had placed a witness at a slaughterhouse because he had borderline personality disorder and it was the only job he couldn't get fired from for killing his coworkers. But that meant Stump had to join him until the trial.

A single word had yet to be typed, but he already knew that copywriting beat the snot out of jabbing cattle in the ass with an electric prod and mopping up junkie barf.

Stump began improv-ing immediately by leaning back in the copywriter's chair and affecting a self-satisfied look. He was an advertising natural. Brad paced like he was waiting for a public defender to spring him.

"It's bullshit because you're not a copywriter. You're a bodyguard. You can't just plop yourself down in an Aeron chair and declare yourself a writer. There's skill involved in advertising. I earned my title. This is an art. You are not an artist."

"I'm a U.S. marshal who needs to stick close to you until the trial is over. Besides, how hard can it be? Everyone knows the words are the easy part."

Dammit. He had a point.

Inmate
4-0-8-Z-G-Fucking-N

This was nothing. Frank Fortunato had been in worse situations. But would it kill them to put Wi-Fi in this dump?

As he sat in his private cell in Rikers, it occurred to Frank that this business of locking him up for Carmine's death wasn't fair. The drug trafficking, point shaving, prostitution, political bribery—putting him away for all that he could understand. But this? He had been handling something that had nothing to do with the police. A personal matter between him and Carmine. An errand. And they come busting in to arrest him. Right when things were starting to go his way. What happened to honor?

Well, this wasn't over by a long shot. They still had to convict him on this bogus charge. That meant a grand jury. A trial. Testimony. Evidence. A jury of regular shmoes. Many variables. A lot could happen between now and then.

"Mr. Fortunato, sorry to interrupt. Everything okay?"

Frank looked up to find the guard who was being paid very well to make sure his stay was a pleasant one.

Everything was and wasn't okay. Frank wasn't thrilled about being in jail, but it gave him plenty of time to think. And plan. And make big decisions. The new big decision he had come to was that his reputation was what counted now. He knew full well he had very little time left on this earth, and he had zero intention of finishing the race in jail. Great and powerful mob guys didn't go out like that. They went out in a blaze of glory. Or surrounded by their crew and family in Gold Coast mansions. Or getting blown by a stripper. Something with dignity.

The point was he wanted everything on his terms and he wanted to control his legacy. Which was possible, but it meant he had to take care of a few things and doing so involved some degree of risk. But, he was thinking big picture here. Time to go all in and play the cards he'd been dealt as best he could.

He nodded to the guard.

"Yeah, great. No wait, bring me more cigarettes. That's all anyone cares about in this place."

Stalker Love

Malcolm was on his third hot chocolate of the morning and dreading the sugar crash that was now inevitable.

But it was a small price to pay for the chance to accidentally bump into The Cougar again. He had been at the Cup 'n Mug long enough that he felt like a silly schoolboy, but not long enough that he was willing to sacrifice the hunt to save a little self-esteem. He had to pee in a bad way, but the thought of missing her wouldn't let him stray from his vigilant, if pitiful, perch by the door.

Malcolm had been back every morning since that fateful day in the hopes she would show up. A few key details were still in question: Was this her regular coffee shop? Was she single? Would she ever be back? If she was, what should he say? Would she remember him? Was this the kind of thing he had missed out on for years because he didn't drink coffee? And most important, who was she?

Maybe just one more hot chocolate. Work could wait.

"WelcometoCup'nMug.WhatcanIgetyoutomakeyourdaybetter?"

Malcolm ordered his drink and tried to ignore the curious looks of the staff who were forced to mumble this cheery statement to keep their jobs. Working in a high-volume shop like this, they quickly learned to overlook the quirky behaviors of their customers. But four small hot chocolates in an hour raised even the weariest of eyebrows.

"Dollar eighty-five."

Malcolm pulled out his wallet and found only a dollar left. He hadn't planned on spending so much today. Of course they took credit cards, but it seemed silly to charge such a tiny amount. Then again, he did pay off his card every month, so it wasn't like he would incur interest on the charge.

"That's a dollar eighty-five, sir.

From the other end of the counter an equally disinterested voice called out.

"Small hot chocolate, ready for pick up."

Malcolm pulled out his credit card and then wondered if he had enough change in his pocket to supplement the single dollar and avoid the hassle of a credit card.

"One moment."

He dug in his pants, pulled out a few coins and started to count them. There was more than enough here, so the question became which combination would leave the least volume in his pocket as an end result of his payment.

"You again? Jesus H. Take a little longer, why don't you?"

There was no mistaking the voice that yanked him right out of his thought spiral. It was The Cougar. Right behind him. He turned to find her in all of her on-the-way-to-the-gym splendor. Oh boy. How should he introduce himself? Is it inappropriate to approach a woman in a coffee shop before ten A.M.? Should he determine some sort of six-month plan to ask her out? That would put them in summer. Do people date in the summer? What if it's too hot?

"Hello. I was about to—"

"Sir, your hot chocolate is one eighty-five."

"I thought perhaps—"

"I have a hot chocolate. Rrrrready. For. Pickup."

The Cougar couldn't take it anymore.

"Excuse me, would you mind speeding it up. Some of us need our fix."

"Hot chocolate, still ready for pickup!"

"One eighty-five."

Malcolm turned around, whipped out his credit card, and handed it to the cashier.

The Cougar ordered her usual as Malcolm stood casually (in his mind) near where the finished drinks where handed out. Of all the things he had considered while dreaming of this day, his current choice of location was one he knew would pay off. Naturally, the coincidence that it was called the pickup counter was lost on him.

Ideally, there would be a nice lag time between when she ordered her drink and when she picked it up. Time for Romeo to say something clever. Or dashing. Or debonair. One of those.

The Cougar paid up and grabbed the coffee handed to her by the cashier and walked over to the condiment bar. Not the pickup counter. Of course. She hadn't ordered a fancy drink that would be handed out later. She had ordered a regular coffee. Damn the details. He hadn't planned on this. Now what? This was a whole other plan of approach. Should he come from the left or the right? Should he wait until she was done and follow her outside, or perhaps interrupt her stirring with some witty remark? Better yet, why not—

"Hey, Hot Chocolate. You got a name?"

In his flash flood of introspection, he had lost track of his prey and she had snuck up on him. Actually, she had walked right over to him.

"Malcolm."

"Malcolm. I'm Lola. Would you like to join me?"

Malcolm's only hesitation this time was to take a moment to smile.

"Would you mind if I used the facilities first?"

They sat at an open table in the back.

"All right, so you're not gay. What are you?"

Yes, Malcolm's first impression as a squirrelheaded non-homosexual was pretty bad. The second one, again clogging up traffic, not so great. But, once he was able to fill in some blanks for Lola, his third impression went pretty well. Being a tenured federal judge carried a lot of weight with women who were always running into guys claiming to be some sort of *macher*, only to find out they were middle management drones. Lola listened closely and liked what she heard. Malcolm knew enough to keep it short and sweet before turning the conversation back to his tablemate.

"Lola, tell me everything about yourself."

Lola was once divorced, once widowed. She loved her gym and her granddaughter whom she spoke with at least once a day, and she was considering piano lessons.

"So, look. I've got a hot box class in ten minutes, but I'd like to continue this conversation. Here's my number. Why don't you give me a call sometime? Maybe we could have dinner."

YESSSS! What a dream come true. Couldn't have planned it better yourself, Malcolm. Looks like you've still got it. Still got the old magic.

He carefully folded the paper and slid it into his pocket.

"I'd like that."

Brittany Returns

"Brad. Were you . . . exaggerating a little bit last time we talked about what you saw?"

It wasn't hard to see that Brittany already knew which way this conversation was going to go. Her way. She was hungry for a conviction and clearly intended this exchange to be one that pointed her in that direction.

She had called ahead to let Stump know she would be coming to Tucson and waiting for them when they got home. No point in getting her neck broken for the sake of dramatics.

". . . Uh . . ."

There was the distinct possibility that she was coming on too strong. Then again, that could be exactly what Brad needed. She had given him leeway in their first interview and he had given her back a Bollywood remake of *Magnum, P.I.*

"Maybe you were trying to tell me what you thought I wanted to hear?"

Her words said, *Don't worry, I'm your friend.* Her tone said, *Maybe you haven't heard, but I'm a badass.* She thought it struck a nice balance.

". . . Yes?"

Jarvis had actually made a little progress in the last week. Brittany's casual threat to hand the job off to Eidelsberg lit a great big nerd fire under him. Jarvis worked day and night, called up old professors, picked the minds of software engineers in the private sector. So far he had recovered another eight seconds of video that consisted of a smiling Brad trying to make eye contact with Carmine in the elevator.

Her eyewitness cruising the murder victim wasn't exactly trial gold, but it was more than they had before. And it gave her hope that there was more on the way. What a presentation that would be. Video. An eyewitness. She would have to remember to tell Tom to get a haircut. Every detail mattered. She should probably start eating salads and what was going on with her roots?

"Why don't we go over it again? And this time, let's stick to the facts. I know you're a big, brave cowboy, but we want the truth about what happened in the elevator with Carmine, okay? It's important, Brad."

Brad nodded and indicated to the Handycam set up behind Brittany.

"What's with the camera?"

"I need to get this on video for Frank's grand jury."

"Oh."

Video seemed like such a commitment.

"I can't risk you setting foot back in New York until the actual trial, so I worked out a deal with the U.S. Attorney's office. You testify on video for now and, a few weeks in, we'll set you up on satellite so both sides can ask you some questions. This way we only have to go back to New York once."

"Uh-huh."

Brittany took his answer to mean *Great. No problem.* In fact, it was an acknowledgement of how profoundly unsafe Brad understood himself to be once he translated Brittany's explanation to mean *There are a lot of people trying to kill you, big boy. We don't like the odds of bringing you in twice.* Which meant bringing him in once was a huge risk.

"Shouldn't I wear a disguise?"

"Do you have a disguise?"

Actually, yes. He still had the giant beard and trucker hat Stump had made him wear on the plane ride out. Suddenly, it didn't seem like such a bad look.

Brittany wasn't opposed to the idea. As long as he testified, she didn't care what he looked like.

Brad went back to his room. The beard was buried behind some T-shirts in his dresser. On top of his wedding ring. Hadn't he thrown that away? Apparently not, but for the life of him, he couldn't remember why not.

Gracie was the best lawyer he knew and she could have told him exactly how to handle this. She would have at least trimmed the beard to make it look less Park Slopey. But he was on his own here. Thanks for nothing,

Gracie. He slid the ring into his pocket and told himself he would toss it out the window the next time he and Stump drove anywhere.

As he closed the drawer, he caught a good look at the scared little man in the mirror. Brad had easily lost five pounds, despite his new omnivore diet. Those crow's feet were definitely not there two weeks ago. And it wasn't just that he had forgotten to pack his Clinique for Men Age Defense Hydrator. How many years was this whole affair shaving off his life? This was real stress. Not the bullshit kind like when the client asks what you think of their son's idea for a tag line. This was the kind of stress that affects your body on a cellular level. The kind that happens to other people.

He hadn't testified yet. It wasn't too late to hop out the window, steal Brittany's car, and live the life of a nameless drifter. It seemed like a pretty decent lifestyle if the Disney movies of his childhood were to be believed. Maybe he could learn to play the guitar by campfire light and get adopted by a Sandra Bullock–type character who would encourage him to play football *his way*. Probably not. Also, he didn't have the first clue how to hotwire a car, and he had heard the Arizona hitchhiking laws were pretty strict. Better just to play along. For now.

Brad slid the beard on and jammed the hat onto his head. Honestly, it worked with the crow's feet.

Brad sat back down.

"Maybe an accent? Should I do an accent? Indian or hillbilly or something? Jack Nicholson?"

"I think the disguise is enough."

Brittany clipped a mic on Brad's shirt and hit a button on the remote to start the camera recording.

"So why don't you introduce yourself."

As if it were connected to his head via some psychic Ethernet cable, as soon as Brittany hit the record button, Brad's brain went white with panic.

What did she know? Holy God, what did she know? Was she on to him or just under some judiciary, red tape deadline? Is that how the FBI worked? There was no way to know.

On top of those worries, the only story he could think of was the two-hundred-million-dollar tentpole he had dreamed up in the shower. That wasn't going to work. In fact, it was probably a great way to raise Brittany's suspicions of his fundamental intentions. No one needs a delusional narcissist on the witness stand.

He quickly cut the story down to its bare bones in his head. Forget the Van Damme splits. No Steven Seagal stare. Maybe the Korean line. The Korean line gave his character depth. No, no Korean line. Just the facts. He had to tell the truth. She could use that, right? She probably already knew it anyway. Were there agents outside the door waiting to arrest him? What was the mandatory sentence for perjury? Did he remember it being fifteen years, or was that for unlawful imprisonment of an animal?

Wait. It can't be perjury. There hasn't been a trial yet. Okay. Maybe it really was time for the truth. Brad replayed the day's events one more time. He went on a job interview. Nailed it. Got on the elevator. Tried to share a little sunshine with Carmine. Noticed a scuff on his shoe. Bent down to rub it off. Two black shoes walked in. Brad sneezed. Carmine was dead.

No.

That sounds idiotic. Who would believe he missed the whole thing? A mob murder happened three feet from him and he didn't catch it? Seriously. That's worse than how he lost the vodka job. He could hear Champ laughing already. Nope, once again, he really didn't have much choice but to lie. This situation called for a carefully curated load of bullshit.

"Hi, I'm Brad Pitt."

Brittany turned the camera off.

"Brad. You can't use your new name. Then people would know your new identity and it wouldn't be a secret anymore, would it?"

"Right. Sorry, I'm a little nervous."

"Let's try it again."

Stump shook his head in disgust. He might have to schedule another trip to the coffee shop.

Brittany hit Record again.

"Hi, my name is Brad Fingerman, and I swear to tell the truth, the whole truth, and nothing but the truth."

"Brad, can you tell us what happened the day of Friday, September eighth?"

"Well—"

Oops. He shouldn't have looked at Stump. Standing there in the doorway watching over the whole exchange, Stump looked at Brad with those preternaturally intense eyes that always seemed like they were dismantling the machinations of his mind like a snobby watchmaker picking over the insides of a knockoff Rolex. This was going to be harder than he thought.

"I had just finished up an interview at Red Light District Advertising in the 1635 building."

"The job you didn't get."

"Yes, Brittany, the job I didn't get. Thank you for reminding me on the public record. But, you know, I really *thought* I did well in the interview. So, anyway I get on the elevator."

"Mmm hmmm."

"And then . . ."

And then he lied lied lied. Not as much as before, but definitely not the truth. He left out the bone-crushing antics of his swashbuckling doppelganger from the initial version of the story, settling instead for a more subdued, early-David-Carradine-esque, Zen approach in which Brad attempted to reason with Frank on a bro level.

"So Frank was crying?"

Brad thought he saw Stump's eyes roll the tiniest bit. He quickly rethought his position.

"No. He had something in his eye."

"Did he tell you that?"

"I could just tell. Anyway, he ran off and you guys showed up before I could chase after him."

And then it was done.

Brittany nodded and turned off the camera. Man, it was quiet in there.

"Thank you for being honest, Brad."

Nailed It Again

She bought it. What a relief. Finally, Brad could get back to his life selling diapers to retirees with weak bowels.

Close Enough

All right, so he lied again. But not as much, and it was pretty believable. A little coaching from an experienced attorney and they would be good to go. Brittany fired up her rental car and headed back to the airport, content with the knowledge that her impulsive trip to Tucson was worth it.

Brad's Zygomaticus Major

Stump had watched the whole thing pretty closely, studying Brad's facial muscles for indications that betrayed what was the truth, what was an exaggeration of the truth, and what was fantastical nonsense. His vantage point was from a side angle and the beard and hat covered a lot of acreage, so he couldn't see every twitch and contraction of Brad's face, but Stump still wasn't convinced Brad was telling the truth.

Based on the gymnastics routine Brad's face was performing, he wasn't even convinced that Brad had been in the elevator at the time of the murder. The lateral pterygoids, corrugator supercilii, and zygomaticus major activity were off the charts. The levator labii superioris and frontalis pars lateralis were all over the place. And what about that depressor labii inferioris? Ridiculous.

It didn't help that Brad had sweat about a gallon while he spitballed his version of the truth on camera. Maybe he was nervous about performing, but this was a guy who sold stuff to strangers for a living. It didn't make sense.

He reminded himself to ask Brittany for a copy of that video. He needed to study it from a head-on angle. Something was up with that guy.

Assure

There are two different governing philosophies within advertising agencies. The first says that the idea is king. The creative directors and copywriters and art directors swagger about and present their work as if it were a gift from on high. They are the holders of the key to the enchanted cave of clever concepts, and everyone else is just support. The second says that creatives are an integral but subjugated part of an advertising machine that serves the god of strategy and account planning as translated by the oracles known as account executives.

Generally, the choice of which philosophy is to be followed is dictated by whoever happens to be running the agency. If it's an account guy who worked his way up through the ranks to become top dog, then creatives look to the account floor for approval. If it's a creative director who successfully made a power play for the chair at the end of the table, then the account execs kowtow to the arrogant creative teams.

Alan Silver liked to think of himself as a creative at heart. A trait he discovered only in recent years. But when he was offered this job, it was with the understanding that as good as an idea is, in the end it's got to satisfy the needs of the people upstairs. The account people.

In other words, no matter how great the work that came out of his department was, if it didn't have an enormous yellow Assure logo in the corner and their cheery tag line *Confident, from the waist down!* underneath, it was going to get dumped on. Getting dumped on was not something that Alan took very well. In fact, it was a great way to trigger the loss of his teeny-tiny patience. And that was the hardest part of Alan's job—not strangling people who dumped on his work.

This was all a little much to explain to Brad, what with them both having the complications of secret identities and sordid pasts. So Alan asked Brad and Stump to follow the creative briefs pretty closely *so we can all leave here in time for happy hour.* That was his little joke that really meant *so I don't have to murder anyone.*

"Can I get a cell phone?"

"No."

"You have one."

"I'm a Federal marshal."

"Can I be a Federal marshal?"

"No."

Brad could tell already, carpooling was going to suck. First of all, the workday started way too early. They were almost at the office and it was only the crack of nine. It was one of those crisp, clean mornings ad guys always try to capture in their commercials but never want to wake up for. And that morning, Brad didn't feel like a leading man. He was tired and irritable and still being followed by this hulking lineman of a government agent.

He never got a break from the guy. Stump was up before he was, went to bed after he did, never stopped hanging around, and now they had to spend their ride to work and the rest of the day together making adult diaper propaganda.

"I just want to call my friend. He's sick. With cancer."

"No, he's not."

"All right, he's not, but I'm an adult, goddammit. I have rights."

Stump pulled into their new assigned parking place in the Assure lot and shut the car off.

"After you testify. Until then, it's too much of a risk. Cell phones can be listened in on, tracked, all sorts of stuff. I can't risk you divulging some important information on your location."

"What if I promise I won't do that?"

Stump got out of the car and shut his door. He waited for Brad to get out, and they walked into the building in silence.

Grand Jury

Malcolm was a little distracted. The majority of his brainpower had lately been devoted to devising plans to not screw up this budding relationship with Lola. Even using the term *budding* made him nervous. They had not even been out on a date yet. Did the five-minute coffee thing count? Probably not. Technically they hadn't shared a meal. And the table by the Cup 'n Mug bathroom hadn't been the most romantic spot to chat. Then again, he understood that coffee dates were the big thing these days. They were an easy test drive with a minimal initial investment and very effective for weeding out the nutjobs. So maybe he had inadvertently played that one just right. He had started with the coffee date and gotten the seal of approval to move beyond the potential whacko level.

If only he had asked her first. That would have really been something to tell Mother about. He tried to put that out of his mind. What's done is done. Focus on the results. Focus on *anything* actually.

Since he'd had an actual live conversation with Lola, he had been driven to distraction. Malcolm had always been one to analyze things to the point of exhaustion, but his compulsion had worsened in the days since The Cougar cast her spell on him.

Deciding on dinner had become a nightly dilemma. Choosing a book before bed was a Herculean effort. And forget about getting dressed in the morning. The idea that he might accidentally bump into her on the street sent his mind reeling. Suit and tie? *I am a federal judge after all.* Business casual? *I'm so powerful I dress however I feel like and men fear me.* Jeans and a button down? *Oh, I'm just plain folk doing my duty for the American public.* The truth was he wore a big black robe at work and could have gone commando if he had really wanted to. In the summer, some judges did. He settled on his usual khaki pants and polo shirt. Like a baseball player with Asperger's, he was not going to blow a streak like this by changing up his routine.

Malcolm had been purposefully vague with his answer when Lola had asked him about getting together again. He claimed he needed to check his calendar. He didn't want to commit to anything and then have to reschedule. He couldn't tell if her smirk was one of affection or a knowing look born from seeing right through his sad little ruse. Truth be told, he could have checked a *TV Guide* to figure out which night was best to get together. His social calendar was emptier than Justin Guarini's voice mail.

His plan was to wait a few days so he didn't seem too eager. Then he would ask her to dinner. The only thing left to decide on was which restaurant to go to, which sweater to wear, what time to go, should they have drinks beforehand, what wine to order, should he bring flowers. Actually, there was a lot to think about.

While Malcolm turned the intricacies of senior dating over in his mind, the rest of the courtroom waited patiently for his decision. The question on the table was whether or not the prosecution had his permission to proceed with the video testimony of their key witness.

"Your honor?"

Malcolm started.

"Yes?"

"May we proceed?"

Malcolm bought himself a little time by readjusting his reading glasses and pretending to read over some papers on his desk.

It took him a moment before it all came rushing back to him. The video. The witness in protection. The whole Frank Fortunato murder trial. Right.

Federal grand juries were the casual Fridays of the law world. Yes, important work got done here, but the real show was the trial. Grand juries are essentially a formality to ensure defendants aren't prosecuted solely because the prosecutor says they're guilty. There needs to be enough evidence to justify a trial, but in most cases that's easier than finding a mullet at a prison rodeo.

In any other courtroom in the land, this would have been over. But Malcolm had had some questions for those involved.

He spent the morning hearing arguments as to why a video of a witness should and should not serve as a valid replacement for a live witness. He had been assured that this witness was key to the prosecution's case. Three jury members had fallen asleep already. Perhaps it was time to move on.

"Yes. Please."

The assistant United States attorney hit Play and a video of Brad appeared on the monitor Brittany had arranged for. As fake-bearded Brad wove his tale, the jury perked up and became interested. It wasn't exactly *12 Angry Men*, but it was a good enough story that when it was done, they murmured amongst themselves.

"Is there anything else to be presented?"

"Your honor, there will be surveillance video from the scene of the crime and a few other witnesses, but we feel this is more than enough to compel the jury to decide to move forward."

Malcolm could feel his thoughts drifting back to the delightful Lola, and he didn't feel like stopping them. He had real decisions to make.

"I agree."

Check, Check, and Check

Three FBI agents. One eyewitness. Surveillance video.

From his prime courtroom seat as defendant numero uno, Frank Fortunato calmly and methodically catalogued the evidence presented against him as if it were a list of sundries he needed to pick up at the Walgreens, and then kill and bury in a Jersey swamp.

Not long afterward, the grand jury decided that there was indeed enough evidence to move forward. A trial date was set and Frank moved a little closer to dying in prison.

The New Guys

"Knock knock? You guys free?"

Of course they were free. It was their first day of work. And nine thirty A.M. The friendly face belonging to the energetic body darkening their doorway was Overly-Confident-Account-Guy. Also known as Mike D.

There was another Mike in the office, Mike P., but he was the mentally challenged mail guy and also Filipino. Mike D. was white. And wore a tie. There was no chance of mistaking the two. But that's how they rolled at Assure.

"Mike D., account manager. Nice to meet you two."

Stump, standing by the door, offered his hand and took on an uncharacteristically outgoing persona.

"Nice to meet you, Mike."

"Mike *D.*, as in Determined."

He punctuated his correction with an energetic wink.

"Ah-huh. I'm Christopher. This is my partner Brad."

Brad leaned over his desk and shook Mike D.'s hand.

"How you doing, Mike D.?" *As in Dillweed.*

"I'm doing great. Welcome to Assure. Hope we're not too crazy for you around here."

And then he laughed one of those laughs people use to imply a deeper meaning but usually mean something lame just happened.

Brad smiled.

"So far, so good."

"Great! Well, listen, I hear you guys are the new creative geniuses around here, so I wanted to get your help on an exciting project we've got coming up. Sound good?"

It didn't, but they said it did and Mike D. handed them each a creative brief for a brochure that needed to be done. The piece was destined to live in the waiting rooms of doctors' offices, presumably for patients hitting that tipping point of boredom when they're willing to read just about anything.

"The piece needs to be engaging and memorable. We're okay with whimsy, but generally, the serious stuff works best. But smart, you know. We like to keep the bar pretty high. Also, you'll see there are some bullet points we need to hit. You'll find a library of images on the server, and I know Alan was hoping to see something in a couple of days. Sound good?"

Mike D. was very concerned that everything sounded good.

Stump had never been in a creative briefing before. He looked to Brad for his cue.

"Sounds good, Mike."

"Mike D."

Cuh-rist.

"Sounds good, Mike D."

Mike D. thanked Stump and Brad for helping him out, as if they had a choice, and reminded them to call him if they needed anything or had questions. One more check that everything sounded good and he was out of there.

Brad had told Mike D. that things sounded good, but the truth was they sounded kind of sucky. A couple of days? Who gets work done that fast? What was this, an iPhone factory? Brad was an artist. And he was just supposed to crank out something beautiful like a regularly scheduled bowel movement? WTF?

As soon as Mike D. was gone, Stump dropped the peppy persona, eased back into his understated self, and checked the blinds for any black hats sneaking up the back way.

"So how does this work? You make the pictures and I write some words? Sounds pretty simple. Let's take a look at the picture library he was talking about."

Brad sighed in the face of what looked like a very long day ahead. So now on top of making an informative brochure for folks in danger of crapping themselves, he had to explain the fundamentals of advertising to Stump. Super.

"I'll take care of it. You keep watch or something."

A bit about Brad's process: It usually began with a bit of online research on the subject at hand. Or gossip blogs. From there it was an internal brainstorming session that looked a lot like watching YouTube videos. A nice long lunch to keep the brain tip top and then the afternoon was spent figuratively throwing ideas against the wall to see what stuck, running things up the flagpole to see who saluted, and tossing furniture into the pool to see what splashed. You know, bullshitting with his coworkers.

But this tried-and-true process would have to be altered somewhat, as Stump wasn't allowing Brad unrestricted Internet access for fear that he would e-mail someone something he shouldn't and inadvertently compromise his existence. So no blogs, no videos, and the nearest restaurant was the Fridays two exits away. That left actually working. Brad started with a classic chestnut.

"We should do something with old people acting young."

"Sounds kind of easy. What else you got?"

Um, what? Who does this guy think he is? He's a friggin' cop. I've been doing this for almost ten years. I'm the Molotov Vodka guy. Unbelievable.

"Let me take another look at the brief."

Now this was uncharted territory. Briefs rarely rated a first look, much less a second. Brad reread the document and found that it actually made some sense. Mike D. could put a sentence together. Appropriately enough, it sounded good. Good enough to inspire Brad.

"What if it wasn't a brochure? What if it was a bookmark?"

"You can do that?"

You could at Overthink. That was one of Brad's favorite moves. Didn't like the media? Change it to something smarter. That's how print ads became microsites and how e-mail blasts became guerrilla wild postings.

"Sure. It's basically the same thing. And we're talking to an older set that tends to read a lot. If they're in a doctor's office, there's a good chance they brought a book with them. This way, we make sure they take our info home with them."

Stump nodded.

"That's good."

Brad opened up the server files and started looking through the library of the stock imagery they were stuck with.

"So how come you told Mike D. your name was Christopher?"

"Because my name is Christopher."

Brad pulled up a few shots of some seniors sitting together on sand dunes looking at the sun set on the horizon of the Pacific. Yes, very hack stuff.

"But everyone calls you Stump."

"Everyone involved with witness protection calls me Stump. But at Assure I'm undercover."

"Do you have a new pretend last name?"

"Flint."

Brad stopped clicking through the images and looked up.

"What?"

"Flint. Christopher Flint. I kept the first name so I didn't slip up."

"Yeah, I know why you kept the first name. Why do you get to pick an awesome last name? How come it's not Jerkoffsky or Walken? Why aren't we Brad Pitt and Christopher Walken?"

"I'm a marshal. I get to pick my own name."

Brad went back to sifting through the shlocky shots. Yep, this was bullshit.

"Besides, Christopher is a generic name that doesn't stick out. Stump is memorable. That reminds me, don't use it while we're here. When we're here, I'm Christopher. You never know who's IM-ing or e-mailing with their friends back East. They mention it innocently and it gets passed on and before you know it, we've got a couple of bullets in the back of our heads."

Ah, right. The whole bullet in the back of the head thing. Brad was so fired up about the bookmark idea, he had almost forgotten what he was running from.

Brad and Stump spent the rest of the morning creating concepts for the bookmark. Brad came up with a few hip looks (as hip as you can get with geriatric models) and Stump wrote some decent copy. Turns out the words really were the easy part.

Brad suggested sushi for lunch and then remembered he was in Way-Away-from-New-York-or-L.A.-Land, so they settled on the Assure cafeteria on the third floor. They were in luck. The day's special was chicken fingers. Sort of like sushi.

The Assure cafeteria was nicer than you would expect for an office park building. Hot lunches with new menu specials daily. Premade sandwiches and wraps on the refrigerated shelves. A continuously busy brick pizza oven. A grill churning out thick burgers and fries. And the token unused salad bar that ended up serving as more of a museum dedicated to green leafy vegetables and the creamy dressings that drown them. Something for everyone. It was a key element in some efficiency expert's comprehensive plan to make Assure run as smoothly as possible—keep your employees on the premises. Car trips to Chili's take longer than elevator rides to the third floor. And not as many people get drunk at lunch.

This was the only time Stump sat down the entire day. Brad assumed it was because standing and constantly sweeping the room for furtive movements or sniper scopes would have been a little out of character for Christopher Flint on his lunch break.

"So how is it that you never seem to sleep?"

"I sleep."

"I never see you sleep."

"Why would you see me sleep?"

"You never shower. Or shave."

"I shower every day. And shave. You just miss it."

Well, that was true. Stump didn't stink, and he never had so much as a two o'clock shadow. Brad couldn't figure it out, and instead of trying he finished his meal and went back to work.

It's Not You, It's the Nielsens

"Thanks for understanding, Brian. I know this must be hard for you."

Brittany prepared for this conversation by imagining she was Julia Roberts in some new movie about a tough, independent woman who plays by her own rules and has to make a difficult choice. She hadn't worked out what the character did for a living or what that tough choice was, but she knew it affected her movie boyfriend and she could see the way her movie self would grimace/smile when she realized that, despite her fondness for her true love and his teen-idol dimples, she had to break up with him or some terrible, yet-to-be-determined thing would happen, probably to children. It was sort of charming and hard to hate in an opening-weekend-box-office-gold kind of way.

"Umm, okay. So then, we're definitely off for next Thursday? I want to make sure I can sell your ticket."

Next Thursday? Poor Brian. He just didn't get it. She was talking about a major life change and he was worried about unloading her seat to *Sleep No More*.

Brittany saw herself as brave for instigating this preemptive breakup. Also thoughtful. What kind of life would Brian have with paparazzi following them around snapping pictures at inopportune moments, the rags throwing him in the Worst Beach Bodies issues just because they needed filler, and all the other pressure that comes with being a celebrity boyfriend? It would be too much. And such a stereotype. Unless he had some sort of plan to turn his incidental coattail riding into fame of his own, their relationship was doomed. She had to be strong for both of them.

"We're off for next Thursday. I'm headed back to Tucson Thursday. And then when I come back, we'll be off forever."

"All right, then. Thanks for calling."

"Take care, Brian."

They had only been seeing each other three weeks and that only involved two dates, but Brittany wasn't taking any chances. The road she was headed down lead to stardom, and she didn't need any baggage when she got there.

Sal smiled as he listened to the girl let the boy down via a wiretap his crew had set up. Didn't really even seem like the breakup was worth the effort. He was pretty sure he had heard the guy mutter "Oh, some girl" to whoever was in the room with him as he hung up the phone.

But what he was positively sure he heard was that the FBI agent responsible for the witness that claimed to have seen Frank murder Carmine was going to Tucson next Thursday. Jackpot.

Frank was going to be so proud of him.

Yo

That afternoon, Brad and Stump hammered out a couple of traditional brochure layouts as a backup to their more creative attempts in alternative media. As uninventive as the work was, Brad felt better losing himself in the task. Nice to be back in the saddle, even if it was strapped onto a broken down donkey instead of the wild palomino he had been riding five weeks ago.

They printed out their work, laid it all out across Brad's desk, and picked a few favorites. Brad knew they had something relatively good because he started to feel the urge to show Alan. He felt like showing off. That was the litmus test. Stump must have felt the same way, but demonstrated a painful lack of understanding of how advertising worked.

"We should stop by Alan's office on our way out and show him this stuff."

"Are you crazy? We can't show him now. It's way too soon."

"But we're done."

"He doesn't need to know that. Mike D. said we have a few days. If we're done too fast, they'll expect it that way every time. I'm not letting them know how good we are yet."

Stump raised his eyebrows at the brochures and bookmarks they had created to sell diapers to the elderly.

"*This* is how good we are?"

That certainly put a fine point on it. Brad realized he had fallen victim to ad-guy myopia. The stuff was 4A. Good *for a* brochure to help people who are worried about soiling their golf pants.

"I don't want to work here."

"Okay."

"Okay, you'll get me another job?"

"No, okay, you don't have to work here."

"Where will I work?"

"I don't know."

"How will I get a job?"

"Uhh, interview?"

"But Brad Pitt doesn't have any work experience. What job could Brad Pitt possibly have?"

"Maybe you could be a movie star."

"It's not funny."

"It's a little funny."

Brad stared at their work, now disgusted as he realized it comprised the entirety of his new portfolio.

"You're welcome to look for another job. You'll need to fill out some paperwork and we'll want to check out the company. But it's your life. Do what you want."

What Brad wanted was that primo job at Red Light he interviewed for a lifetime ago. It was the only thing he knew how to do. But his résumé was now a blank piece of paper. Soon it would be a piece of paper that read, "Brad sold diapers!" but he couldn't imagine that would be of too much assistance.

"I'm gonna take a dump."

"Good start."

Brad did not need to take a dump. The truth was he needed to get away. He turned and walked down the hallway as if he had somewhere important to be. He continued purposefully straight past the bathroom and made a left at Skinny-Jeans-Emo-Haircut-Guy's cubicle.

Brad needed to breathe. Alone. He managed a weak smile as he passed Uptight-English-Account-Planner-Girl's office.

He needed to get this stress out of his system. When he passed Perky-Gay-Assistant-Guy's vacant desk, he stopped.

He needed to tell someone. He needed to talk. And there was Perky-Gay-Assistant-Guy's cell phone. Just sitting there. The universe was giving him a sign. Probably.

Brad checked over his back before he nabbed the phone, shoved it into his front pocket, and kept walking. When he came to the elevators, he found one waiting for him. Empty. Perfect. He stepped in and hit the highest floor there was.

Ahhhh.

Brad watched the floor lights go up. The building was only nine floors, but that would do. He was headed for his own private conference room on the roof.

Ding. Dammit.

The doors opened on the sixth floor and Perky-Gay-Assistant-Guy looked in.

"Going up?"

For the love of God.

"Yup, going up."

"Great!"

Perky-Gay-Assistant-Guy stepped in and hit the button for seven.

Really? You couldn't spare the calories?

Ding. The elevator slowed to a stop almost as soon as it started. Perky-Gay-Assistant-Guy bounced on his toes in anticipation of spreading joy on the seventh floor. Finally, the doors opened.

"Have a great day!"

"You too—"

Brad was interrupted by the muffled "Single Ladies" ring tone coming from his front pocket.

"Oh my God! I have the exact same ring tone! We should go clubbin—"

Mercifully, the elevator doors cut Perky-Gay-Assistant-Guy off before he did the ring-tone math.

Ahhhh.

The view on the roof of Assure Worldwide wasn't quite as magnificent as the one on top of Brad and Gracie's apartment building. It was a sweeping view of the office park in all its redundant glory. Five identical buildings, each composed of red brick and dark glass. It gave you the feeling that someone had decided to save some money by reusing

the same architectural plans for each new address. Brad's building sat
on the south edge of the park, its rear parking lot butted up against
a golf course. He headed around the structure that housed the stairs
to the golf course side, pulled out the phone, and dialed a number he
knew by heart.

He needed to have someone else share this burden. Why should he
be in this mess alone? It was a risk and he knew it, but so was using a
Kindle in the bath and that had always worked out for him. He just
had to be careful.

Gracie picked up on the third ring. He couldn't tell if she was working or sleeping or confused by the Arizona area code he was calling
from. He couldn't tell because she didn't say hello. She just picked up
the phone.

Brad may have been brave enough to call Gracie, but he didn't have
the guts to say a single word to her. And if he did what would that word
be? Something nasty? Something conciliatory? Something admonish-
ing? He realized he probably should have thought this out a little more
before calling. Perhaps jotted down a few notes.

". . . Brad?"

Whoa.

Brad hung up immediately. She had known it was him. Or is that
how she answered the phone every time it had rung since he left? Was
she heartbroken? Was she repentant? Did she want him back? Did
she hate him? Did she want to make everything better? Did she want
to start over or join him in Tucson or tell him she was wrong about
everything? Did she know he knew?

He was dying to know the answer to even one of these questions,
but his reptilian brainstem forced him to end the call before any
deeper feelings were evoked or he was stupid enough to say something
out loud. Like "Hello" or "God, I miss you."

That was close. He was white hot with adrenaline.

What was he thinking? Why did he just do that? Hiding from the
Mafia was hard enough on its own. What was with the unnecessary
self-torture?

Brad dug his wedding ring out of his pocket. He had been carrying
it around since he discovered it in his dresser drawer but hadn't found

the perfect stretch of road to dispose of it yet. Not in all the nine miles of the South Nogales Highway between his home and the office.

The ring sat there in the palm of his hand, staring back at him. Daring him.

What are you looking at, pussy?

The band of gold was no different than the stupid phone call he just made. He got worked up every time he saw it and he had no idea why that was so pacifying.

Brad clenched the ring one last time and then hurled it as far as his moderately exercised arms would allow. It landed somewhere just over the golf course fence, in the rough of the fifth hole fairway. If he wanted to badly enough, and if there was a metal detector rental place around here, he probably could have found it, but he knew that wasn't ever going to happen. That ring was gone.

Brad dialed Owen's number.

"Hello?"

"What's up, you lazy shithead?"

"Dad?"

"Dude."

"Brad? Holy shit, what are you doing?"

"Going crazy. I need to talk to someone."

Owen was polite enough to not interrupt the silence that followed while Brad figured out something else to say.

"So, how's work?"

"Same. But there's some new guy who just doesn't get it."

"He doesn't get handing out fliers?"

"He almost got into a fight with a cop. Some people aren't cut out for this kind of work."

"Nope."

"But, hey guess what!"

"You passed your test? You're gonna work for the city?"

"Yep. I start in a few days, and I already have my assignment. That's like going straight to the big leagues."

It was so depressing to hear that life in Manhattan was moving forward without Brad.

"Wow. I'm really impressed. Congratulations."

"Yeah. I guess it doesn't matter the new guy isn't Chicken Shack material. Not my problem anymore, right?

". . . Owen, I didn't see anything."

"Well, how could you? You're out of town. Trust me, the new guy is a loooo-ser."

"The murder. I didn't see the murder I'm testifying about. I didn't see Frank Fortunato murder Carmine."

There was that weird beat where someone pauses while they wonder what's wrong with the person they were listening to.

"But, you said you did. To the FBI."

"Look, I was in a weird place. I tried to tell them I missed the whole thing, but they wouldn't believe me and then a bunch of stuff happened and I said I saw the murder so I could get into the Witness Protection Program because no one would hire me in New York and I'm pretty sure my wife is having an affair. My story is complete bullshit and to top it all off, it got me nothing. Now I'm stuck in Tucson making diaper ads."

"You could have crashed with me."

"Uh . . . oh."

Well now, that would have been a simple solution, huh? Brad told himself that things were complicated and Owen just didn't understand.

"I don't know what I'm going to do."

"Come clean. Tell the truth."

"No. Something else."

"I don't see a lot of options here."

This was not exactly turning into the motivational seminar Brad had hoped it would be.

"All right, whatever. Never mind. I just have to be convincing on the witness stand."

"Well, how hard could that be? You were there when it happened, right?"

"Right."

"Well, you must have seen something."

"No, nothing. That's what I'm trying to tell you. I was cleaning my shoe. I didn't actually, technically see the murder. I'm lying to the FBI."

"You can't lie in court. That's . . . sacred."

"I can't go back to my old life."

"Oh man, this is bad."

Brad sort of wished he had called an Indian tech support line instead. At least they would have the decency to lie to him and say everything was going to be all right.

"I gotta go. Take care, Owen. I'll steal another phone soon."

Brad hung up and took a moment to stare at the golf course, now golden in the setting sun. Some people would call it wallowing.

"That's some fucked up shit."

Uh-oh.

Brad rounded the corner of the stairwell housing to find a man leaning against the wall as if it were the east side of Union Square Park. Baggy jeans. Huge white T-shirt. Lit joint hanging loosely from his lips. When he spoke, Brad noticed a few gold teeth.

"Lying to the FBI. Mmm."

There were a few different ways to handle this situation. Pretend his new friend misheard what had been said and explain that he was talking about a movie he once saw. Beg the eavesdropper to not say anything about what he definitely heard. Be righteously indignant and demand an explanation for this sneakery. But Brad was too aggravated to act any way other than the way he was feeling. Pissed.

"Who are you?"

"Yo."

"Hello. I said, who are you?"

"I'm the guy who heard all your dirty little secrets."

Brad quickly realized that he had blown his cover in less time than it took to generate the documents that supported it. But he couldn't help indulging in a tiny bit of frustration. Can't a guy have a simple, super dangerous, mission-compromising conversation without someone listening in? Now what? He'd have to go into Witness Protection Protection?

"Yeah, well, marijuana's illegal."

Weed Guy chuckled and took another deep puff. He kept it in and held the joint out to Brad.

This decision was an easier one. Brad took the joint and inhaled deeply as well. Weed Guy finally exhaled.

"Well, I guess we both know something about each other then, huh?"

Brad exhaled. Now that was some helpful therapy. He figured since he was smoking the guy's herb, he might as well introduce himself.

"I'm Brad. I'm the new guy."

"I know who you are."

"Have we met?"

Brad passed the joint back. Weed Guy took another major hit.

"Nope. I'm Dr. Yo."

This guy did not look like a doctor. He was wearing cornrows, for Christ sake. Maybe a PhD from state university, but even that was a tough sell.

"What are you doing up here?"

"Same thing I do up here every day."

Dr. Yo stubbed what was left on his shoe, stuck the roach in his pocket, and headed for the stairs.

"Later."

What Sal Heard

"My friend is going to get some air."

"Your friend is going to get some air."

"But he's not going to get it in Zone B."

"Okay."

"And he's not going to get it in Zone C."

"Not Zone C."

Sometimes Sal was so bad at talking in code it made Frank's forehead hurt. He was fine with pronouns. The guy with the thing at the place. No problem. Frank could decipher that without thinking twice. They had been talking like that for the better part of thirty years, so understanding that particular dialect of Sal-speak was easier than Frank Jr. flunking algebra. He and Sal had more interpretations of the words "thing" and "guy" and "place" than the Eskimos had words for snow. And the feds could never crack it because it only made sense to the two of them. It was a beautiful system. As long as they were talking about a thing or a guy or a place.

But when it came to putting other symbolic words into the channel, Sal was awful and usually indecipherable. So, as they sat there in the Rikers visitation chambers talking over handsets, it took all the self-control Frank could muster to not derail the conversation by calling Sal a fucktard and focus on figuring out what valuable information was being delivered.

Not going to Zone B for air. Not going to Zone C for air.

"My friend is going to get some air in . . ."

Not B. Not C. Why did he skip A? Ah. He's going to get some Air in Zone A. Arizona God, that was a long way to go for a code word.

"Got it. Any particular place in Zone A?"

Sal looked around to see who was listening. Like that's how the feds did it. Sneaking up with a cup against the door or pretending to get a drink at the water cooler and hoping to overhear your murder plot instead of picking up a backroom extension of the line they were on. What an idiot.

"Well, I'll have to ask my son about that. Not my number one son, though."

Charlie fucking Chan over here with another prizewinning riddle. Not number one son. So . . . his number two son. Number two son. Ah.

"Got it."

"You want that I should set up a *scholarship* for my friend?"

Wow, was Sal a bad actor. He even tilted his head down and raised his eyebrows when he said "scholarship."

"No. Don't do anything. I'll handle the scholarship or whatever."

"No, Frank, not a real scholarship. A scho-lar-ship."

"Yeah, I understand. Scholarship. I'll handle it. I don't want you touching anything for a while, okay? Stay clean."

Sal was visibly hurt by this perceived rejection. Here he was bringing information that could shoot a big hole in the conviction that was looming and Frank's treating him like a fat stewardess.

"I just thought . . ."

"I said I'll handle it. But I still want you to go see about that thing."

"The guy with the thing or the thing at the place."

Frank grimaced and cocked his head at Sal as if he should know already.

"Oh, that guy. You got it."

Yo, Yo

Brad held firm that they shouldn't show the work any earlier than was absolutely necessary, effectively earning him and Stump six hours of dicking-around time the next day. He was pacing himself.

They filled their time with Stump-approved Internet gossip sites, online chess, and a passionate debate (on Brad's side) over the merits of paparazzi rights. Stump couldn't have cared less, but it was fun to push Brad's buttons.

"What if they're putting innocent lives at risk?"

"Celebrities are not innocent. If they didn't like risking their lives they wouldn't eat at The Ivy."

"Knock knock!"

It was Mike D., as in Determined, to interrupt their fake work process.

"Hey, guys! How's it going? You kicking some killer ideas around?"

"Brad thinks TMZ is the Bible."

Mike D. stood there, D. for Dumb.

"Were you looking for something, Mike D.?"

Mike D. snapped to.

"Oh, yeah. I wanted to see what kind of progress you guys were making on the brochure project. We've got a status call with sales tomorrow, and I'm hoping you can go over stuff with Alan and make revisions before then so we can keep this thing moving. Have you shown the big guy anything yet?"

"Not yet. We were going to stop by after lunch."

"But it's done?"

"Yeah, it's all done."

"Sounds good."

This was an unusual protocol for Brad. He was used to the more creative-driven agencies where his department conducted activities in Opus Dei–like secrecy and let the account team know when they were good and ready.

Now, why the hell was Mike D., as in Doofus, still standing in the doorway, smiling?

Oh.

"Sounds good, Mike D."

"Thanks, team!"

Mike smacked the doorframe like it was a right tackle's ass and set off on his merry way.

Just for that, Brad decided to make the account team wait a few more hours by making Alan wait a few more hours.

"Lunch?"

"Don't you think we ought to see if Alan's free?"

"Later."

Stump shrugged. Not his problem.

Brad opted for the bacon cheeseburger and garlic cheese fries. Sort of an extended toast to Gracie. Stump joined him at a table in the middle of the large seating area of the cafeteria after piling two plates full of vegetables and tofu.

"We should figure out how to frame the work."

Stump knitted his eyebrows. Huh?

"How we're going to sell it to Alan. How we set it up. So he buys it."

"Can't you just show it to him?"

"Mmm hmm. Sure. We'll walk in, dump it on his desk, and leave. That's how all the great salesmen do it. 'Somebody order some ads?' Let's make it a point to do it in thirty seconds or less. I hear that goes over big."

Brad stuffed his mouth with fries and talked anyway.

"We have to make him love this stuff. And in the process give him the tools to go sell it to everyone else."

"So they can sell it to the public."

"Right."

"What if it's the wrong stuff and you're just really good at selling it to your boss?"

This guy had no idea what he was talking about. Brad took a beat to compose himself before he started explaining the complex world of advertising to the cretin sitting across from him.

"You can't be honest with people. That never works. You have to figure out an angle. For instance, with these brochures and bookmarks, we didn't just create some offline marketing tools. We thought about it and asked ourselves, *What do old, incontinent people do and what do they really need?*"

"No, we didn't."

"I know. But I'm just saying. It's a good way to set up the work. We asked the question and the answer was *If you haven't discovered Assure yet, you probably spend a lot of time on the can . . . reading.*"

"Ah."

Across the hall, Brad noticed Dr. Yo standing by the exit, calmly observing him. Yo gave him the universal man chin bob, acknowledging that they had seen each other. Brad returned the gesture, but flavored it with a bit of question. Yo flicked his head sideways, *follow me.* Brad nodded. Yo turned and walked out. Stump didn't see Yo's half of the conversation and thought the head movements were somehow an acknowledgement that he and Brad were now on the same page.

"Got it."

"I'm going to go grab some more lemonade. I'll meet you back at the office."

Brad got up and moved toward the drink section before detouring and heading out the exit after Yo.

Down the hall to the left, Yo stood waiting. He opened the stair doors and went in. Of course, Brad understood that following the gentleman who was essentially a stranger into uncharted territory without his bodyguard's knowledge was behavior that Stump would frown upon. A lot. At the same time Brad realized that if Yo were the hired assassin a suspicious mind might suppose him to be, Brad would have been dead on the roof already.

He trailed Yo down six flights of stairs to find him holding the door open in the second subbasement. The floor was white and sterile like some secret government lab. Down the hall were a series of doors, each secured with a security card lock.

"Yo."

"I know. You told me. I'm Brad."

"No, I mean Yo, as in hello."

"Oh. Yo, Yo. Where are we?"

"I'm gonna show you something. Come here."

Yo ran his security card across the scanner on the lock to his office and the light above it turned green. He opened the door and welcomed Brad to the dark room where he spent his days.

Yo closed the door and slid into his chair in front of the desk that held four monitors for the computer tower below. Brad looked around and let his eyes adjust to what little light there was.

"So, what is this?"

"This is what I do for a living."

Brad was still adjusting to the darkness.

"Okay, so what do you do for a living? Develop negatives?"

"I watch people. I'm the head of liability security."

"Are you going to sell me some insurance?"

"No. I have cameras. I read everyone's e-mails. Listen to their voice mails. Monitor the websites they go to."

"You get paid for that?"

"Someone's got to do it. It's an easy way to keep the company safe from intellectual property theft, harassment suits, corporate espionage, bullshit like that. My main job is to protect Assure from losing money, IP, or being sued for someone doing something stupid."

"Adult diapers have intellectual property?"

"And it's all digital. But everyone lives on the computer now, so it's easy for me to keep track of pretty much everything that's going on."

"Why?"

As he spoke, Yo cycled through a number of feeds from cameras in the building.

"Liability. Cost efficiency. Most companies with more than fifty employees have someone like me watching. It's a minor investment compared to what they could lose. We got guys watching porn all day when they should be working. Grown men stalking ex-girlfriends. Harassing them with e-mails. Calling them forty, fifty times a day. People spending more time managing their fantasy football teams than doing their job. Guys cheating on their wives. Wives cheating on their husbands. People planning divorces. Managers losing their salaries to online gambling. Anything you can think of."

"Why don't you stop them?"

"Some we do. Some we don't. Liability and cost efficiency. If it looks like an employee is engaging in behavior that could get themselves or someone else hurt or, more importantly, cost the company money for negligence or failure to interfere, I let my boss know and somebody stops them. Sometimes you just need to goose 'em. Have a manager to stop by a little more often so they'll calm down. Sometimes you disguise your voice and call up pretending to be from IT wondering what's up with all these calls to the same number."

Yo brought up someone's computer desktop on his left screen and called up the security cam in the same office.

"See Daniels here on screen three? He's going to be arrested tomorrow morning as soon as we get all his files and records of his Internet activity backed up. He's been trying to sell some company secrets to a competitor. See ya, Daniels."

"Holy Jeebus."

"Most people we leave alone. They're not hurting anyone, just making their friends and family crazy."

"You watch me?"

"Please. I already know your deep dark secret. I heard you on the roof. You're on the run from the goodfellas."

"That's it?"

"And you pick your nose a lot. You have allergies or something?"

"Fuck, there's a camera in *our* office?"

"Sure, take a look."

Yo punched up Brad's office to find Stump sitting alone. Brad seized the opportunity.

"What about him?"

"Nothing. Straight arrow. He checks the weather online. That's pretty much it. Most of the time he just sits there like he is right now. Is he asleep?"

"I don't think the guy ever sleeps."

"He's your boyfriend?"

"No, he's the marshal assigned to me for the Witness Protection Program."

"Ahh."

"Why are you showing me all this? Isn't this super confidential?"

"Oh yeah. I'd be fired on the spot if anyone knew you were here."

"So?"

"So, I haven't told a soul in the five years I've worked here. You're the one person in the world I know isn't going to say a word. Plus you'll probably be dead in a few weeks. So why not?"

Brad spent the next half hour in Yo's office peppering him with questions about the worst things people did at work (masturbate, sleep, and hold down second jobs). A good twenty minutes of that was spent watching Mike D. flit around the building as he checked in with almost every office.

Finally, Brad realized he should probably get back and present some work to Alan.

"Thanks for showing me all this. It's amazing."

"Any time. It's not like you're busy, right?"

Brad couldn't help smiling. It was weird being able to be totally honest with someone.

Before he left, he turned to Yo. Brad was building a new life for himself. At some point that should probably include relationships with people who weren't assigned to him by the government.

"You ever play PlayStation?"

"I'll kick a fool's ass on PlayStation."

"So, yes?"

On the way back to the office, Brad popped into the men's room and found an open stall. The solitude lasted approximately twelve seconds before the bathroom door blew open.

"Pitt?"

It was Alan.

Whoa. Time out. Wasn't the shitter off limits? Can't a man crap in solitude? Wasn't it understood that, all advertising jokes aside, what an art director did in there didn't constitute work and therefore shouldn't fall under the jurisdiction of his boss? Was there no decency? Apparently not.

"Pitt. I saw you walk in here."

Alan charged the stall next to Brad's, stood on the toilet, and looked over the divider.

"There you are. Listen, you guys have some brochures to show me? Mike D. is up my ass and I can't keep those guys waiting."

"Um, yeah. We're going to show you some stuff in a few. It's good. Exciting."

Alan lit up.

"Yeah? It's good? Tell me about it."

Really? Right here on the throne looking up with my junk all tucked between my legs like a tranny? Is there some other place we might find in say, two minutes?

"Can I come down to your office in a few—"

"Broad stroke it for me."

Brad really hoped he was talking about the work.

Alan waited.

"Um, well, we took a look at the brief and thought to ourselves 'What do old, incontinent people do and what do they really need?'"

"Uh-huh."

"And then we figured out that if they haven't discovered Assure yet, they probably spend a lot of time on the can . . . reading."

"You're not reading."

"I'm not incontinent."

"That's it?"

Brad continued and as he went further and further with his explanation of bookmarks versus brochures, he noticed Alan's face getting redder and redder. Unsure if this was because of building excitement over his pitch or because Alan was struggling to maintain his position looking over the stall, Brad tap danced even faster in his framing. Finally, he ran out of steam.

". . . So that's it. A bookmark?"

"Uh, yeah. And some brochures."

Alan hopped off the toilet and marched out of the bathroom.

"You're not going to believe what just happened."

Brad breezed into his office ready to tell Stump the whole men's room invasion story only to find Alan and Mike D. poring over his layouts with Stump taking them through the work.

". . . so that's why we felt that treating the copy like this made a lot of sense."

Mike D., as in Didn't I mention that I was going to tell Alan you were done with the brochures? looked up.

"Hey, buddy! Great work. Really creative. Love the bookmark thing. Waaaaaay out of the box."

Brad snuck a look at Stump who raised his eyebrows to indicate he didn't have much of a choice but to show them.

"Um, thanks."

Alan, face still flushed like a beet choking on a piece of popcorn, turned around to Brad.

"This is fucking great stuff. Well done."

"Oh, right, yeah, well we thought that understanding the target market's need—"

Alan looked to Mike D. for approval.

"Perfect, right?"

"Sounds good."

Mike D. high fived Alan and nobody got strangled.

A Visit with Giggles

"Don't worry about a thing. I'm going to file so many motions, they're going to need a snorkel to get through them all. Years. That twat lawyer is going to retire before we even get to opening arguments."

The tabloids had described Tommy Gigliani as "a rumbling carnival show of legal shenanigans," "a human law library slash frat house with a Little Italy address," and "a coldblooded litigator who preferred fistfights to debates." And he was okay with that.

Say what you will about his professional ambition and predatory behavior in the courtroom, Tommy was on balance a fairly laidback guy. He tended to laugh things off pretty easily and often used that laughter as a trick to lull an opposing counsel into a state of overconfidence. Then he cut their balls off.

The papers called him "Giggles." The public dug him. He was the Wolf Boy of lawyers. A Giggles cover always sold out.

Standing only five feet five inches tall and weighing well over two hundred and fifty pounds, Giggles was almost a perfect circle and, based on the seemingly flawless memory he possessed, many hypothesized that the volume of his person was created by law theory and case studies that went in and never came out. He was a legal killing machine with supercharged instincts. So he was surprised by Frank's reaction to his plan.

"Fuck that. No motions."

Giggles giggled while he thought about the best way to tell his good friend the murderer that he was way off base on this one.

"Frank, they've got video. And eyewitnesses."

Yeah, no shit. None of this was breaking news to Frank. But he had some thoughts on these issues. In fact, he had to finish up this business with Giggles and get to a meeting he had with the Aryans.

As soon as Frank had entered prison, he set up shop. He didn't plan on being there long, but to keep his legacy creation on schedule, a few key things had to happen. As much as it sucked to have to sleep in an eight-by-six cell every night, prison life did offer certain advantages to a man who had needs as specific as his.

His first move was to convene Skinny Al, Big Fredo, Moldy Tony, Pete the Phone, and Johnny Pancakes, also known as The Boys—a crew of inmates who used to work for Frank on the outside and had the good sense to keep their pie holes shut when they got busted. They were the suburb to Frank's city family. A Mafia cul-de-sac in a really bad neighborhood.

Prison was a lot like high school—a dense population of mixed interests carved up into a bunch of little fiefdoms. Only with more butt-rapery. There were an assortment of factions around the facility involved in different activities and, therefore, with varying levels of power and influence.

The Boys filled him in on who was moving the good drugs, where the various cells of power lay, and who owed favors to the Maraschino prison family. At the top of the list in all three categories were the Aryans, led by a charmer named Mitchell.

In the real world, Frank wouldn't be caught dead talking to a skinhead sporting a large forehead tattoo of a cartoon penis protruding from a giant swastika. But the Aryans had strong outside ties and didn't mind killing a man for money. To them, it was just another business exchange. And they liked killing people.

This would have been a Sal thing on the outside. But Frank understood that since his was being billed as yet another lengthy "trial of the century," every one of his capos and soldiers was being watched very closely lest they try to thin out the witness herd in an untimely manner. No, this would have to look like it had nada to do with Frank Fortunato. A freak accident. A random murder. It could look like gender reassignment surgery gone horribly, horribly wrong for all he cared. It just couldn't look like it was done on his orders. So the Aryans got the nod.

It was time for Frank to give Giggles the heave ho.

"Yeah. Eyewitnesses and video. Listen, I have a right to a speedy trial, right?"

"Okay, sure. You also have the right to pay good money for front row seats at a Josh Groban concert, but I don't advise you do that either."

"Forget years. I want this thing wrapped up in a few weeks."

Giggles giggled again.

"You're a funny guy, Frank."

"Just make it happen. And don't worry. I know a few things about a few things."

"I don't know what the fuck that means, but don't do anything stupid. I have to tell you, the feds are out for blood. We can beat them, but you have to trust me."

"I trust you. Now, get me into the courtroom, do your job, and don't fuck it up."

"Frank . . ."

Frank hung up his receiver and walked away.

Giggles stopped giggling.

"Twenty percent on the cheebah deal and you look the other way on the laundry room thing."

"Five percent on the cheebah deal and I get a taste of the laundry deal."

"Fifteen and a taste."

"Seven and a taste. Final. That's a good deal, Mitchell."

Goddamn he was a cheap fucker. Killing three FBI agents and a key witness to a mob trial for what Frank was offering? That was a terrible deal. But Mitchell, the Swastika-Boner Aryan, didn't have much of a choice. Fortunato was too powerful.

Mitchell would take the offer. After the meth deal went down and Chuy turned the laundry room over to him, the Aryans would have a little more clout around here. Then, we'll see what happens, Frank old buddy.

"Fine. Seven and a taste."

There it was. Frank knew Mitchell was a reasonable man.

"The main guy's in Tucson. The rest are around."

"No problem."

Frank nodded and walked back across the yard toward The Boys. Mission accomplished.

Mitchell watched Frank amble off and then swept his eyes across the yard. The agents were local guys, so no big whoop. But if Frank was gonna pay shit, then the Aryans would farm the other thing out.

Where was . . . Ah, there. He made eye contact with the cat who ran the Yakuza wannabes, Jin. Jin shuffled over to stand next to Mitchell for an invisible chat.

As a favor to Mitchell, Jin took the job in exchange for a few hours of phone time. He promptly handed it off to the Mexican Mafia who owed Jin for the showerhead incident. The Mexican Mafia turned to the Bloods for some help. As consideration for the Mexican Mafia's assistance in TV room riots, the Bloods agreed to accept the assignment. They passed it on to the Nuevos as part of a truce agreement. The Nuevos were a little short on guys in Tucson, so they subcontracted the job to a reliable fellow outside the gang who had done some work for them in the past.

Brad Fingerman was as good as dead.

Isn't It Bromantic?

The whole bookmark affair had worked out so well that Alan proclaimed Brad and Stump his new favorite creative team, and piled the work on. Trade ads. Whitepaper tweaks. Promotional materials. The stuff of nightmares for a former rising star like Brad Fingerman became the daily grind of new hire Brad Pitt.

But that didn't seem to matter so much, now that he had found a new friend in Dr. Yo.

"'Sup, Terminator?"

"He's in the living room. Ready for your date."

"Man, this isn't a date. I came to humiliate someone. Yo, Brad-LEE!"

Yo walked into Brad and Stump's house like he owned the place. He had been dropping by regularly for the last week to hang out and beat Brad soundly at whatever PlayStation game they had in the machine.

If Stump had his way, Brad would have sat in his house and stared at the walls until the trial. But that wasn't realistic. He knew how much trouble witnesses with nothing to do could be. That's why he always got them jobs.

Jobs were the easy part of the program. Whenever he needed to place someone, he called up a placement from years earlier and, if they were still alive, Stump knew they could keep quiet about the important stuff. Like his new placement. It was a simple, but effective test. The more people he placed, the more favors he could call in. After so many years of making witnesses disappear, he had more contacts than he could ever use.

New friends of witnesses, on the other hand, were a very different matter. It was a difficult task explaining why Stump was always hanging around, watching. Some would call it lurking. He didn't drink and was on constant lookout for potential danger. Not exactly the ideal third wheel.

If the witness was female, he could pass himself off as a jealous boyfriend by giving her an occasional stern look. That worked well, except for the one time he was placing a seventy-two-year-old woman. In hindsight, overprotective grandson would have been the smarter play.

But with guys, it was tougher. They're a suspicious bunch anyway, and when you're spending most of the social hour standing quietly right behind the witness and their new best bud, they don't love it. Stump found it was usually easier to buy the beer. Get a case, ice it down, and let them drink themselves silly. Soon they stopped paying attention to him, which left him free to keep an eye out while monitoring their conversation.

Dr. Yo, on the other hand, was an entirely unique situation that Stump very much liked. Here was a guy who was clearly tightlipped. Brad had explained the context of their meeting (although he had swapped "secretly making a phone call" for "really had to clear my head") and Yo's unique position at the company. Truth is, Yo probably would have found out about Brad on his own anyway. Better that Stump was aware of who knew the details of their circumstance.

Stump chatted him up a few times and, once he got a bead on him, gave Yo the thumbs up. Yo was a pretty smart guy, despite the fact that he smelled like Shaggy and Scooby's van. And while no one is completely trustworthy, based on the muscle action in his face, Yo seemed to be on the up and up.

Brad and Yo began what would likely be an entire evening sitting on the couch with game controllers.

"You check out that girl on four?"

"The whale or the scarecrow?"

Yo shook his head in disgust.

"No eye for talent."

It was quite the bromance Brad and Yo had begun. Arrogant, white New Yorker meets mellow, black suburbanite. They got along easily from the start and unlike most of the male babysitting Stump did, this friendship actually helped matters. Yo stopping by meant Brad would be safely occupado for hours.

"I'm about to beat you like you owe me money."

"What's your cell number? I want to text you when I get to the end zone."

There was plenty of empty trash talk, but as they sat there in the tractor beam of the PlayStation, completely mesmerized by their game, there was a tremendous volume of real and honest conversation. Defenses came down and their life stories flowed easily. Plus, Yo had really great weed. Not the shit Brad would occasionally smoke in Manhattan, but sticky Purple Haze. And Yo loved to chat when he was high.

Yo had dropped out of society proper six years earlier, forsaking his given name, credit score, and position on the fast track to the American dream in the process. He had a bachelor's degree in economics from Yale, a master's from NYU, and was on his way to a doctorate from Berkeley when he discovered the wide and wonderful world of conspiracy theories. Shadow governments. FEMA internment camps. The truth behind 9/11. Voter-machine fraud. New World Order. And don't get him started on the Masons. Or Amway.

It was his belief that we are all being set up, and that it won't be long before the civilized world and every sucker putting money into a 401(k) and buying MP3s online will be subject to some horrible new global totalitarian government that's been in the works for centuries. According to Yo, the same government that was so busy spending seventy-five million dollars on a bridge to nowhere had simultaneously been helping to unify jurisdiction of every country on the planet under an elite group of foresighted leaders.

"If they're so smart, why does the DMV take so long?"

"That's their front. You're falling for it."

"What about the Witness Protection Program? That's run by the government."

"I don't know about them."

Yo snuck a look back at Stump.

"But I'd watch my back."

Since becoming "aware," as he referred to it, Yo had remained completely off the grid. There were records of his existence, but only up to 2009.

He didn't have a bank account, rented a room from a half-deaf widow who didn't ask too many questions, and used the Internet only from the safety of his office at work, and then always under an encrypted alias. He had no driver's license. He didn't vote. He paid no taxes. Yo had, in effect, set up his own Witness Protection Program.

He had talked himself into the job he currently held with a fake ID and somehow arranged to be paid off the books. Every check he got from Assure was taken to the bank from which it was issued and cashed within an hour of receipt, and each time at a different branch.

When the pizza guy rang the doorbell, Yo reached into his pocket and pulled out a roll of twenties the size of a baseball.

"I got it."

"What's with the pimp roll?"

"That's from my side job."

"Spying on your coworkers isn't fulfilling enough?"

"On the weekends I drive a tow truck."

"Why?"

Yo shrugged.

"Free money."

Yo had bought an old truck at a junkyard and fixed it up on his own. He cruised around Tucson looking for illegally parked cars and then took his time hooking them up.

Nine times out of ten, their owners came running over, crying for him to give them a break. He would let them beg and plead, and then tell them there was nothing he could do. After all, he could lose his job if he took their car off his truck. It was *company policy*. Eventually, every one of them offered to pay the tow charge in cash and Yo would accept. Somehow this morality play didn't compromise his job. Some tow escapees were so grateful, they even tipped him. He could clear two or three grand in a weekend.

And as an added benefit, the cops never ever stopped him regardless of his plates being out of date and the truck not being registered.

"They just wave when I drive by. I'm on their team."

"Why spend your weekends doing that, though?"

"It's only for another two years. 'Til my mattress gets full."

"What happens then?"

"I disappear."

Stump had done his share of undercover work (*My, that's a large towel boy*), eavesdropping (*Wow, Stump! How did you know I'd be at this particular drag queen showcase?*), and plain old spying (*Somebody's been in my underwear drawer!*), but he had never learned so much so fast as when he simply stood behind Brad and Yo and listened to them yak.

Stump made a few calls back East to find out what he could, but this Yo guy didn't show up anywhere, although "a security guy named Dr. Yo" wasn't exactly a lot to go on. Apparently Yo knew what he was doing.

Maybe he really would disappear one day.

Sal Gets the Call

Switching that wireless phone plan was the smartest thing he had done in years. The overage charges were killing him, and his wife had been going over every line on the bill to find out why it was so high. It was getting tough to explain all those calls to Jersey City.

How the hell did so many guys keep their wives in check so well, anyway? Bobby Oatmeal never had this problem. He just told his old lady to mind her business and go make him a sandwich. Big Pete smacked Gina around a little bit a few years back and she learned some respect. Concrete Jimmy had that look he gave his wife and, oh Nelly, she wouldn't say a word.

Sal had tried the look. Marie asked if he was having a seizure. He told her to mind her business and she threw her compact at his forehead. Three stitches. He hadn't hit her yet. It was under consideration, but he wanted to work things out through diplomatic channels if at all possible. He wasn't an animal.

All it took was switching plans. Now instead of a two to three hundred dollar bill, he got more minutes and a consistent ninety-nine dollar bill. She left him alone.

He also figured out that in case she did look closely at the bill before he could throw it out, he'd give her the seizure look and she would start panicking and dial 911, forgetting all about the Jersey calls.

Now when his phone rang three weeks into the billing cycle, he no longer winced.

"Hello."

"Sal?"

"Who's asking?"

"A friend of Tiko."

Yes! Sal was in debt up to his eyeballs, even before the whole cell-phone crisis. That friggin' gumad was expensive. What was it with twenty-six-year-old women and handbags? His Maraschino crew couldn't steal enough to cover the cost of this new relationship, so he took on the occasional freelance job. Pretty basic stuff. Collect some money from this guy. Burn that guy's garage down. Break some other guy's collarbone. Work for hire. It wasn't going to get him anywhere politically since it was overflow from other gangs and if Frank ever got wind he'd be pissed. But what was he gonna do? Keep living paycheck to paycheck? Fuck that.

"What can I do for you?"

"Tiko's wondering if you'd like to sit down with him."

"I'll be there in twenty minutes."

Sal took the meeting at Tiko's restaurant up in Spanish Harlem. The greasy-spoon dump of a diner served as a front for the New York City chapter of the Nuevos. Which explained why every employee in the place had the same tattoo on their neck. Nobody really came for the food.

Over Cuban sandwiches and juice coolers, Tiko explained that some friends of his needed Sal to kill a man located in Tucson, Arizona. They had already dug up a picture and the address of where he was probably staying.

"Tucson?"

"Yeah, why?"

"Nothing. It keeps popping up lately is all."

"I hear it's an up-and-coming city. Great schools. Solid real estate value."

Sal shrugged off the coincidence. He wasn't one to overanalyze. It usually didn't help and he wasn't that smart anyway, so what was the point? That's what made him such a good soldier.

The only issue Sal had with the job of murdering a perfect stranger was leaving Frank. His best friend was sitting in prison facing life, and here was Sal running off to raise a little cash that would inevitably be used to buy earrings for the dumbass stripper he was banging. That wasn't exactly the stuff of blood brothers. And then he got a call from Jersey City.

The dumbass stripper had a few dumbass friends from the club she danced at sleeping over at her house. They were pretty drunk already and she asked if he could pick up some coke and drop by. Odds were there was going to be a foursome.

Sal took the job.

Brad Kneels

The debate was whether or not the pretzels were worth it.

Brittany was down five pounds and loving the way she was looking. But she hadn't eaten since yesterday's lunch of miso soup. Was this really hunger, or was it boredom from sitting in a forensic edit bay all morning watching Jarvis try to rebuild her lost surveillance footage?

As she stood in front of the vending machine ogling its bounty of processed, food-like products, her mouth started to water. Most doctors would consider the reaction an indication of hunger. Brittany decided it was weakness.

Do you want to eat or do you want to be famous?

She wanted to be famous and famous people were thin. Famous people didn't eat Mounds bars. Famous people looked great on camera when they were testifying in open court on live television. Like she would be in a matter of weeks.

Sorry, fatty. You've got some ell beez to drop.

She put her single dollar away and opted instead for another cup of the anorexic's best friend, coffee.

"Hey, you want to take a look at this?"

Brittany almost dropped her unopened no-calorie sweetener packet into her mug when she heard Jarvis call down the hall from his bay. He wouldn't be yelling if he didn't have something to look at, right? He would have kept working if he still had a bunch of digital cubes and fuzz and buzzing, no?

She grabbed her steaming cup of dinner and speed-walked back to Jarvis.

"So, this stuff you've seen. He's in the elevator making goo goo eyes at Carmine. Then we drop out for a while. Then there's this . . ."

Jarvis slowed the footage down so Brittany wouldn't miss a thing and walked her through what he had made out so far. On his monitor, the digital detritus turned to his latest recovery, a fairly clear picture of Brad standing next to Carmine.

"Okay, then they stop."

In the elevator, Brad bent down on one knee and leaned forward toward the ground as the doors opened. The screen turned to a mess of digital artifacts.

"That's what I've got so far."

"What's he doing?"

"I don't know. Maybe he dropped something."

Or maybe he was ducking because he knew what was coming.

Brittany had to assume it wasn't the lightheadedness from her rigid diet that sent her reeling. She knew what she saw. She just wasn't sure what it meant. Had she grabbed an accomplice and convinced herself that he was a witness? Had she shot herself in the foot because she was overambitious? Was she limiting herself to four hundred calories of pure protein a day for nothing? She sat down to compose herself and review the situation.

She had spoken to Brad. Looked into his eyes. Rifled his stuff when he was out of the room. She really thought she knew him. And now maybe he was in on the murder?

Impossible. She was too good of a judge of character to make a mistake that big.

Brittany Calls Stump

"Do you think Brad is lying?"

Brittany didn't sound nearly as surprised as Stump might have expected.

"Maybe."

"Well, why didn't you say something earlier?"

"I was going to. I just had to write this headlin—Hey, wait, why are you asking, anyway?"

Not quite the call Stump expected to get, but exactly what he had been wondering himself. Aside from punching up the copy on those instructional inserts and tightening the disclaimer on the new sport-package mock-up, Stump's to-do list included calling Brittany to discuss a few things that had been bugging him since they put Brad on video.

"We found something wonky in our recovered surveillance footage. Either Brad is lying or he might be epileptic. Have you noticed him acting epileptic at all?"

"Not really. But tell me about the lying part."

Brittany told Stump about Brad's furtive movement and the suspicions it had raised. She probably exaggerated the nefariousness of it a little too much, but it didn't matter. Bending over can only look so evil.

"That's it? He took a knee?"

"Yeah. I saw it clear as day."

"So his partner could shoot Carmine."

"Right."

"Then why would Frank even have Brad there in the first place? How does bending over help the big plan?"

"To . . . keep Carmine there."

"In the elevator."

". . . Yeah."

While Stump had the sneaking suspicion that something was amiss with Brad's story, he doubted that it would turn out that Brad was a mastermind criminal accomplice. He wasn't mastermind material. This was another piece of a puzzle, but not the puzzle Brittany was trying to put together. He would keep it in mind, but chances are it was as useless as a third earring hole. She sounded like she was under a tremendous amount of stress.

"Are you sleeping?"

"Not really."

Stump could see Brad down the hall, returning from his seventh trip to the "bathroom" this morning.

"Look, he's on his way back. I don't think he was in on it. But I do have a few questions about some things. Can you get me a copy of his grand jury testimony video?"

Malcolm and Lola's First Date

Lola caught the bartender before he started making her second martini. She happened to see Malcolm approaching the bar and thought better of ordering another drink without him. Besides, the first one was humongous. That ought to at least tide her over until they sat down. Just in case, she whispered to the man behind the bar.

"Keep an eye on me."

He nodded knowingly. Lola loved a good bartender. She dropped twenty dollars on the counter and turned to pretend to be surprised to find Malcolm there.

"Well, hello there. Don't you look handsome."

"Good evening, Lola."

As she stood up, she realized exactly how drunk she was.

Lola was certainly not Malcolm's type. Not his specific type, anyway. She was pretty and straight and not a practicing Nazi, so she definitely fit into a general category of women that he was attracted to. But she seemed so wild and outgoing. That wasn't Malcolm at all.

He wondered if perhaps when people say, "She's not my type," what they were really referring to was not their type of opposite sex, but rather their own type. Maybe they were really saying, "She's not exactly like me. She doesn't do and believe the same things I do. She wouldn't react the same way to news that the Magnolia Bakery had burned down." What narcissism.

No, Malcolm was convinced he had had a breakthrough. Maybe going out with Lola wasn't such a crazy thing. Maybe it was a really smart thing. She wasn't his type. Perfect.

He had suggested his favorite sushi restaurant because he felt the Japanese lent a certain sense of mystery to the evening. The sushi restaurants in the city were always so dimly lit. More important, this one was quiet. He had no interest in yelling his hometown and favorite movies across the table at her.

Approaching the restaurant, he had told himself to calm down and relax. This was another date, just like the one he had two years ago that turned out to be a distant cousin. Nothing would come of it.

Nevertheless, Malcolm felt an extra spring in his step as he entered the restaurant and found Lola waiting for him at the bar.

For two people who had lived such remarkably different lives, Lola and Malcolm had a surprising amount in common. Over appetizers they discovered they both loved Greek food (Lola's second husband was Greek; Malcolm kept an account at the Thermopoulous Diner on the first floor of his building), F. Scott Fitzgerald (both had read everything he'd ever written; Malcolm had taken the Long Island literary tour), and Labrador Retrievers (Lola had one at home; Malcolm always wanted one but could never decide on a color and now with labradoodles added into the mix of options, forget about it).

During their entrees, they discovered even more overlapping interests. Malcolm had majored in Latin studies at Columbia. Lola had a tramp-stamp tattoo of a winking margarita. Lola's desert island item was an insta-hot. Malcolm had a mug of India Spice tea every night before bed. Lola found Malcolm's dry-as-sand sense of humor adorable. Malcolm liked Lola's manners. And she had big fake tits. To be fair, he noticed them earlier.

"I have to admit, I felt a little silly sitting in that coffee shop waiting for you."

"Don't worry about it. I've dated stalkers before."

"Really?"

"No. Actually, you're my first."

"I'm honored."

He sipped his wine.

"I was going to ask you out, you know."

"I know."

"So why did you ask me first, then?"

"Because it would have taken you months."

True. He smiled the tiniest bit. Yup. Malcolm thought this woman who was definitely not his type was dynamite sticks.

Frank 1, Hot Dog Agent 0

Hello, rat.

According to the "reliable witnesses" quoted on the front page of the national paper Stump read as he stood on the front porch of his and Brad's model home at sunrise, those were the last words heard by special agent Mike Collington before he was gunned down in broad daylight.

This brazen execution was of special interest to Stump, and by extension Brad, as Mike Collington had only a short time before played the role of Hot Dog Vendor Guy in Project Fancypants. He was also going to play the role of Witness in the upcoming Frank Fortunato trial. Not a key witness, but one of a series of special agent witnesses who would testify they saw Frank enter the building in which Carmine was murdered. It was overkill, but this trial would not be about finesse. It would be about winning.

Stump folded the paper back up, walked across the front lawn, and dropped it into his neighbor's recycling can.

As Brad readied himself for another big day of advertising adult incontinence products, Stump took a little time to stretch his back. He had spent the previous night hunched over his laptop, studying the video Brittany had posted. He had been over and over the footage, pausing and rewinding to see Brad's internal pterygoids, levator palpebrae superioris, and orbicularis oculi. There was no longer any doubt. Brad was lying.

Brad hadn't told Frank to make things easy on himself by dropping the gun. He never noticed Frank's pulse pumping through his jugular. And you didn't have to see his levator anguli oris to know that Brad definitely did not almost throw himself in front of Carmine but then decide it was a little too show-offy. But, having lived and worked with Brad now, these were all things Stump could have told you without looking at the video. Brad was no hero.

The interesting thing about the video was not what Brad was lying about, but what he was truthful about. He was definitely there. He definitely saw *something*. And he definitely had to pee when he asked for the bathroom break.

Stump would let Brittany know. But not yet. With all of his rewinding and frame-by-frame examination, he had only made a close study of about a third of the footage. No point in alarming her until he knew the whole truth. Maybe it wasn't so bad.

Chutzpah

Frank made a decision. Everyone should see what happens to a rat.

He had been watching a bunch of online videos while awaiting trial. He really liked the ones where someone falls off the backyard trampoline or women at weddings slip while fighting for the bouquet. What's wrong with those people? They never seem to learn.

But the videos that really struck a chord were the ones in which Peruvian drug lords made threats and put price tags on their rivals' heads, or L.A. gangbangers recorded themselves giving new recruits a beat down to show them how much they love them. That was chutzpah. That's not drunken tough-guy talk. That's documentation for the world to see. All of the world. Now that was something Frank was interested in.

He headed over to the yard to tell Mitchell the Aryan that whoever he had sent for Brad should bring a camera.

A Crisis of Incontinence

"I feel like *strangling* someone."

Alan's face got extra red when he said the word *strangling*. Like he enjoyed even the thought of it.

Stump had seen this look before and knew where it could lead. His eyes narrowed as he watched Alan pace around the office like an oversized toddler. Alan caught his eye and stopped pacing.

"That's a figure of speech, Christopher. I'm not actually going to strangle anyone."

Mmm hmm.

Brad and Stump had been called in to Alan's office first thing that morning. They had been sitting there for a full two hundred Mississippi already and, aside from serving as an audience to the worst production of *Stomp* ever, had no clue as to why.

"Jack just fired the New York agency."

"Who's Jack?"

"Our CMO. Upstairs. Smart guy. Used to run account services for that erectile dysfunction pill company, until they went under. You know what I mean."

"Why did he fire the New York agency?"

"We have a New York agency?"

Brad wanted to kick himself. It made sense that they would have a New York agency. Why hadn't he thought of that before? His back-door reentry into big-time advertising was right in front of him. Assure was a major player in the world of super-absorbent disposable briefs. Of course they would look to the heavy hitters back East to craft their most visible marketing while the schmucks in the in-house agency did the shit work. He was already wondering if someone back there had seen the work he'd been doing here, and if they'd been impressed.

"What happened?"

"The top guy, the CEO creative director, ran off with a receptionist and ten million dollars."

"Whoa."

"And he erased their entire server. The whole agency is ruined. He left a note. Said it was a test."

Ding. Fucking Geoff.

Brad didn't acknowledge his familiarity with Red Light. No point in associating with losers.

"So what does this mean?"

"It means we've got to pick up the slack. They were working on the spring campaign. That's the big one."

In his pre-interview research on Red Light, Brad had not discovered that they were the agency of record for Assure adult diapers. Seems poopy pants were not considered a trophy client.

"What kind of slack?"

Alan had picked up a letter opener and clenched it in his huge angry fist. Stump couldn't take his eyes off of it as Alan waved his arms around to emphasize his words.

"Slack! The whole pile of pancakes. They were flying out to present to Jack on Thursday. Print ads, TV spots, digital. Now it's all gone. The media is all bought and paid for and we can't run the old ads because they don't feature the new packaging. Jack asked me to come up with a Band-Aid campaign to run until he can find a new agency. First round is due in two days. God, I hate pressure."

He whipped around to face Brad and Stump, letter opener in one hand, sweat seeping through his shirt. He looked like a terrible cat burglar.

"So, you guys up for making some magic?"

Brad shivered at Alan's pitiable attempt to rally the troops. There's nothing less inspirational than an unimpressive leader attempting a One-for-the-Gipper speech. The best you can hope for is that they have a heart attack before they actually tell you what they need from you.

Whether they were up for making some magic or not, everyone got the nod to start work. Brad and Stump, über-cerebral-writer-guy, j-pop-retro-punk-look-art-director-girl, goth-by-Hot-Topic-interactive girl. Even perky-gay-assistant-guy was asked to contribute what he could creatively. This was an emergency. They had two days to come up with an amazing campaign. Something magnificent that positioned Assure adult diapers in a unique manner while emphasizing the brand's breakthrough design and world-class customer service. Or at least something that filled thirty seconds of airtime and prominently featured the logo and tag line.

In Brad's old world, this sort of ambush assignment wasn't unusual. This is what separated good creatives from great ones. The ability to make magic on command. And putting several teams on one assignment was pretty standard practice at Overthink. But here in the land of misfit toys, it was unheard of. These were people who were used to spending their weeks honing technical copy about the proper application of waistband adhesive to prevent embarrassing accidents. Layered wordplay? Clever art direction? Huh?

As far as Brad was concerned, this was cake. And maybe one last shot at greatness. If nothing else, a chance to flex a little muscle and rub some payback in Geoff's face.

Yes, you turned me down, Geoff, but here's the news, chump: You failed MY test! Look at the award-winning campaign that your agency didn't do and mine did. IN-HOUSE! HA! Chew on that! . . . as you have sex with your super-hot receptionist girlfriend in the Bahamas on a bed made of ten million dollars.

All right, maybe this would be just for Brad, but still, he felt good about at least getting back in the game on some level besides grunt work. This was as big of an opportunity as Brad Pitt might ever have. One last at bat in the majors. He was going to the show.

"You probably just thought something like *I'm going to the show* didn't you?"

"No."

Stump's observational skills could be downright annoying sometimes.

"Oh, right. You've probably had tons of opportunities like this. All those national campaigns you sold in New York? This is old hat. Just another notch on the belt, huh?"

"All right, fine. Look, Brad Pitt has no experience, but this could be it for me. This could get me back on track.

"You can't go back to New York, you know."

"I can go to San Francisco or some other town with real agencies and restaurants that aren't Applebee's."

"You can do that."

"I'm going to crush this thing."

Everyone stayed late that night and ordered pizza because they had seen ad guys in the movies do that. It made them feel more creative. Unfortunately for Brad, they also thought it would be a great idea to bring all the food into the conference room where he had no choice but to interact with his coworkers.

This would be Brad's first real-life test. His first run out in the wild among civilians. Über-cerebral-writer-guy took the first shot.

"So, Brad? It's Brad, right? Where are you from?"

"Back East."

Fingerman scoring early.

"Oh, where?"

"Um, Boston."

"I grew up in Boston. What part are you from?"

Stump watched patiently as the truth predictably tied the game and then took a commanding lead.

"Um, the northern south part of the . . . It's a subdivision just out-side of . . . You know where the Garden is?

Stump let Brad squirm a bit before jumping in to distract über-cerebral-writer-guy by playing the part of enthusiastic coworker.

"You're from Boston, too? You a big Red Sox fan?"

"I don't really follow baseball."

"I do. I was there when they won their division and . . ."

And on and on Stump went about baseball and all the players and stats no one in the room cared about until everyone present had forgotten how they got on the subject in the first place and found an excuse to grab another slice, head back to their office, and leave Brad and Stump alone to finish their fascinating baseball conversation.

"Thanks for jumping in there."

"Yeah, you might want to put some thought into a backstory."

"I'll do that."

It was nine thirty by the time they pulled into their vanilla subdivision. They rounded a corner and headed down their generic street. Stump drove past their prefab home without so much as tapping the brakes.

"What are you doing? That's our house back there."

"I know. Someone's inside."

"How do you know?"

"I left the hall light on this morning. It's off now."

"Maybe it burnt out."

"It's halogen."

Stump slowed the car to a stop at the end of the block and pulled his gun out of his ankle holster.

"You carry a gun to work?"

"I am a U.S. marshal. Stay here. If you see anything suspicious, drive away as fast as you can. I'll find you."

Stump hopped out of the car and made his way into the shadows of the suburban landscape before Brad could protest.

"Fucking kill you motherfuckers!"

Stump recognized the voice just in time to not shoot his unexpected house guest in the back of the head.

"Yo."

He holstered his gun as Dr. Yo waved from the couch without looking away from his first person shooter PlayStation game.

"I almost put a bullet in your brain. What are you doing here?"

"Saving the world. Where the hell ya'll been?"

Either Yo was used to being almost shot or just didn't care. Stump couldn't tell.

"Yo, why are you here? This is our house. And it was locked when I left."

"Oh, yeah. I made a key the other day. It's a hobby of mine."

A byproduct of his paranoid security persona, Yo had a catalogued collection of keys that filled several drawers in his kitchen. Whenever he got the chance, he would lift someone's keys and copy them. You never knew when they might come in handy. Armageddon. Zombie apocalypse. Or when you've got a real jones to hit the PlayStation and your buddy is late. Like tonight. He had even been so kind as to return the favor and made a copy of his own apartment key for Brad. In Yo's weird world, it was a real bonding moment. Stump just thought it was dumb.

"You're out of soda, by the way."

Stump went to get Brad out of the car, beating himself up for the security breach the entire way. It worked out to be a harmless mistake, but it could have been a painful one. That's what he got for letting Brad have his own key.

Brad Wakes Up

Brad woke up happy the next morning.

This in and of itself was not groundbreaking. Historically, plenty of members of the human race have awoken with a song in their heart.

It was the context of the realization that merited examination. With all the worry about losing his job and hiding his unemployment and making sure his thirty-percent-off-wings fliers were finding the right people and the rash the chicken suit gave him and his wife treating their marital vows like the adult diapers Herr Fingerman was now hocking and Frank Fortunato trying to unfriend him in the most painful way possible, Brad had come to be unhappy as a matter of normal course. It had become his natural resting state over the last several weeks. Occasionally he would use the methadone of despair as a crutch, but, in general, depressed was his baseline emotion.

This morning, however, his waking thought was not *Why me?* but rather one of anticipation. And this wasn't a matter of whistling past the graveyard. Brad was actually looking forward to going into work and accomplishing something. Granted, that something was the pea-cockery of advertising, but nevertheless, it was *something* to look forward to. A tiny beacon of meaningfulness. Hope.

Not being the terribly introspective type, the significance of the change was lost on Brad. Instead he looked at it through the myopic vision of a morning DJ.

I'm baaaaaack! I'm back in the saddle again!

It was maybe the worst Steven Tyler impression ever and those were the only words he knew for the song, but it served its purpose. Brad initiated his own rally cry and sang his heart out in the shower.

He had a new name. He had a new job that was giving him a second chance. He had a new friend. Sure there was a trial to get through and some over-the-shoulder looking to be done for the foreseeable future, but his life was better today than it had been yesterday. And that was something that hadn't happened in a good long while.

Maybe things really were going to work out.

Frank 2,
Brittany's Agents 0

Hello, rat.

As usual, Stump had gone out for the paper before Brad woke up and this morning the headlines informed him of another Fortunato-related death. This time it was on video. Someone had killed a gentleman by the name of Alfonse Amorelli, formerly known as the FBI agent who ran the fake three-card Monte game outside 1635 Broadway on the day Frank Fortunato was arrested. He was also scheduled to testify on behalf of the prosecution against Frank. Once again, not a major contributor, but definitely a guy who could put Frank in the building when a murder was committed.

His killers had strangled him with his own belt and captured the whole thing on a video they posted on YouTube under the title *How to Kill a Rat.* Then they tagged it with popular search words like *sex, porn, tits, funny, twerk, Cyrus, Kanye, Angelina,* and *Kardashian ass.* It had over two million plays before it was removed for breaking indecency rules.

Which made it front-page news, even out there in the sticks of Tucson. Stump dropped the paper off in the neighbor's recycling bin. He would have to keep Brad focused on work today.

Things Look Brighter for the Lifer

When the news of the killing—and more important, the posting of the video—hit the Rikers grapevine, Frank couldn't help but preen a little bit. His stock shot up immediately as the beginning of his master plan came together. Even the Samoans looked at him with new respect.

The news channels squawked about the obvious connection to the trial. Public servants demanded action. But the truth was that the Aryans had done an excellent job covering their tracks. Not a tattoo in sight for the whole video. Nothing identifiable aside from Alfonse's crooked teeth as he fought bravely. Sure the FBI would investigate, but they wouldn't get far.

Frank took a nice, leisurely victory lap around the yard to let everyone know who was in charge. He made sure to give a knowing single nod to Mitchell as he passed by. Nice doing business with you.

Malcolm's Missed Cue

Is it possible to consume negative calories?

Ever since Brittany found out about Frank requesting a speedy trial, she had been in a panic. Her case was solid. Her eyewitness was hidden. Jarvis was still making progress recovering surveillance footage. But she hadn't lost the last five pounds. How was this fair? She finally got the perfect break, but couldn't fit into the skirt that showed off her calves so well. It was maddening.

Her grandmother told her to find a bra that squeezed her breasts up high and tight, and the rest would fall into place. Who would be looking at her legs? But Brittany wanted that skirt.

At least her grandmother had someone to keep her busy these days. Not that Brittany was looking for a grandfather figure or anything. She just wanted Lola to be kept occupied. And stop calling so much. Actually, Brittany didn't care what Lola did as long as she stopped dialing her up every ten minutes to tell her that men don't like smart women, so open her top button.

Maybe this new guy was just the thing. He was a bit of an enigma to Lola. They had been on a few dates and she had been dropping hints like they were care packages over the Congo, but he hadn't acted on any of them. And Brittany knew firsthand that her grandmother's hints were tough to ignore. Lola's innuendos were as subtle as a cable network promo and as tasteful as an art sale at an airport hotel. This guy was either a real gentleman or a deaf mute with a head injury.

According to Lola, the happy couple had been out for another date last night. She had used the old *I feel a real chemistry here* line, pretended to sprain an ankle so he would put his arm around her on the way out, and even suggested a quick nightcap and backrub at his place. Nothing. He had checked his breath but claimed to not smell any chemistry, warned her of the dangers of high heels, and mentioned something about his mother needing her sleep for a colonoscopy the next day.

The details were a little fuzzy, thanks to one too many martinis, but the gist of it was that Lola had tried to bump uglies with Malcolm and he had instead walked her to her door, shaken her hand, and left. What an asshole.

The unfortunate series of events was described to Brittany in excruciating detail while she sat with her cell phone to her ear in Jarvis's bay, watching the back of his balding head as he reconstructed all the unimportant parts of her surveillance footage and she continued to not lose enough weight for primetime television. It was like the whole world was against her.

The Fire Drill

At least the crisis of firing the New York agency gave Brad something to do at work besides bitch. Stump could tell Brad was thrilled to stretch his creative claws because he had been quiet all morning, assuming the role of Relax-I've-been-here-before-guy and burying himself in the vast library of awful stock photography in the hopes of finding some gem that he could turn into a campaign. So far he had only lifted his head a few times to float some not-so-impressive ideas.

"What if we did, like, a fashion week thing and all the models were wearing diapers on the runway and Tim Gunn is there and he's all 'Mmm! Make it work, girl!' and then we have a line like *Assure, the next big thing in accidents* or something like that?"

"I don't think so."

"Why not?"

"Models don't wear underwear."

It was pretty light lifting for Stump, which was fine by him. He wasn't really a copywriter and was far more consumed with his real job.

Two agents related to Brad's case were dead. That meant someone was looking for Brad like he was the last bowl of Chex Mix at a locals bar. They would find him. And if they were willing to kill agents, they wouldn't think twice about offing a civilian. Or a marshal. And there would go his perfect record. He had to be on his toes.

Of course, after three hours of being on his toes while staying in character in the middle of a quiet building at the center of a lonely office park, Stump got a little bored.

He slid on some ear buds and pulled Brad's testimony video up on his computer. Perhaps a little facial action study to break the monotony.

He had already broken down more than half of the footage and had made extensive notes on practically every word Brad had spoken.

They broke briefly to grab lunch from the third floor and brought their food back to their desks to eat while they worked. It was self-serving, but unintentionally inspired the other teams. Über-cerebral-writer-guy took his soup to his desk. J-pop-retro-punk-look-art-director-girl canceled her trip to Chipotle and grabbed a burger from the cafeteria. Goth-by-Hot-Topic-interactive-girl wasn't eating anyway because she was body dysmorphic and the hunger pangs made her feel in control.

By the end of the day, everyone had something to show for all their hard work. Except Stump. He had picked out a few more insignificant lies from Brad's testimony, but that wasn't the kind of thing you share during a creative gangbang.

Alan paced. He had called everyone together that morning and reminded them he was presenting the work to Jack the next day, which meant he needed to see something at the end of today. Tomorrow was all about revisions and tweaking for Jack.

Mike D. had been kind enough to come down to re-brief the teams and make sure everything sounded good. Everyone claimed to have understood their mission and scuttled off to get to work. Here it was eight hours later. They had better have gotten it goddamn right.

Alan's no-choking policy had served him well so far. A few close calls, but nothing serious. Certainly no behavior that would indicate Alan was about to squeeze the life out of someone he worked with. But he had never been tested during a time as stressful as this one. He stashed his letter openers and scissors in a desk drawer, just in case.

"You ready for us, Alan?"

Brad and Stump were the last to present. So far, über-cerebral-writer-guy and j-pop-retro-punk-look-art-director-girl were the frontrunners with a campaign featuring an anthemic flagship spot that played a gospel choir soundtrack while seniors participated in family activities tinged with a patriotic vibe. Occasionally, the old people would laugh at some unheard joke and high five. Their overarching theme for the effort was *Dry Is Why*, a chorus that answered various rhetorical, empowering questions asked by the stars of the ads.

Alan thought it spoke to the emotional connection consumers can have with a product. Also, it implied confidence to venture more than fifty feet from a toilet. People really responded to that. Mike D. had blessed it as well.

"Right on the money, brother. You're saying if they don't wear our product, they might crap themselves during church and then where would they be, right?"

Über-cerebral-writer-guy hadn't really über-thought of it like that, but sure, why not?

"Something like that."

Mike D. slapped both hands on the work in a simian display of ownership.

"Dig it. Alan, I dig it!"

"Then I dig it, too."

So the pressure was somewhat off by the time Brad and Stump made their way into Alan's office to show him what they had come up with. Alan already knew he had a safe campaign to show Jack that would at least fill the inside cover of *Parade* magazine and half a minute of airtime during *Jeopardy!* Everything else was gravy.

"All right, guys, what do you have?"

Brad had done a yeoman's job on the project, conceptualizing the campaign, laying it out, even writing all the lines. He had run them by Stump who had grunted an approval, but that was the extent of any outside influence. This was all Brad.

"Well, we've got five campaigns to show yo—"

"Five?! What the hell are you talking about?"

"Uh, we just wanted to make sure you were covered."

Alan checked his watch. Always a good sign when you're presenting work.

"All right, let's see them."

Brad took Alan and Mike D. through the campaigns. There was a wide variety of thought, ranging from surreal executions of metaphors to clever slice-of-life banter to straight-talking authority figures.

"So then he looks into camera and says, 'We put the *Sure* in *Assure*.'"

"Go back to the other one."

"*Full Load*?"

"No, the one before that."

"*Code Brown*?"

"That's it."

Yes! Brad had a winner. Maybe. Alan studied the campaign featuring wide-eyed seniors in crowded rooms.

"Mike D.?"

Mike D. squeezed his mouth to one side of his face, unimpressed.

"Meh. Back pocket."

"Yeah, I agree. Not quite on target strategically. We've got *Dry Is Why* and the testimonial thing we saw earlier. Let's back pocket this one. Thanks, guys."

Back pocket?! Fucking Mike D., as in Douche Nozzle, had torpedoed Brad's one shot at greatness with Assure with a simple *Meh*. Did he even get the bigger concept behind the campaign? Didn't he understand the subtext of the dialogue? Had he missed the whole joke? How dumb was this guy?

"Alan, don't you think you might want to present something a little more conceptual? To sort of round things—"

"Nope. Done."

Alan stood up, completely satisfied with himself, and brushed some imaginary dirt off of his hands.

Brad's work wasn't even going to be presented unless some sort of disaster happened. Nothing short of the entire gospel-singing population of America getting struck by lightning during a volcanic earthquake would get any of Brad's campaigns presented to Jack. Nope. Done.

Yo was waiting for them when they got home, warming up the PlayStation. Brad spent the evening on the couch next to him, sulking his

way through Madden. Three straight losses playing as the Cowboys
didn't help matters much.

"This guy knows nothing about advertising. He couldn't creative
direct a ham sandwich and *he's* telling *me* I was off strategy?"

"Seems like a lot of effort just to sell diapers."

True. But this was the microcosm Brad had chosen to care about.
He had woken up happy about it that very morning.

"I'm just saying."

"If it makes you feel any better, he compulsively sniffs his armpits."

It didn't.

Brad's sleep was fitful and if it's possible for sleep to be spiteful, it
was that too. His psyche was saturated with disbelief and anger. By the
time five thirty the next morning rolled around, he'd had enough of
the battle and dragged himself out of bed.

Frank 3, Holy Shit

Brad had an angry shower, followed by an angry shave, and considered a little angry masturbation, but, honestly, was just too tired from tossing and turning all night. Instead, he made some coffee and resumed his fuming about getting shut out of the Assure in-house advertising World Series. Did they have any idea who he was? Actually, no. He couldn't show them his résumé. He couldn't hype himself up by dropping the names of agencies he had worked at or the campaigns he had sort of worked on. All they had was the work that Alan and Mike D. had so politely passed on. And by end of business today, the whole thing would be a done deal. Jack would have all the work and would probably go with that hacky choir thing. Brad considered his options.

A bomb threat? It's been done. Stealing the work and burning it? Kind of baby-ish. Beating them by doing better work before five o'clock today? It was crazy but it just might work.

Quality ideas that did a better job of selling diapers than a non-denominational singing group and preternaturally happy seniors. Sneaky. But that was the kind of renegade thinking that sometimes birthed miracles.

Brad sipped his coffee and thought of the implications. That would mean working his second full day in a row. It would involve the distinct possibility that Alan, and worse yet, Mike D., would once again dismiss him out of hand and move forward with what they had already approved. It could result in further rejection from an even greater authority, and tattoo him with the stigma of the high-rolling loser. Or it could mean some redemption.

Fuck it. Brad didn't like the vine he had been given so he would make his own. And he would tell it where to go. Right back to

I-Deserve-This-Success-Ville. Oh yes, today would be a big day. Forget being happy or unhappy. Brad was going to be the motherfucking man. This day would set the tone for the rest of Brad's life. He would dig deep. He would zig and zag and give one hundred and ten percent and all sorts of other clichés it was too early to think of. He would own this fucker.

So he had to reinvent himself. So what? Hadn't people weaker than him done it? Al Sharpton used to wear track suits to court! Of course Brad could do this.

He stared at himself in the mirror and looked deep into his own eyes. If only someone was there to play some heroic montage music as he promised himself a new and better Brad. He would stand tall. He would make the world take notice professionally. He would rebuild himself in the manner he chose. Brad Pitt, advertising giant. And once this trial worked out, assuming it ended favorably in terms of Brad's primary goal of staying alive, maybe he could find his way back into real advertising with his new name and some sparkling new Assure work as his calling card. *Brad Pitt Saves Major Diaper Account!* It was no vodka job, but it definitely merited attention. Between the new name, the new work, and perhaps some strategic facial hair, maybe Brad could even reintegrate himself back into New York advertising. Start over. Take over. God, it would make a great anonymous Twitter feed. He just needed some brilliant work.

But first, he would check his horoscope on the crapper. Why not start the day off right?

On his way to the front of the house to grab the paper, he passed Stump's open door. Brad never woke up before eight on any given day, which meant normally Stump was up well before Brad stirred. But today, he lay stiff as a board on his practically undisturbed bed as Brad tiptoed past and quietly guided the front door open.

The sun was creeping up over the horizon, adding a sort of surreal light of optimism to Brad as he greeted the day. Unfortunately, that light didn't do much for his stunned face as he read the front page headline: AND THEN THERE WAS ONE.

Holy eff-ing Jesus-on-a-corn-dog shit. This was not the throne reading Brad was hoping for.

According to the article, an agent by the name of Thomas Henry Lewis (also known as the guy who walked Frank down the stairs of 1635 Broadway on a certain fateful day) was not only garroted in a parking garage, but the entire event had been captured on video and put online as a warning to the one remaining witness in the Frank Fortunato case.

And he wasn't the first one this had happened to. According to leaks from inside sources (leaks!), there were four key witnesses— three minor players who were now dead and one major eyewitness who would be delivering the most damning testimony of all. According to the blabbermouths from inside the Justice Department, the eyewitness was in hiding, although authorities claimed to be "concerned" about the situation.

We are utilizing a vast network of resources to maintain both the anonymity and safety of certain individuals involved in the Fortunato case. We are confident in the abilities of law enforcement officials and look forward to seeing justice served.

Vast network? Where was the vast network when newspaper-guy, hot-dog-guy, and three-card-Monte-guy were killed? Did they have their own Stumps? Weren't they supposed to *be* their own Stumps? If they couldn't defend themselves, what was *Brad* supposed to do? And by the way, this had to happen on the day he decided to take control of his life? Thanks a fucking lot, universe.

Okay. Brad could now officially check Experience Relentless White-Hot Fear off of his bucket list. He took a deep breath. There were a few alternatives to consider.

He could run. Stump was still asleep. Brad had Brad Pitt's credit cards and driver's license. He could just disappear. Of course, that wouldn't be that much different from what he was doing right now, only without the help of a professional bodyguard protecting him. Meh. Back pocket that one.

He could refuse to testify. And then what? No more killers after him. Probably. Maybe. And no more help from the marshals. No more job at Assure. And no job anywhere in New York. Not much of a future. His back pocket was filling up quickly.

He could man up.

Wait. What? Keep going with the morning's plan?

Yes. He could just pretend he never saw this paper. If they kill him, they kill him, and would that really be so terrible? He had lived a reasonably long, mildly interesting life. Maybe someone would find those half-finished still-life sketches he left in his old apartment and think they were brilliant, and he would get some sort of recognition posthumously. At least that would be something.

Yes, Brad had chosen this path and there was no turning back now. Plus, why let a perfectly good self-generated pep talk go to waste? Whether or not there were Italian-surnamed boogiemen hiding behind every corner, he still had the opportunity to re-create himself in the mold of his choosing. If it helped to flavor that mission statement with the notion that he was the bravest coward ever, soldiering on through life like some tragically flawed, but epically noble, Nicholas Sparks contrivance, then so be it. In his mind, it gave his character depth. Brad imagined the movie poster of his life. A shot of him looking off into the distance. A woman, clearly mourning his tragic demise, super-imposed over him. Some sort of female-friendly prop down below, a diary maybe. All set against the beach. Or snow. In sepia. Mmmm, yes. That helped.

He dropped the paper back on the front porch as if he'd never touched it and went back inside to rethink his approach for today.

Stump's eyes popped open exactly twenty minutes after he closed them. He quickly surveyed his surroundings, checked the placement of his gun (still under the small of his back), and listened for anything out of the ordinary.

Brad was up before him. Odd. Probably had a tough night after that massive fail yesterday in Alan's office. But, things could be worse. Let him sweat the little stuff like office politics. Stump would focus on the big stuff like making sure there weren't any red laser-sighting dots on

Brad's forehead. The trial was coming quickly and things were heating up.

He brushed his teeth and, when he came out of the bathroom, found Brad dressed and ready for work.

"I thought we could go in a little early today."

"It's six thirty."

"A lot early."

"To do what?"

"Work."

"Work."

"What, are you busy doing something else?"

Stump couldn't figure out what the heck was going on here, but it didn't really matter. His job was to make sure Brad stayed alive through the trial, regardless of whether he was at home as usual or at work super early.

"I'm just going to grab the paper."

Crammers

The early morning sun welcomed them as they pulled into the Assure office park. Brad concentrated on steering his energies toward creating greatness. He would be a machine. The Terminator. Today he wouldn't stop until he had absolutely wrung brilliance out of this assignment. Or someone killed him.

Their drive over had been utterly silent.

Brad spent the entire time psyching himself up and trying to ignore the fact that he was the biggest target in the country.

Stump quietly reviewed the facts of the news story and internally translated them into how they could affect their lives. Someone was coming. He would have to be on guard every second. Thank God Brad didn't know. That would have complicated things.

Stump pulled into their assigned space and Brad was out of the car and marching toward the front door before Stump could get his seat belt off. He scrambled and caught up just as Brad swiped his security card across the scanner next to the locked door.

This time Brad really did go rogue. Not at first. In the morning he played it strictly by the book, translating Mike D.'s creative brief into a series of concepts, each one better than the next. He truly believed that not only was he going to win this game, he was going to do it playing by the rules. A daring gamble for a creative like Brad.

The nagging steak knife of fear that had been jammed behind Brad's ear served as an unlikely motivator. Anytime he had visions of Luca Brasi sneaking up behind him, Brad forced himself to think of another image involving adult diapers. His first few campaign ideas involved concrete boots and decapitated horses, but eventually he got into a groove.

There's a zone that good copywriters and art directors can get into if they focus. On those rare occasions when they sit their lazy asses down and really concentrate on what they're doing, the ideas just flow. First comes a germ of an idea. That germ blossoms into a concept. Then that concept bounces off the walls of their brain and turns into something else a little bigger and a little better. And that bigger-and-better something else generates spin-off ideas that start bouncing off brain walls as well, and there ends up being a snowball effect that leaves a trail of concepts and scraps of campaigns. And at some point in this creative tornado, there will be one massive idea generated that leaves all else in its dust. The leftover, also-ran concepts and scraps can be crafted into campaigns on their own and presented along with the one big idea, but they are straw dogs. They will be outshone and disregarded. Whenever the one big idea is in the room, nothing else matters. The other ideas disintegrate like German soldiers at an Ark of the Covenant opening.

Brad silently worked himself into one of these frenzies, and by lunch he was in such a good place he allowed himself to drift away from the rigid constraints of Mike D.'s creative brief.

And boom, he had the big idea.

Big enough that he stopped what he was doing, leaned back in his chair, stretched, sighed, and said one sentence out loud.

"I've got it."

He wouldn't explain what "it" was to Stump. There was no time. If it was going to be presented and sold to Alan before he went to Jack, Brad would need every second. He hunkered down and started laying out print ads and storyboarding rich media flash banners and writing television spots as fast as his mind would work.

What he wanted to present had not a thing to do with Mike D.'s brief. Didn't matter. The idea was too huge. It was bigger than Mike D.'s creative brief. Bigger than that moronic anthem. Bigger than the product category itself. He had abandoned all hope of competing on a level playing field with über-cerebral-writer-guy and j-pop-retro-punk-look-art-director-girl. He was playing an entirely new game and he would either win big or lose big. All or nothing.

Maybe it was the lack of sleep or the immense pressure of his impending testimony in a major Mafia trial, or more likely the stress of having an enormous price tag resting on his sort-of-innocent head, but Brad was convinced that he was doing something that would change the world of diaper advertising as we know it. God's work.

By four forty-five, he had done enough to get his idea across in a thorough and meaningful manner. It was all printed, organized, and the whole collection tucked under his arm as he and Stump marched down to Alan's office.

"So should we do the joke about the guy with the white pants?"

"I like it. I think it breaks the ice. Really sets the tone for the rest of the stuff."

"All right, then let's lose the all-you-can-eat joke."

"Sounds good."

Brad knocked on the doorframe of Alan's office as if he were a vampire who needed to be invited in. Alan looked up from his preparations with Mike D.

"Hey, buddy. We're kind of busy getting ready for Jack. Can we talk tomorrow morning?"

"I have more work."

"We have the work. We're all set. Remember, *Dryyyyyy Is Whyyyyy?*"

Alan had a terrible singing voice, but Mike D. started snapping and back up dancing from his seat on the couch anyway.

Brad watched calmly as he screamed in his head.

LOOK, GUYS! I'M GOING TO BE DEAD BY TOMORROW MORNING! LET ME SHOW YOU SOME SOON TO BE POSTHUMOUSLY CELEBRATED WORK.

When Alan was done, Brad spoke calmly. Almost like an adult.

"Just give me five minutes. I guarantee you'll like this."

Alan looked to Mike D. to see if they had five minutes. Mike D. checked his watch. Sure, why not.

"Okay, this is a bit unorthodox. I know you're expecting to see diaper ads for seniors with incontinence problems. But I veered slightly off that path. What I'm proposing is creating a new revenue stream from existing assets."

Alan leaned back. This should be good.

Stump hung back out of the way as Brad went on to make the second-best presentation of his life. It involved a complete redesign of the Assure packaging to create a new product line, an entirely new branding effort, a whole new tag line, and a totally new target audience. The new product was called Crammers! The new target audience was college kids. The new tag line was *No, thanks. I'll wait.*

The television spots, print ads, and banner ads involved college kids frantically preparing for exams, too busy to stop for something as petty as a bathroom break—they had finals!

Brad read through each ad and each spot with enthusiasm and charm. He pointed out the benefits of positioning themselves as the new best friend of a target market that renews itself every four years. And he reminded Alan and Mike D. that no one would actually buy these for studying. Road trips and nonstop partying on the other hand, definitely. *Why stop to pee when you can keep on trucking? Keg stand? Sure, I'm wearing Crammers!*

Brad finished presenting, sat back, and finally relaxed. There was nothing left in his tank. It had taken exactly five minutes.

"So, what do you think?"

Mike D. didn't say a word. He looked a little stunned. Alan became more red than anyone in the room had ever seen him. Finally, he stood up, grabbed all of über-cerebral-writer-guy's work, scooped up all of Brad's Crammers! work, and stomped out of his own office.

Mike D. took a deep breath and stood up.

"Okay. Thanks for that."

Meanwhile, at Brad's House

Hello, rat.

Or should it be something new? Sal felt like the whole rat thing had been played out. He'd heard other guys were using it when they did someone. This must be how LOLcats started. One guy does it for years and then someone finally notices and starts doing it also. They do it in front of people who matter, it catches fire, and soon the whole nation is burning out one catchphrase like, *You're fired!* or *That's bananas!* or some other whitestar trend.

Maybe he should try something new. *Time's up, pigeon. Game over, squealer.* Then again, *Hello, rat* was a classic.

Sal kept looking for a plug. Of all the things he had to take care of, charging up his goddamn phone should have been top of the list last night. For whatever reason, recording video of the killing was important to Tiko. But Sal fell asleep with his phone on his chest. Now, if Brad came home too early, he'd have to keep it on the charger cord and that would be awkward.

Uh, could you just move over this way a little bit? That's kind of a weird angle to kill you at and my cord is only so long. Thanks so much.

He decided that next time he would bring one of those extra power things he saw in *SkyMall*. And a tripod. Ooh, and lights! Dammit, why didn't he think of these things earlier?

Sal began to plan for the worst. Okay, Brad is most likely going to come home with his big caveman bodyguard and head for the kitchen. To do that they'll have to pass through the laundry room from the garage. Plugging the phone into the outlet just inside the living room would give him enough slack to get the drop on the marshal and still capture the magic.

He checked the lighting in the room to make sure it would suffice for his cinematic standards. It worked, so he decided he'd go with his plan, plugged in, and waited. The sun was starting to set and, not that he had ever held a straight job to use as a frame of reference, Sal imagined Brad would be coming home within the hour.

He pulled out the picture Tiko had given him. The Nuevos were thorough. They had tracked down a recent picture of Brad, his current address, and even found out who his marshal was. Guys who do a lot of meth can sometimes be overachievers.

There was a jingle outside as a set of keys slipped into the front door lock. Sal's little brain clicked into the dumb guy's version of overdrive. Fuck! This was not the plan. The phone wasn't charged up and there was no way the cord would reach far enough for him to get a good angle on the front hallway. He hadn't even checked the lighting there. Who knew what kind of shadows he'd have to deal with in there? What about the framing and composition? None of this had been planned out.

All right. Sal decided he had to wing it. He would ambush his prey first and worry about the video later. The killing was the important thing here, right?

The front door opened and a figure entered into the darkness of the front hallway. Sal tiptoed over to the corner inside the kitchen, gun drawn.

"Yo! Who's here?"

Dr. Yo entered the living room and flipped on a few lights.

"Guess I'll just have to get this bitch started up myself."

He pulled a fat joint out of his pocket and lit it before grabbing a PlayStation controller, plopping down on the couch, and turning the TV on.

"All right, who wants some?"

Okay, Sal wasn't ready for this. The guy on the couch looked very different from the one in the picture. The guy in the picture was the same height and weight, but had lighter hair and blue eyes. Also he wasn't black. And where was the Marshal? Sal was pretty sure this wasn't Brad Fingerman. He double-checked the address on the back of the picture with some mail on the counter. Yup, this was the place.

He couldn't just stay in the kitchen and wait. Brad and the marshal might come home and walk right in. The whole element of surprise would be gone, and even if the phone was charged up by now, what kind of video would that make? A terrible one is what kind.

"Yo."

Sal walked in from the kitchen, gun drawn, to find the guy who was not Brad Fingerman too immersed in his game to respond.

"I said, yo."

Yo flicked his eyes over to Sal briefly before returning them to his game. He assumed Sal was another marshal here to help out and figured Stump must have briefed him on Yo's identity. He mumbled a greeting.

". . . whassup."

This was completely not going as Sal had planned. He cleared his throat loudly. Nothing. This guy really loved video games.

BLAM! Sal shot the PlayStation console.

Yo stopped focusing so much on the television and looked over to Sal.

"You're not a marshal, are you?"

"And you're not Brad Fingerman, are you?"

"Who's asking?"

BLAM! Sal shot the couch.

"Where's Brad?"

"I don't know any Brad."

Sal figured he'd ask a few more times nicely and then start putting bullets through various appendages in Yo's body. It usually took two or three before the really tough guys gave up their buddies. And then he noticed a folder on the table next to the couch.

Yo was smart enough to keep staring forward at the smoking remains of the PlayStation as Sal walked over and looked at the new employee benefit folder on the table. He kept his gun on Yo as he flipped through.

"Hmm. I think I know where Brad is."

"So we're cool?"

"No."

Sal stuffed the employee benefits folder in his pocket, reloaded his gun, and unplugged the phone from the wall. The PlayStation had begun to smolder quite a bit as he gathered everything up, but that was hardly his concern. He had killed Yo as soon as he realized he no longer needed him, and that meant his time here in Tucson was limited. Sal had to get busy.

Hello, Rat

Today was one of those days Alan wished he still drank. He had spent the day worried he was going to choke someone out before nightfall, thanks to all the stress of the creative fire drill. Then the thing with Brad piling on at the last minute. God, a nice strong belt would have helped then.

He had not only kept it together but also sold the shit out of that ridiculous choir campaign Mike D. insisted on presenting. And Jack loved it. Shook Alan's hand. Patted him on the back. Used his first name. Mike D. had tried to worm his way in there for some credit, but Jack froze him out. D., as in Don't even think about it. Jack knew who the creative genius was around here.

Alan was the man. Things went so well with the first campaign, he took a risk and floated Brad's idea of a new product line. Jack bit. He dug the idea. He bought the entire program without changing a thing. He was going straight to the board with the whole project. This could mean millions for the company.

Alan had not only pulled off the impossible in less than forty-eight hours by delivering a spot-on campaign but he had even thrown in a genius, alternative revenue-generating idea. Jack had mentioned the word "promotion." It may have been in reference to a coupon they were going to offer at certain grocery store chains, but Alan let himself believe it might be an upgrade in his title or a better parking spot. Ah, success.

Immersed in self-satisfied silence in the elevator, savoring the glory of his magnificent win, Alan smiled to himself. Then he remembered that he hadn't pressed a floor button and had been standing there without going up or down for almost five minutes.

"Just a little bit longer."

Stump nodded. The office was as empty as a conversation between two runway models. Except for Brad and Stump. Alan had gone upstairs an hour and a half earlier, and they were still waiting.

Stump stood guard at the window, looking out over the parking lot. Brad sat at his desk staring at his old comps and discarded ideas. Sooner or later Alan would come down. He would have to pass by their office to get to his own, and they would be able to find out whether Brad's big gamble had paid off. In the meantime, there was nothing to do but sit and wait. And think.

Now that Brad didn't have the challenge of reinventing diaper advertising to distract him, there was nothing on his mind but the unknown killers sent to track him down and kill him. On video. Obsession would be too mild a word to describe his thought process. As his mind raced with possibilities, he wondered if instead of concepting ads for diapers he should transition to wearing them. Who knew what would happen when he came face-to-face with his would-be killer? Hopefully, he could keep it to some quiet pleading and crying, but no sense in not being prepared.

Brad watched Stump at the window. What did that guy know anyway? He picked up the paper this morning. Didn't he read it? Did he have no opinion on it? Why hadn't he brought up the top story? And what about the previous reports? Was he so used to reading about all the people slaughtered on the way to Brad's house that he simply took it all in stride? Or was he hiding it? Yes, of course. Stump hadn't even brought the paper in this morning. Just like the times he claimed it was stolen or the paperboy must have overslept or it was a slow news day so they didn't publish anything. Of course. Stump had been protecting Brad from seeing the ugly truth. The bastard.

"Do you think someone is going to try to kill me to keep me from testifying?"

Stump had been through this before. As trial dates got closer and closer, witnesses became more and more preoccupied with their own mortality. And for good reason. There was no point in trying to talk them out of believing there were killers after them. There were. That's why they were in the program. So he tended to be completely honest with them. Except for the part where he threw out the paper that mentioned other witnesses getting killed.

"Probably."

"Well, what are you going to do about it?"

Stump lifted his palms a little bit away from his body and raised his eyebrows at Brad's reflection in the window as if to say *I'm doing it.*

"But what if they send fifteen guys?"

"They won't."

"How do you know?"

"Because that's not how they work. And they don't need fifteen guys to kill you. They usually only need one."

Oops. That didn't come out like he meant it to.

"But I can handle whatever they send. If they can find us. Which they won't."

"Is there anything I can do?"

"Your job is to tell the truth."

Brad definitely did not like the way that sounded. He had been under a lot of stress lately and had certainly worked himself into a lather today, but that last comment sounded like it might have had an extra meaning or three.

"I'm going to tell the truth."

Stump looked out at the landscape. All quiet out there.

Brad couldn't let it go.

"What did you mean by that? Why wouldn't I tell the truth?"

"I never said you weren't going to tell the truth."

Brad stared at Stump's back. A guilty conscience can be a powerful thing. And sometimes it can look a lot like righteous indignation.

"Do you think I'm lying about what I saw?"

Stump kept his gaze out the window.

"Because I saw everything. I saw Frank Fortunato kill Carmine."

Stump resisted the temptation to turn to look at Brad's face as he spoke.

"I saw it with my own two eyes. I saw Frank in the elevator. I saw him with the gun. I saw him pull the trigger. I know what he was wearing. I know how he moved. I know what he said before he murdered Carmine. I saw every detail and I'm going to testify in a court of law and Frank is going to go to jail until he's executed and I'll be a hero."

Stump considered calling Brad out on his bullshit, perhaps lecturing him a bit on the subtleties of Facial Action Coding and/or weak storytelling but then stopped. He racked his focus to the reflection in the window of the office door. Uh-oh.

"Hello, rat."

Stump whipped around to find Sal standing in the doorway, gun pointed calmly at him. Brad swiveled around to see Sal.

"Shit."

If he had spent his time walking down to the product supply closet instead of interrogating Stump, Brad would be well prepared for this moment. As it stood, he was just going to have to trust his sphincter with his dignity.

Sal was too far away for Stump to effect any damage with his years of martial arts training. Sal's gun was out and cocked with the safety off, so there was no chance of Stump pulling his own weapon out of his ankle holster without getting shot six or seven times. And he was too far away from Brad to throw himself in front of him as a human shield. Sal had played it perfectly. There was nothing left but negotiation. Diplomacy. Begging.

"Let's talk about this."

Sal grimaced as he struggled to keep his gun trained on Stump while opening his camera app.

"All right look, I don't have a lot of battery left, so we're gonna have to make this quick."

He tucked the phone under his arm, snuck a peek at the back of the picture of Brad he had in his pocket, and then looked Brad over.

"Brad Fingerman?"

"Yes, and . . ."

Stump rolled his eyes. All their training. For that?

"Great. Thanks."

Sal tucked the picture back into his pocket and turned his attention back to the phone.

"Oh, hold on. I had it on still picture. There, video. Is the red light on? That means this is recording? I don't see a red light."

Brad looked at Stump. What the hell was he waiting for? An invitation? *My good man, would you mind being so kind as to perform your sworn duties? I have an appointment to be alive in half an hour and I don't want to miss it.*

Or should Brad do something? Holy God. What if he jumped the guy with the gun? Created a distraction so Stump could disarm him? Did something/anything on his own behalf? Was there a stapler he could throw? An end table he could flip? A joke he could tell?

Sal lifted the phone to face Brad.

"I think this is autofocus, so we're good."

Stump's mind raced, calculating the speed at which he could get across the room and put a finger through Sal's eye socket versus the time it would take Sal to move his attention away from his stupid phone and pull the trigger of his gun. It looked like negotiations were out. This was going to be another viral video and no amount of smooth talking or bargaining would get them out of it. He would have to act, and if he got gutshot in the process, at least he would go down swinging. He tensed in anticipation of springing the next time Sal blinked.

"Pitt! Flint!"

Stump froze. It was Alan. This could be the distraction he needed.

Alan popped his head into the office and flashed a big smile.

"You guys got a minute for some great news?"

"Beat it, shitbag."

Sal kept his gun on Stump and gave Alan a quick once over.

"We're busy."

"Excuse me?"

Sal pointed the gun at Alan.

"I said we're busy, asshole. Now, get out of here."

This wasn't the first time Alan had a gun pointed at him, so it didn't have quite the effect Sal was hoping for. Instead of screaming like a Lane Bryant cashier and running to hide in a bathroom, Alan gritted his teeth and his face got very, very red.

"Who the fuck are you?"

Not that he would have answered Alan seriously, but Sal was tackled by Stump before he could get a word out. They tumbled to the ground and rolled around, each trying to gain a dominant position.

The newly reinvented Brad watched in horror as his bodyguard risked life and limb to protect the government's most valuable witness. The result of this wrestling match would determine a great deal of the rest of Brad's life. If Stump won, Brad could keep running, now fully aware that he was not nearly as well hidden as he had been led to believe. The choice to be made, of course, was whether or not to include Stump in that running. Certainly Brad appreciated the passion Stump was now displaying, grunting and straining to subdue the tubby hitman on top of him. But, restraining gunmen shouldn't even be an action item on Stump's to do list, should it? Brad was supposed to be unfindable. If it could happen once, it could happen again. Hmmm. He and Stump would have to have a long talk about all this before he made his decision on who rode shotgun with him into the future.

On the other hand, if Stump lost, well, that story pretty much wrote itself.

Dammit. Why couldn't Alan have come down earlier? At least Brad would have known if he were going to be remembered as a brilliant mind taken too soon or a cheap hack who was going to be fired anyway. Oh God. Imagine that funeral. Who would come? Alan? Yo? J-pop-retro-punk-look-art-director-girl? No one? Would no one come? Would the program tell Gracie? Would she care? Would she come? Would she bring a date?

Is this how it ends? Brad Pitt dies and no one gives a shit?

He felt as if he should maybe cheer or yell encouraging words to Stump, but decided that might be bad form. Besides things were moving quickly and it looked like Stump really knew what he was doing.

Stump forcibly flipped Sal over and yanked one of his arms back to the point where it came a little out of the socket. Unfortunately, it was not Sal's gun arm and that's what he used to shoot Stump in the face. Stump died before he hit the floor.

Well, that settled the riding shotgun issue. Brad watched, frozen, as Sal shoved Stump's body off of him and grunted his creaky bones back up to face Brad, irritated by the imposition of the attack.

"Why does everyone have to get involved?"

He noticed Alan still standing there, steaming. Civilians were so annoying.

"What are you looking at?"

Sal reached down for his phone and when he came up, found Alan's hands coming at him. Before Sal could react, Alan latched on to his neck and squeezed like there was no tomorrow. Sal brought his gun up to shoot Alan in the chest, but Alan threw him against the wall, cracking several Mafia ribs in the process. Alan never lost his grip on Sal's neck.

"You come into my office and interrupt my *workflow*?"

Sal tried to bring his gun up again, but Alan threw him into the door, breaking Sal's other shoulder and popping the gun out of his hand.

"I AM TRYING TO GIVE MY COWORKERS SOME FEEDBACK!"

Alan spat when he yelled. Sal's face transformed into that confused look people get when they're dying.

"I WILL NOT TOLERATE UNPROFESSIONAL BEHAVIOR!!!"

And then Sal was dead.

Alan released his grip and Sal melted to the floor. Alan stepped back and looked at what he had done. It was very disappointing for a man who was making every effort to avoid this exact kind of thing. He slapped a hand on the back of his own head as if he had forgotten where he had parked at the mall.

". . . Dammit, Alan."

He shot Brad a quick, ashamed look and turned to leave. When he got to the door, he turned back.

"Congratulations on the Crammers! thing. Jack loved it."

Then Alan ran out of the office.

Brad sat in shocked silence, trying to make sense of the last ninety seconds. He was about to get killed and then someone tried to save him and they got killed and someone else killed the killer and now here he was, alone. Oh, and his brilliant idea had been not only accepted but resoundingly applauded as a career-making game changer. Except that his boss had become a murderer and blown both of their Witness Protection Program covers in one fell swoop.

Through the window, he could see Alan run through the parking lot, scale the fence to the golf course, and scamper off across the fairway. Probably safe to say that Brad wouldn't be working at Assure any longer.

Brad had started the day with the resolve of a Persian soldier at Thermopylae and was ending it with a muddling of confusion and probably tears. All he had wanted to do was sell some diapers.

He looked back at Sal and Stump lying on the office floor in a bloody mess. The two sides of his life. The killer and the savior. Neither of whom could get the job done.

Now who was he supposed to lean on? Who was protecting him? He would have to make his own security decisions. Out here in Arizona where he knew nothing and had no history. Jesus.

The more he thought about it, the worse it got. Brad had no idea if Sal had come alone, or if other hired killers were watching. What if Stump was wrong and Sal was part of a team? What if there were more on the way?

Brad gathered himself and started to run out when he realized that Stump had the keys to their car in his pocket. He forced himself to rummage through the pockets of his dead former bodyguard until he found them.

On his way out he stopped to grab Sal's gun. He had yelled, "Take his gun!" at too many bad cop movies to not pick it up. He probably wouldn't shoot it, but he might point it in the general direction of anyone threatening him. Suddenly selling diapers didn't seem that important. Or advertising in general, for that matter. What seemed really, really important was figuring out how to stay alive for the foreseeable future.

Brad jumped into his rental car and started driving without even thinking.

Fifteen minutes later, he pulled into his subdivision and was making the turns to get to his street when he had a painfully obvious realization.

If that guy with the gun found his office, wouldn't he also know where Brad lived? What if that's where the imagined team of henchmen were waiting for him? Should he really be going back to the house? On the other hand, everything he owned that he wasn't wearing at the time was back there.

He made the turn onto his street and quickly found out that it was a moot point. His house was surrounded by fire trucks, ambulances, and neighbors who would no doubt later refer to Brad as a quiet man who kept to himself and was probably gay with the big guy he lived with. The model home was burnt to the ground. Firefighters had kept the surrounding houses safe, but Brad and Stump's temporary housing was gone, gone, gone. He pulled into a driveway a few houses before his own and turned around before anyone noticed who he was.

Dr. Yo's room was rented from a lovely eighty-six-year-old woman who lived about seven minutes from Brad's subdivision. It was another layer of secrecy in Yo's effort to stay off the grid. He had given the old lady a little help filling out the lease and, in the process, put her name in the lessee's name space. The lease he signed had effectively leased Gertrude Abernathy's apartment to herself. Gertrude's eyes were failing and Yo had paid a year up front in cash, so she didn't look too closely anyway. Considering even telemarketers couldn't track Yo down, Brad thought it might be the one safe place to hide from the platoon of Mafia killers scouring Tucson for him.

He parked behind the house, scurried past the detached garage and up the stairs to Yo's back entrance. The windows were dark and there was no answer when he knocked. Where the hell could Yo be?

Brad used the key Yo had made for him and let himself in, figuring he would hide until Yo showed. He sat down on the couch and soaked in the quiet stillness of the empty room.

Holy crap. He had just witnessed a double murder. And this time he really did see everything. And then Alan ran off to who knows where. Which meant Brad was the only witness. Again. No way he was testifying this time. He had seen how well that worked out.

Brad took a moment to ask the universe to hold on just a goddamn minute.

How was this fair?

Losing his promising career, his magnificent New York City life, and the mirage of a loving wife was supposed to have been his rock bottom. That would be anyone's rock bottom, no?

The whole point of starting your life over was to make it better. This was not better. It was decidedly worse. He was now on the lam from being on the lam. This was not the picture Brittany and Stump had painted for him only a few weeks ago. Who approved this new extended rock bottom with the dead partner and the blown cover and the rapidly dimming hope for a future that involved breathing? Not Brad.

Brad wanted the afterschool special version of rock bottom. The one where a tough but likable authority figure stops you from throwing that rock through the window of the abandoned factory and then bonds with you over a story about when he was a kid growing up in the hardscrabble black-and-white-film days. Not the rock bottom where someone chases you forever and ever and very much wants to cast you as the lead in a low-budget snuff film.

How is it possible that he was missing his unemployed, cuckolded, guy-in-a-chicken-suit days? This was the worst vine ever.

And where was Yo? If anyone could give him advice on disappearing, Yo could. Maybe they would go together. Ride off into the sunset, never to be heard from again. Like Butch and Sundance. Or Thelma and Louise. Or that robot from *Iron Giant* and the Great Pumpkin. Brad's analogies became more and more disjointed as he drifted off to sleep, overwhelmed by the day.

Malcolm's Sordid Past

A bit about Malcolm's history with women: He had never had sex with any of them. Never with a date. Not with a one night stand. No vacation tryst. Nothing.

There had been no wild nights out with the boys. No one had ever set him up with their loose cousin. Even during the post-birth-control-pill/pre-AIDS period of his high school and college days, he couldn't get the job done thanks to eight years of crippling shyness.

His romantic backstory included a total of seventy-four first dates. This evidence is presented only to validate the effort he had put forth. It wasn't that he didn't like women. He did. In fact, he had had the nerve to ask well over a hundred women to join him for a drink after work or perhaps a night of dinner and dancing. Seventy-four had accepted.

None of the encounters had amounted to anything of value and certainly none had ever begged for an encore presentation, although there had been a few sympathy second dates. There had been girls he had liked. And presumably some who had liked him. But Malcolm had simply not run into the right girl at the right time in his forty-one dating years. Yes, he had ridiculously high standards. No, he had not compromised those criteria as time had marched cruelly forward.

But he kept trying. Naturally, it took a tremendous amount of time before he would broach the subject of dinner or even coffee with a woman. He had to think things over first, consider the smartest plan of attack. Occasionally he would run a background check. He was the opposite of spontaneous and that had worked out to about one point eight dates a year. For a man as secretly passionate as he was, it was maddening. But for a man as patient, disciplined, and scrupulous as Malcolm, it was necessary.

Of course he had never bothered with prostitutes, believing that was the sport of a lower class and wouldn't put him in the best light once he did settle down with the woman he was sure to fall in love with. Besides, most whores didn't have the kind of time it would have taken Malcolm to answer the question, "What are you looking for tonight?"

And that was why Malcolm Middleton was still a virgin.

He knew the mechanics of sex and presumed himself to be a natural at the act of intercourse. He had seen a few racy French movies and had accidentally-on-purpose clicked onto a couple of off-color websites when his mother went to bed early. But that was the extent of his experience with seeing a naked woman in the same room.

He had high hopes for Lola. She was an entirely different venture for him. She had asked Malcolm out. He was positive there was a meaningful connection. They had already successfully completed a second date that he was sure had gone swimmingly, and he was planning on asking for a third. A third!

He had let a little time pass since they last met so as to not look too virgin-y, but he felt in his heart that finally the time was right. He picked up the phone, called Lola, and asked for the very first third date of his life.

She said yes before he finished the question.

The Latest News

Brad woke up on Gertrude Abernathy's couch four hours after he sat down on it. It was almost eleven and Yo still hadn't shown up. Brad did not have a good feeling about this. Or maybe he was super hungry from not eating all day. He wondered if Yo kept any food in his fridge.

He did. Brad whipped up a sandwich and popped open a beer to help with stress management. He sat back down on the couch and turned on the television.

As he flipped through the channels, the reality of the situation started to sink in. Brad was in big trouble. His bodyguard had been killed. Very bad people still wanted him dead. Someone in the government he had trusted with his life had leaked enough information that he had been found. And it was all nowhere near over.

He had almost no money. His car was rented on a card that would no doubt be either canceled in the next few days or used to track his whereabouts and, either way, someone was probably scouring the streets for his license plate number right now. He was a fugitive, and he wasn't guilty of anything besides straying from a poorly written creative brief.

The local news came on and cleared a few details up. A very concerned reporter described a bloody shootout at an office park Brad was familiar with. A promising young copywriter had been killed along with an unidentified man. Police didn't have any suspects, but they were looking to question one Alan Silver. In other news, a fire burned down a house in a neighborhood Brad had recently visited. The house was a total loss and there was one fatality. A man about Brad's age had been killed in the blaze. Firefighters were assuming the dead man was one of the residents, and were still trying to determine the cause.

A neighbor commented that the dead man had always been the silent type and she hoped his boyfriend was all right. Up next, the newscasters promised some super-helpful diet tips for eating healthy in Chinese restaurants.

Yo was dead.

Brad realized Sal's first stop wasn't the office. It was his house. He had found Yo there, probably playing video games, and killed him. Yo probably thought Sal was a member of some elite hit squad commissioned by a shadow government his conspiracy theories were so fond of. Chances were, his last words were "I fucking knew it." Brad took some comfort in the fact that Yo died basking in the warm glow of self-validation.

Brad was alone.

This would have been an awesome time to get some advice from someone who knew something about situations like this, but anyone who could advise him had recently passed away or was part of the organization that revealed his location. So he would have to figure something else out. On his own.

At least when he lost his job at Overthink, he still had Gracie. And when he lost her, he had the program. And when he lost Stump, he still had Yo. But now?

No vines. Nothing.

Brad was all by his lonesome. And not in the fun, Wander-the-Earth-Like-in-*Kung Fu* kind of way. Not in the Boy-It's-Lonely-Being-the-World's-Most-Handsome-Man way. Alone in a The-Hounds-of-Zaroff way. Yes, Brad was going to have to earn his Save Your Own Ass merit badge tonight.

Compounding the issue was that, aside from a goldfish and some cherished sitcoms, Brad had never before faced the death of a loved one. Seeing a human friend killed in front of his very eyes had shocked him to his core. But as the reality of the situation settled in on him, what struck him like a Bob Sapp nutpunch was how close he had become to both Stump and Yo without even realizing it. As different as the two friendships were, they were both based on the most honest interactions Brad had ever had. Stump and Yo really knew him. And they liked him. They had inadvertently become his best friends and now they were gone.

When he really thought about it, it wasn't the living alone part that scared him. It was the dying alone part. There was the distinct possibility that Brad would end up as an anonymous pile of ashes whose only eulogy would be his butchers' debate over which fast food drive-through they would stop by once Brad's remains had been consumed by an industrial furnace.

Was this it? Would his only real contributions to the world be a few minutes of commercials, a bit of brief hope for an ambitious FBI agent, and some hardly needed inspiration for frat boys to binge drink? Probably.

Brad stopped himself. This momentary sigh of self-awareness was as philosophical as he would allow himself to become. Self-improvement had a time and a place. Currently, there was the matter of self-preservation to be considered. Regardless of how well attended his funeral would be, he needed to do something immediately to forestall that event. If he could just get out of the city and settle down into a simple blind panic, he would consider that a good start.

Brad took inventory of his current assets. Half a sandwich. Sal's gun. Sixty-three dollars in cash. His shoes were in pretty good shape. He looked around Yo's tiny room for anything that might be useful. He dug around under the mattress just in case Yo's reference to his retirement fund wasn't a figure of speech. There was nothing, of course. Yo was too smart for that. Brad assumed that cash was quietly hidden in the Caymans and not terribly accessible to him at this hour. Okay, what else? Books? Nope. Yo's stash of Purple Haze marijuana and petty cash to buy more. Yes. Pornographic DVDs. Maybe. Car keys. Ah-ha.

On a hook by the door hung a set of car keys. Could these be an extra set of tow truck keys? The key ring was emblazoned with a vintage Buick logo. Does Buick even make a tow truck? Even Yo's keys were in disguise.

Yo's truck. Cops never stopped him, and he made good cash by shaking down innocent drivers. Perfect for Brad's new life on the run. Or not.

Yo would have driven his truck to Brad's house. It should still be there sitting in front of the charred remains of Brad's fake life. Could Brad sneak back to his house on foot and make off with Yo's truck? Who would look for a runaway art director in a tow truck?

Brad pulled the window treatments back a millimeter or two. The alley behind the Abernathy estate was fairly well lit, thanks to its proximity to the side street. As far as Brad could tell, there was no Mafia hit squad lurking outside.

He slipped the keys off the hook, cracked the door open quietly, and slipped out. As he quickly tiptoed down the stairs, he noticed something very important. No gunshots. So far, so good. Just another forty years of this and he was set.

He hid in the shadows of the house and took a good look around at the terrain he was about to head out over. Late-night suburbia. He figured the distance to his french-fried house was about three miles as the crow flies, or four and a half as the marked-for-death witness runs. Was this his best plan? Should he instead stick with his rental car until he hit the Mexican border, walk into Nogales, and hope he picked up the language? That was only supposed to take two weeks if you really immersed yourself, right? And his sixty-three dollars would go much further there. Or he could grab the tow truck, head for Canada, and grow a mustache. How hard could passing for Canadian be? He just had to act unambitious and gullible. Boom, Canadian. It was nice to have options.

Brad snuck along the side of the house to avoid appearing in any type of light until the last possible moment. The detached garage had a long set of shadows that would take him right out to the street. He crept along the darkest parts, plastering himself to the wall, until he passed a window.

Weh-heh-hell. What was this?

Inside the garage was a car. A big, boss muscle car. No way the real Getrude Abernathy spent her weekends working on that. Brad seriously doubted she drove this bad boy to her weekly bridge game. He snuck back to the door at the front of the building. It was locked, but he checked one of the keys on the chain and it slid right in, unlocking the door as if it were expecting him. Brad slipped into the garage and looked at the car. It was a Buick.

1970 is considered by many in the car world to be the year of the American muscle car. It was also the year that Buick released the GSX, but only six hundred seventy-eight of them.

Brad didn't realize it as he drooled and prayed to sweet baby Jeebus that one of the keys he was holding fit the car he was looking at, but he was standing before a meticulously refurbished GSX, complete with functional scoops, front and rear spoilers, color-coordinated headlamp bezels, TH400 turbo transmission with a Hurst shifter, power disc brakes, a Rally Ride Control package (featuring rear stabilizer bar, front and rear firm ride springs, and rear lower control arm assembly), and the eight-track player that the previous owner had used to wear out Zeppelin's fourth album. It was a spectacular feat to have re-created such a monster of a car to this level of perfection, and it had taken Yo the better part of two years to do so. Sold on the open market, this masterpiece could fetch well over one hundred thirty thousand dollars. But this was all lost on Brad.

As far as he was concerned, it was what looked like a fast car that no one would associate with him. And that made it beautiful for reasons most car enthusiasts never consider when judging refurbished 1970 muscle cars.

He slid into the driver's seat and tried the key. VROOOOOMMM. The powerful engine fired up, so smooth. The gas tank was full. Even the air freshener had recently been replaced. He turned the car off and checked the glove compartment for a registration. The car had been registered three months earlier to one Gertrude Abernathy. All part of Yo's planned anonymity. Brad imagined Gertrude wouldn't mind if he took it out for a spin.

Six hours later, the sun began its predictable rise in front of Brad as he motored along Interstate 10, trying to look as inconspicuous as he could in a pristine, Saturn-Yellow GSX. He had made it past El Paso and still had no plan as to what he intended to do or where he was going to end up.

Canada was out. Too cold. Mexico was out. Too exotic. Like so many American desperados before him, he was headed in the general direction of Florida. If he was going to get hunted and killed like an animal, perhaps he could get some snorkeling in first. It beat waiting for death in some landlocked redneck town. Hopefully.

His six hours on the road had given him time to think through what had happened pretty thoroughly, and to make some big decisions regarding the rest of his life. So far, he had figured out that he was going to get as far away from Stump and Yo's murders as he could, he was going live a quiet life under an assumed name he had not decided on yet, and he should have bought a muscle car a long time ago. Beyond that he was wide open and fascinated by the idea that the future was entirely in his hands.

The adrenaline he had been overflowing with earlier in his escape had begun to subside, and he started to realize just how exhausted he was. Coffee and beef jerky could only keep a man going so long. Brad pulled into a truck-stop parking lot and eased the GSX to a stop between two eighteen-wheelers. He turned it off, climbed into the back seat, and fell fast asleep.

Brittany's Pickle

No wonder Stump didn't check in last night. They were supposed to discuss what he had found while studying Brad's video testimony. That's what Stump had thought anyway. Brittany had finally managed to squeeze into her skirt and bull-effing-shit if she was going to the Justice Department and tell them Brad was changing his story now. There was too much at stake and she was totally ready. Mostly ready. Jarvis hadn't really gotten much further and all of her other witnesses had been killed. But as long as she had Brad testifying, she was fine.

But Brittany had gotten a call first thing this morning from the Tucson police department telling her about the double murder at Assure and the fire at Brad's house.

"And you're sure the body at the house is Brad Fingerman?"

"We're not aware of a Brad Fingerman, Ms. Marinakos. Is this someone we should be considering a person of interest in this investigation?"

"No, no! Please, don't."

Brittany thanked the Tucson officer and excused herself from the call without using the word "Fingerman" again.

Dammit. Brad was dead. She had kind of liked him. He was doofy and a terrible liar, but Brad was a nice guy and definitely deserved better than dying under an assumed name in Tucson. Poor thing.

Speaking of which. Now what?

The trial was in twenty-four days and she had no witnesses left. Give up? Fat chance. Move forward with only Brad's video testimony? Would Justice go with that? It was such a long shot, but Frank Fortunato was a big catch. To pull out now after all the press would be nothing short of embarrassment. And it's not like any new evidence was going to come along.

It was settled, then. If they were going to get Frank for Carmine's murder, they would have to do it with what they had. Fine. She decided to fight with Brad's video testimony, her agents' affidavits, and her own testimony serving as circumstantial evidence. Brittany was on a mission and even something as crippling as Brad getting himself killed wasn't going to stop her. It was what reality show contestants refer to as "time to step up."

There was still a job to be done here. Frank would go down. Brad would be avenged. That G.D. skirt would be worn on national television.

And right then, Jarvis called.

Happy Frank

It didn't take long for the news to work its way back to Frank. Prison gossip is a very efficient machine. He was thrilled his plan had worked and even shrugged off the lack of video documentation. The important thing was that he was going to get off and enjoy the remaining years of his life, God willing, in his own home, with his friends and family and a few girlfriends.

When Frank congratulated Mitchell the Aryan on a job well done, it sort of looked like Mitchell was surprised. Maybe he wasn't used to gratitude. Maybe appreciation was considered a sign of weakness in here. Whatever. That no-good rat was dead along with all the other scumbag agents. Burned to death! Totally untraceable to Frank. That's what mattered.

He had to pay a little extra since the assassin had died in the process, but in Frank's mind it was a minor penance. He told Mitchell to put it on his bill.

Back with The Boys, Frank told Pete the Phone to have Moldy Tony get the word out that everybody, everybody including Sal, needed to hit the mattresses until after the trial. He wanted to make sure nothing screwed this up now that it was practically a done deal.

He also had Johnny Pancakes make arrangements to anonymously send Brittany a dozen roses along with a *Sorry for your loss* card. God, he was in a good mood.

Brad's Blowout

Brad was awakened late in the afternoon by the honking of a trucker angry at him for taking up a primo eighteen-wheeler parking spot with the GSX. It took a few moments for him to shake off the confusion of where he was and why he was sleeping in his clothes in the back seat of someone else's car. He hoped it was some sort of buddy road trip that involved a sorority, but as the cobwebs cleared, he remembered the whole murder-witness-on-the-run-from-bloodthirsty-killers thing.

Brad looked around to find himself still sitting in the rest stop parking lot, no longer protected by the trucks he had hidden between this morning. His bright yellow car was sitting out in plain sight, blocking valuable truck parking.

He cranked down his window to hear the driver behind him.

"This is for trucks only, asshole."

"Right, sorry."

Inside the truck stop, Brad gnawed on another piece of jerky and chased it with a sip of maybe the worst coffee of his life. The question was how much of his cash should be allotted for food. The more he ate, the less he had to spend on gas and chances were when he ran out of gas money, he was staying wherever he was. For a brief moment, as he stared at the moon pies on the counter next to the cash register, he thought maybe he could trade Sal's gun for some snacks. This was Texas, after all. They loved guns here. But then, based on his current status of Guy Running For His Life, he decided against it and erred on the side of spending his cash on gas in the hopes of coasting into

Florida on fumes. He did allow himself one indulgent purchase. A prepaid cell phone.

When you called Owen's home and he wasn't there, the outgoing message played a recording of a high-as-a-kite Owen saying, "Yoooooou know what to do . . ." followed by a minute and a half of Owen channel surfing before saying, "Is this still on—(BEEP)."

Brad called hoping to talk to the one person in the world he knew he could still trust. But he got the machine instead. He didn't leave a message because it wouldn't have helped anything to drop his problems on Owen. So that left Brittany.

Despite the fact that someone in her agency had ratted him out to Frank, Brad still felt like he could maybe/kind of trust Brittany. And he really needed to talk to someone. If nothing else, to get the truth off his chest. It's not like he was going to testify in Frank's trial now. Maybe it would help if he had one less burden to carry around. Maybe if he came clean with Brittany, they could start fresh and she could wire him fifty dollars or call a cousin who lived in Orlando so Brad could crash on their couch instead of at another truck stop or Walmart parking lot.

Brittany sat on the edge of the couch in Jarvis's bay, once more watching him peck away at her surveillance video. He had come up with something interesting in the footage after Brad bent down. Brad had sneezed. She didn't know what to make of this detail, but wondered if it wasn't significant. He had never mentioned the sneeze before and according to her calculations based on the timing of the shots, the sneeze had to happen just before Carmine was shot. What did that mean? How did it affect the story Brad would have told if he weren't blackened Fingerman right now? This would have been so great to have had two weeks ago.

As Jarvis fiddled and tweaked, Brittany distracted herself with a phone call from her grandmother. Listening to her blather on about her next date was excruciating, but would hopefully one day get Brittany into heaven.

Brittany almost ignored the call on her other line when she didn't recognize the number. Not that she didn't want an excuse to get rid of her grandmother. The details of senior-citizen Brazilian waxing were way beyond the point of too much information. Lola was planning "something big" for her new boyfriend, and felt like some girl talk with her granddaughter. How could this help anyone? As if having Brittany's best marshal killed and her star witness burned to a crisp weren't bad enough, Lola started in on how some overly hot wax gave her a blister that could ruin her whole evening. Brittany shivered in disgust, interrupted, and clicked over.

"Hello, Brittany. It's me, Brad Pitt.

When she heard Brad's voice, she almost made in her pants.

"Where are you? I'll send marshals."

"I can't tell you where I am. And I don't want any marshals."

"Look, Brad, I know you're scared, but we can protect you."

"Uh, no, I think we tried that."

Brittany bit her lip, hoping some intense pain would help her think. What could she possibly offer Brad to save the trial of the century and, let's face it, her television career?

"I'll come get you myself."

"Look, I just called to talk. I could only afford like four minutes on this thing."

"Brad, I really need your testimony. All my other witnesses are dead."

Oops. Maybe she should have bitten a little harder.

"Funny you mention that. I have something I have to tell you. You know, about being a witness."

"That's great. Let us come pick you up."

"I didn't—"

"Brad, if you don't show up at the courthouse in three weeks, my case gets thrown out and I lose everything. I've worked too hard on this to lose it now. It's my whole career."

There it was. She laid it all out. Almost. "Oh, and Frank will get off. Don't forget, Frank will get off."

Brad drove in silence for a moment. He really felt bad destroying Brittany's career, but there was the gaggle of Mafia trigger men to consider.

"I just called to tell you—"

BOOM!

Brad dropped the phone and scrunched down for cover. The car began to swerve violently and he struggled to maintain control.

Holy Christ, they found me. That trucker must have sold me out. I hate truckers!

It took a few moments before he realized he was not, in fact, a victim of trucker backstabbing, but instead, a flat tire.

"Brad? Brad, what happened? Brad, Jesus, are you all right?"

He picked his phone up and hit the Off button. Obviously, he was not meant to confess to Brittany just yet.

Brittany barked into her phone a few more times, but got no response. The last thing she had heard was a loud noise (gunshot?), a bunch of commotion, and then silence.

Really? He's killed and then he's alive and then he's killed again? How is that fair?

She tried calling his number back, but guessed there wouldn't be an answer. She was right.

Brad glided the car to a stop and sat in silence. And then he cried. He cried for being alone and helpless and having no idea what to do and for not just telling Brittany he hadn't seen anything in the first place and for not knowing if he was going to have to live like a scaredy-cat baby the rest of his life or even if he was going to have a rest of his life. And then he got mad at himself for crying. If the truckers hadn't turned him in before, they definitely would if they saw him like this.

Brad pulled himself together. Enough already. If this was to be his life, then he needed to accept that. So what if two months ago he was married in Manhattan with a great new promotion and one of the coolest jobs of anyone in his chosen profession. That was over. Someone had different plans for him. It was time to nut up and figure out his next step. Forget New York. Forget advertising. Forget his old life.

There was no sense in trying to re-create what was gone. There were bigger fish to fry. He was now a nobody with nothing and nowhere to go. If he were ever to become a somebody with something and some-where to go, he had to make something happen himself.

But first, he had to change the tire.

Brad popped the trunk and found it as tidy as the rest of the car. He pulled the pristine carpet up to find a full sized, Armor All-ed spare tire and jack. He moved the fireproof lockbox out of the way and started unscrewing the wing nut that held the tire in place.

Wait.

Why was there a fireproof lockbox in the trunk of Yo's car? Brad pulled the box out and sat back down in the front seat with it. It was heavy. And it was locked. Okay. So you're a paranoid conspiracy theo-rist with something of value you need locked away. Where do you put the key?

If anything, Yo was a practical man. He wouldn't have kept the key to this presumably valuable treasure trove in the same place as the lockbox. But if he kept the box in the car he maintained to perfection but never drove, the box was probably never touched either and meant to be used only when the car was used. Brad checked the key chain. There were a few smaller keys next to the ones for the garage, ignition, and trunk.

He tried the first. No match. He tried the second. Didn't work. He tried the third. Click.

Brad opened the lockbox and looked inside to find the meticulously laid plans of Dr. Yo.

"Whoa."

The game had changed dramatically once again, so he dialed up Owen's number one more time in the hopes of getting some advice. He succeeded without even speaking to Owen. This time, when Owen's answering machine told Brad he knew what to do, he hung up and did it.

Brad Fingerman Is Alive

"I want every available agent on this. I want his credit cards tracked. Both identities, real and program. Also check Stump's cards just in case he's using those. Check the hospitals. I want roadblocks and face checks and cavity searches at every bus stop, train station, and airport if we can get them. If he's still alive, I want him."

Brittany pulled every resource she could onto the case. As long as there was a glimmer of hope, she planned to use up whatever favors she had within the agency.

Two and a half weeks later, Brittany's key witness was still missing. Brad had called from a disposable phone bought somewhere in West Texas. Local agents scoured the highway, found the phone where he had tossed it out his car window, and that was where the trail had ended. No more phone calls. No credit card purchases. No sightings. Nothing at all.

She never officially told the press that Brad was dead, so Brittany didn't tell them he was possibly still alive.

She did call Justice and let them know the good news. They told her they were looking forward to meeting him and that things were going well with their preparation.

So, there was that.

Malcolm and Lola's Third, Fourth, and Fifth Dates

Malcolm had been paid pretty well in his past life as an attorney in his dad's firm. Babysitting money. Now, as a judge he made $169,300 a year. Which wasn't great by local standards. Unless you still lived with your mother in the same rent-controlled apartment you grew up in before your parents divorced. Then it was pretty good.

Malcolm's two-bedroom, one-bath, three-story walk-up was that mythical apartment every Manhattan resident keeps a secret eye out for, hoping against hope that one day a long-lost cousin, old friend, or father who abandoned them when they were six will ring up and casually mention that they are moving to the suburbs and ask if you'd like to hop onto their dirt cheap, state-enforced lease. It never happens.

What does happen in these situations is guys like Malcolm save the money they don't spend on things like exorbitantly high Manhattan rents and mortgages for the bigger, more-impressive apartments they never moved into, dinners for the third and fourth dates they never had the nerve and/or inclination to ask for, starter wife engagement rings they never bought, exotic honeymoons they never went on, hefty private school and college tuitions for the children they never had, daughters' weddings they never paid for, oh-you-really-shouldn't-have anniversary presents they never bought, spontaneous all-inclusive vacations they never took, alimony for the divorce they never got, and oversized, second marriage, trophy-wife engagement rings they never even looked at. And they end up loaded.

Which is how he could afford to buy Lola such a nice tennis bracelet on their third date. He had never been so spontaneous, but there was something about this woman. Some weird electricity between them had altered his inner being, causing him to feel relatively swashbuckling. He found himself playing racquetball, sleeping naked, and considering R-rated movies. He was a new man.

Their fourth date had been dinner at Manhattan's most expensive restaurant, prime seats at the opera, and a drink afterward. Lola had hinted strongly that she would like to go back to his place and kept humming the Brazilian national anthem. But Malcolm wasn't quite ready to introduce her to his mother. She was probably already asleep anyway. So he politely declined and found Lola a cab.

Later, as he over-analyzed the evening, he realized the real reason she wanted to come home with him. In her usual turnaround of classic roles, Lola was invoking the third date rule. Technically, it was the fourth date, but it was obvious what was going on. It was time to get busy.

Looking back he saw that she had tried to invoke it on their third date as well. Wow. She must have really liked that tennis bracelet.

Malcolm made a life-altering decision. Their fifth date was coming up. He was going to have sex with Lola Marinakos.

Brad Is Back

Brad did eventually make it to Florida. The Keys, even. Down in the middle islands, he found a small, family-owned hotel that took cash and had parking in the back. He stayed in his room for most of the two weeks he spent there, ordering in from various restaurants around town and keeping to himself. He didn't use a phone. He didn't send an e-mail. He barely changed TV channels. Occasionally, when the loneliness was too much, he went to movies at the one theater in Marathon, getting there after the film started and leaving before it ended. Not that anyone in that sleepy town was looking for him. Like the rest of the Keys, Marathon was filled with people trying to escape their own past lives and worrying about someone else's problems just took energy away from worrying about your own, so why hassle with it? And, same as the rest of the year in Marathon, not much happened while Brad was there.

By the time Frank's trial was a few days away, Brad was rested and ready. Hiding out in the islands had given him plenty of time to reflect and plan, and he was quite sure of what he needed to do.

So he fired up Yo's car and drove to New York.

The Morning After

Malcolm was awake before dawn, but he didn't move a muscle. Hopefully, Mother would understand that he hadn't called, as this was a bit of a special occasion.

It hadn't been on the fifth date as he had planned, or even the sixth or seventh. But last night, number eight, Malcolm had finally mustered the gumption to release the hounds.

As the morning light began to creep in through Lola's bedroom window, he allowed himself the luxury of rolling over to look at his conquest. He marveled at her as she slept on her side, facing away from him. The paper-thin skin of her back piling up as it cascaded down onto her mattress. The butterfly tattoo on her shoulder, crisp and flirty in her late twenties, now a faded blob of fuzzy color that looked more like a Rorschach test question. Her hair ratty and matted under her head. Her angled, snore-preventing pillow, stained with the previous evening's make up. Lola farted in her sleep. Malcolm let the gravity of the situation sink in.

Last night had been spectacular. He had presented Lola with his latest purchase. A Birkin bag. He had read in one of the women's magazines that they were quite popular, and after a considerable amount of trouble and expense, he had tracked one down. Lola had been duly impressed with his gift, and he could tell she was about to say something laced with innuendo as she leaned forward and smiled through the haze of her third martini.

"Ooh, I'm getting a little tipsy."

"Shall I call you a cab?"

"Oh, I'm just saying I may have had a little too much to drink."

She smiled a smile that might as well have had "H-I-N-T-H-I-N-T" written on her teeth and it meant that what came out of her mouth next would be unequivocally forward. Malcolm was having none of that. The night was his and things were going to happen on his terms. He seized the moment, grabbed her hands, and looked into her eyes.

"I'm tired of slow dancing, Lola. It's time to *mach schnell.*"

He was pretty sure that was a Jimmy Stewart line. He followed it up with one of his own.

"Let's go back to your place."

His arm was still a little sore from being yanked as she hopped up to leave. It was a bit of a blur, but Malcolm was pretty sure she had thrown a few hundreds on the table and told the waiter to keep it before dragging him out. That was fine. His shoulder would heal.

What was far more important was that he had finally inserted his penis into the vagina of a live and willing woman. The waiting and wondering of fifty-seven years was over.

Who's gay now?

Boy, if this ever came up at work and he had the confidence to say anything and somebody cared to listen, would they be impressed.

He rolled back over onto his back and smiled.

"So this is love."

Brad Turns Chicken

Thank God for Christian-radio talk shows. Rock music is fun to listen to and everybody loves to sing along to Motown, but for pure entertainment purposes nothing beats Christian talk shows on the radio. And, because it's never too late to get the word of God out and dissect it fifty ways to Sunday, they played and replayed the worst of them on at least three AM stations in whatever areas Brad drove through.

How to choose Christian lingerie for married couples? What do we get to eat in heaven? What team would Jesus cheer for? There was no topic too great or too small for Bible-beating hosts who needed to kill an hour of sponsorless air time. Everyone that called in had an opinion they feverishly defended with scripture quotes, quasi-logical arguments, and general glossolalia before capitulating to whatever domineering host happened to be manning the mic. Trying to keep up with these nonsensical debates kept Brad from obsessing on how relentlessly boring his drive was and, more important, kept him from falling asleep at the wheel.

He traveled only at night and timed his drive so that he would make it to the Holland tunnel just before dawn. As he drove out of the tunnel and into the city he used to live in, he felt the satisfying buzz in his soul so familiar to Manhattan residents. It was good to be back.

Brad found a parking garage four blocks away from where he needed to be, left the car and, sticking to side streets as much as possible, made his way back to his old workplace. Thankfully, it was a cold morning and very appropriate to be wearing a hat and scarf.

He checked his watch as he got closer. Six fifty. Perfect. He hadn't worked at the Chicken Shack long, but if he remembered correctly, this was right when they mopped the floors, loaded in the produce, and usually forgot to close the back door. Brad rounded the corner and saw the rear entrance wide open. Things hadn't changed.

He walked up casually and looked inside. Chuck was in the walk-in refrigerator, yelling at some delivery guys for bringing too many onions. Brad crept past the dishwashing equipment and into the changing room where his locker had been. There on the hook, as always, was his old costume. He stuffed the chicken suit inside the oversized chicken head and dropped the whole thing into the trash bag he brought with him. On his way out, he grabbed a thick stack of fliers.

Brad walked out unnoticed as Chuck finished up with the delivery guys and got aggravated that some idiot had left the back door open again.

Brittany Stalls

"You lost him?"

"I'm sure we'll find him. Eventually. Can't you get a continuation? Just for a few weeks."

"Jesus, Brittany. Maybe."

Tim Irakura paced for a few seconds and wondered why he hadn't gone into business with his father when he had the chance. Everybody loves Camaros. But instead, he was an attorney for the government in a case that could very well go down as the most embarrassing in the country's history. Was there a chance Brittany would actually come through? He exhaled loudly and resumed his role.

"Okay. I'll see what I can do. Middleton loves to hear motions. We can probably talk him into it."

Tim hung up without saying goodbye.

Brittany had probably over-promised. Weeks of telling the assistant attorney general that she would have their star witness there on game day, days of claiming that she was just playing it safe keeping him sequestered until the last minute. And the whole time screaming at anyone with a fraction less seniority than her to get their ass moving and find her goddamn witness.

She was a little screwed. She hustled over to the courthouse in the hopes of doing a little damage control.

At the very worst, they could still move forward with her testimony, Brad's video testimony, and the surveillance footage. Jarvis had added time codes along with a couple of freeze frames with arrows pointing out the door Frank had shot through and the bullet holes in Carmine's chest. It looked totally official and, in her mind, very convincing.

The courthouse steps were jammed with reporters and camera crews crafting their ridiculous angles on this massive trial. Thankfully no one recognized Brittany going in and, aside from the big chicken handing out fliers on the way, she was pretty much ignored.

Hi, Owen

The chicken suit was more comfortable than Brad remembered. Well, once you got used to the enormous head. He'd been standing in front of the courthouse in lower Manhattan for over an hour, handing out Chicken Shack fliers to the uninterested reporters gathered for the big trial's opening day. The quickly discarded fliers were starting to swirl around as the wind picked up.

There were probably fifty news crews on the steps. Frank Fortunato had been brought in the building through the back entrance reserved for those making the trip from jail. The best these guys could hope for was a shot of the opposing counsels, ideally a fistfight between Tommy Giggles and some underling from the prosecution. What a shame they had no idea their slam dunk Pulitzer Prize–winning story was standing right next to them, being told to fuck off every seventeen seconds.

Brad faced away from the courthouse, using the large viewing patch of the chicken mouth to scan for Owen. He should have been there by now.

And there he was. Dressed in his bailiff uniform. And a mustache. He was moving quickly as he headed toward the courthouse.

The large-headed chicken on the fringe of the gaggle of reporters walked purposefully to the left of the group and positioned himself directly in the path of the bailiff who looked like he was running late for work.

Brad held out a flier.

"Hey, I need your help."

Owen broke stride out of respect to his former occupation.

"Oh, I know, but you'll get the hang of the job. Just don't hit any cops. Chuck hates that."

"Owen!"

"Oh man, why didn't I ever think of that? Using people's first names is a great way to get their attention. Boy, the business sure has changed since I left. Listen, I have to get to wor—"

"OWEN!"

"Brad?"

"Hi, Owen. Nice mustache."

"You like it? It's fake. Until I grow a real one. I think it adds character. Hey, what are you doing here? Did you know Frank Fortunato is inside? You should testify while you're in town."

"You're still a bailiff, right?"

"Oh, yeah. For weeks now. Things are really happening for me. If I keep pissing clean, one day—hope, hope—*judge*."

"I need a huge favor."

"Oh, I can't get you in to see the big trial. I'm not working the Fortunato thing. I'm helping out another courtroom. There's a guy coming in later who always throws his own poop at the judge, so, you know."

"That's not the favor."

Starbucks bathrooms have their pros and cons. On the one hand, they stink. They are the public toilets of New York City and no matter how often company guidelines say low man on the totem pole has to swab them out, the sheer volume of traffic through their doors makes the task of keeping them clean simply impossible, and getting them to smell not disgusting is a laughable task at best. On the other hand, if you need a nice, wide-open dressing room where you and a friend can trade outfits, and one of those outfits is an unwieldy chicken costume, they're a godsend.

Brad adjusted Owen's fake mustache to appear as balanced as it was going to get. Thank God he shaved this morning. He slipped Owen's tube of mustache adhesive into his front pocket. He looked almost natural in Owen's bailiff uniform and tried to relax the hand that clutched Owen's official bailiff identification. Brad checked himself in the mirror. He looked no more ridiculous than Owen did four minutes ago. So this was it. Do or die.

"Wait two minutes and then come out. We don't want it to look weird."

As if a bailiff and a man-sized chicken hadn't looked weird going *in* to a Starbucks bathroom together.

"You sure you know what you're doing, Brad?"

"No, but I know it's the right thing to do. Probably."

"Maybe you should have stayed in Florida."

"You're the one who told me I should testify in the first place."

"But not disguised as a bailiff. That seems kind of dishonest."

"Don't worry, buddy."

If there was one thing Brad Fingerman was not doing on that day, it was being dishonest.

Malcolm's Bar Mitzvah

Malcolm had given his virginity an honorable discharge. He savored his manly thoughts as he tightened up his tie, smiling at the decisive charmer in the mirror and thinking back on his achievement. He was a changed man. No more bullshit in his life. He had better things to do. Like sex. Holy Christ, did Malcolm have some lost time to make up for. He had heard the stories, but never expected it to be this much fun. Oh, it was time to get busy.

No more second guessing myself. No more hemming and hawing and wondering if I'm making the right choice. That's child's play. Today, I turn over a new leaf. Today, I am a man. I'd like my steak medium rare. I'll definitely take the blue Corvette. Sure, I'd like my sideburns trimmed. Oh yes. That feels good.

One last spritz of hair spray to keep everything in place, and Malcolm headed out to sit for the first day of Frank Fortunato's trial.

Brad the Bailiff

The courtroom was packed. Standing room only. Brad did his best to look official when he entered the back of the room and pressed himself up against the wall.

There were about seven other uniformed bailiffs standing in the back as well. This trial was a hot ticket and even court employees wanted to see the action. Which meant he was just another staffer lost in the crowd.

The attorneys for the prosecution and defense manned their tables at the front of the room, discussing last-minute details with their partners. The judge's chair sat empty.

A door in the back opened and a large majority of the crowd cheered as Frank Fortunato was escorted in wearing an orange jumpsuit complemented by wrist and ankle manacles. Brad did not cheer and, instead, pretended to rub an itch in his eye while taking careful note of everyone huzzahing the man who tried to murder him.

Frank smiled widely and raised his hands as much as he could in his chains. A team of uniformed officers helped him to his chair and parked themselves off to his side.

When Frank was faced away from him, Brad scanned the room for the one person he knew could help. And she'd probably be pretty glad to see him. He hadn't told Brittany he was coming and really hoped this wasn't a huge waste of time. But if he was going to be a part of this trial, there was only one way for it to go down. His way. Complete surprise and no chance of anyone leaking anything. It was a big risk, but the only other option was not showing at all.

There. Across the room, making her way to a seat in the third row. Brittany. Geez, she'd gotten thin. Nice skirt, though.

"All rise. Hear ye, hear ye, the United States District Court for the Southern District of New York is now in session—the Honorable Judge Malcolm Middleton presiding. All having business before this honorable court draw near, give attention, and you shall be heard. You may be seated."

Malcolm walked in from his own entrance and motioned for everyone to relax. He took his seat and looked over his kingdom like a boss.

"Sit, sit."

Brad stared lasers at Brittany as she moved down the aisle to a seat someone had saved for her. Just before she sat down, she looked his way.

Brittany found her seat and tried to ignore the bailiff in the back who kept making really wide eyes at her and motioning with his chin. She wondered if he had some sort of condition. Can you be a bailiff if you have Tourette's?

She returned her attention to the front of the room as her last hope took his seat behind the judge's bench. As hard as it was to believe, Brittany still thought that Brad was alive and that she could track him down. She just needed a few more weeks. Surely he would surface by then. How long can he go without using his credit cards?

She snuck a quick look around the courtroom to see which high-powered media outlets would be covering the trial. CNN. MSNBC. *Access Hollywood*. Nice.

And there was that bug-eyed bailiff making goo goo eyes at her again. Really? Like she would ever be into a guy with a mustache? What is this, 1978?

Up front, Judge Middleton had a couple of questions for his staff before beginning. Brittany snuck another look around.

Are you fucking kidding me? Am I going to have to take off the mustache? How is she not noticing me?

Brad considered whisper-yelling to Brittany, but figured that might be a little too conspicuous. How much wider could he make his eyes before they popped all the way out? He was afraid he was going to pull a muscle. One last try.

Jesus, perv. Get out much?

Brittany was starting to get depressed. Why did she keep looking at the crazy bailiff? Was this attraction? Some crazy instant love match she couldn't resist? Was she destined to live out some awful made-for-Oxygen movie about an FBI agent who falls in love with a civil servant? Even *she* wouldn't watch that. Why was she so fascinated with the bailiff? Was it because he sort of looked like Brad? Or did she just think everyone looked like Brad now because she was so focused on finding him?

Lately she had started taking closer looks at bag boys, the guy at the dry cleaners, her therapist. Double checking to make sure they weren't Brad. Why not? Just to be safe. She had to make sure she was doing all she could, right? Or, she was spiraling quickly into dementia. And if that was the case, why not take a second look at Bailiff Brad?

She turned once more to see him bulging his eyes out and covering his mouth. He whipped his hand away for a millisecond to reveal that he no longer had a mustache. Wow, he really looked a lot like Brad. She leaned back over the bench to get a better look. Bailiff Brad nodded and whipped his hand away again to mouth the word "Help."

Holy shit.

It was Brad. He was here.

Brittany stood up and scootched her way down the row, toward the middle aisle.

"'Scuse me. Pardon me. Court business. Goddamn, dude. Move your knees!"

Her row-mates were not making it easy for her to move fast.

She noticed Judge Middleton finishing up with his staff and preparing to get down to business. It was now or never. She swung her left leg up over the row in front of her, excusing herself as politely as was possible in a situation like this, and stepped up and over. Again with the next row and finally over the small fence that separated the court proceedings from the audience. A team of bailiffs began to swarm her direction, but Tim Irakura waved them off.

"What the hell are you doing?"

"He's here."

"Who's here?"

"Fingerman. Brad Fingerman is in the building."

"Is he going to testify?"

"I don't know. Give me five minutes. Just five minutes, Tim. I told you I'd get him here and I did. Just let me talk to him. Stall. Do some lawyer stuff. Anything."

Judge Middleton looked down from his seat and frowned.

"Is there a problem, Mr. Irikura?"

"Your honor, we have a special circumstance. May I approach the bench?"

Malcolm nodded and Tim walked toward the bench, followed closely by Tommy Giggles.

The crowd murmured amongst themselves and Brittany raced back toward the door that Bailiff Brad had just walked out of.

Brittany Gets a Little Clarity

Brittany stood, flabbergasted, and tried to speak. She and Brad were standing in an empty room down the hall from the Fortunato courtroom. She had a million questions, but one was far more important than the others.

"So . . . ?"

"Frank's guys found me and killed Stump and they were going to kill me but I escaped and then I went off the grid."

"Okay. Okay. Okay."

Brittany nodded, processing everything.

"But, you're here now. And you're going to testify, yes?"

"Brittany, I have to tell you the truth."

"Yes. On the stand. Tell everyone. And if you can work my name in there, so much the better."

"No, you have to hear this first. It's important."

He looked so scared standing there in someone else's clothes, irritated red skin where the mustache had been. Driven by some need to do good, even if it meant he would live the rest of his life terrified of scary guys with knives and guns and those picks ice climbers use. Men who wanted to kill him just for being in the wrong place at the wrong time.

And then it hit her. Reformed drunks have a phrase for beautiful flashes of insight like this—a moment of clarity. That one sacred split second when the world stops being an asshole long enough for you to see things really clearly and realize things like *I should have had children* or *My MBA is kind of pointless.*

In Brittany's moment of clarity, this is what she realized: *It's not worth it.*

Yes, Brad's testimony would maybe possibly convict the leader of one of the most powerful crime families in New York City and in the process land her a Geraldo-circa-1994-size cable news network deal that would set her up with up-yours-Van-Susteren money, but it would be at the expense of this completely innocent man who had already been through so much. *It's not worth it.*

It would have been such a beautiful moment of profound Zen and personal growth had the message not been delivered in her head by her grandmother's voice.

Still, it was true and she knew it. Fuck if she wouldn't have to become famous the old-fashioned way. Infamy. Goodbye, Tyra with a badge. Hello, Marcia Clark with a chip on her shoulder. Unfortunately, Brittany knew there was only one thing to say.

"It's not worth it."

"What?"

"It's not worth your life. They'll never stop hunting you. They killed Stump, for God's sake. What chance do you have? They'll find you and they'll kill you and all you did was get into an elevator at the wrong time. You never asked for this. I bullied you into it. I'm sorry. Don't testify. Tim can take his chances with the grand jury video and my testimony."

Her voice cracked a little when she mentioned the video, but overall, her performance was pretty convincing.

"Wow. That's not what I expected to hear."

"You think I'm such a cold-hearted drone?"

"Well, no, I just risked my life getting here to testify against a mob boss who would like me flayed at the earliest possible convenience and you're telling me *Oh, forget it, we'll just wing it and take our chances.* I mean, ouch."

"Okay, maybe that came out wrong."

"I'm testifying. Either you put me up on stage or I make a Denny Crane entrance and just start yammering to whomever might care to listen in the courtroom. There are plenty of reporters in there."

"Brad."

"It's the right thing to do. That's why I'm here."

There was no way Brittany could have known that Brad actually thought his testimony would be helping Frank Fortunato. No one could have. So it was fair and reasonable that her heart leaped for joy as the dead man in front of her (in her humble opinion) willingly sentenced himself to a life on the run.

Maybe it was worth it.

The Fingerman Issue

The girl from the FBI had interrupted again a few minutes before to introduce a man she claimed to be a missing eyewitness, although he looked like he worked here. Malcolm tried to make heads or tails out of what was being told to him by Tim Irikura while filtering out the jib-jab coming from the terribly agitated defense lawyer.

"So let me understand, Mr. Irikura. Your star witness, the key to your case, was *lost?*"

"Yes, Your Honor."

"But now you found him. And he's here today and you want him to testify?"

"Yes, Your Honor."

Tommy Giggles was definitely not laughing. He was already extremely unhappy with the speed at which this process had moved. They shouldn't be in the courtroom for another two years. And now a surprise witness gets thrown into the mix? One that he had been told was no longer among the living? Outrageous.

"Your Honor, this is absurd. We were told the witness was dead."

Tim pounced before Giggles even finished talking.

"Who told you that, Counselor? It certainly didn't come from our office."

"I know for a fact he was dead!"

"Well, that's something we can take up later. I'm sure I know some people who would be very interested in why you would have thought that. In the meantime, I would remind the court that Mr. Fingerman has been on our witness list since day one."

"Well, we never got to talk to him."

"You never asked."

"Because he was dead."

"Apparently not."

Giggles's head just about exploded. Why the hell was he told Brad was dead when he wasn't? Fucking Frank told him that. That's why they were rushing the trial. It was supposed to be a sure thing. Why was he the only one who did his job right?

Tim pressed harder.

"Your Honor, I haven't spoken to my witness in months. I'm as unprepared as Mr. Gigliani to question him, but he's got something to say and I'm afraid that if he walks out that door we'll never see him again. He's disappeared on us once already, and you can see how good he is with disguises."

Tim, Giggles, and Malcolm looked over at the prosecution's table where Brad stood listening in on the conversation. He indicated to the mustache he had put back on for security reasons and raised his eyebrows a few times.

"So, unless Mr. Gigliani doesn't feel like he's up to the task of asking Mr. Fingerman a few questions, I think you should allow it."

Malcolm considered the issue. Normally, this would have taken a week or so. It was a highly visible murder trial and, traditionally, he was a man who liked to hear every side of the argument before rendering a decision. He was thoughtful like that. Until today.

Malcolm was now a man. A man who made decisions without hesitation or regret. He was the big dog in the room, and he was going to act like it. So he might be overturned on appeal. Fine. He may catch flack in the papers. Screw 'em. He might make the wrong decision.

No, he wouldn't.

Malcolm looked up to see Lola standing in the back of the courtroom next to a large chicken. She looked stunning as she smiled and winked at him. She said she would stop by, and there she was. Here to see her man. And it didn't look like she was wearing a bra. It was all Malcolm could do to suppress the urge to growl or howl or go mark some territory with his own urine. Instead, he marked some territory with his newfound decisiveness.

"I'll allow it."

The courtroom exploded with the murmurs and chattering of reporters and audience members. Oh, this would definitely make the news tonight.

Malcolm sat back, ignoring the whining of Tommy Giggles, and enjoyed his first taste of judicial machismo.

He looked back to Lola and returned her lurid wink. It felt good to be a man.

Brad Testifies

"I, Brad Fingerman, do solemnly swear to tell the truth, the whole truth, and nothing but the truth, so help me God."

"You may be seated."

"Mr. Fingerman, I know we have limited time with you, so I'll just cut to the chase. Can you tell me what happened on the afternoon of September the eighth of this year?"

Brad looked around the courtroom. Brittany sat on the edge of her seat. She nodded encouragement to him. In the back of the room, Owen, chicken head now off to reveal his excited eyes, pumped his fist. The older woman next to Owen appeared to be blowing kisses toward the front of the room, possibly even at Brad. Then she rolled her tongue around the inside of her cheek. How that was supposed to inspire him, he didn't know.

Brad began his testimony.

"On the afternoon of September the eighth, I entered the elevator on the fourteenth floor of 1635 Broadway to find a man whom I later learned to be Carmine Mastramouro. The doors closed, the elevator went down a few floors and stopped."

Brad paused once more to enjoy the last few seconds before he threw his life away. He thought of Yo and Stump and wondered what they might have made of him right then. Stump would have given him a hard blank look before shrugging *Go ahead. It's your life*. Yo would have chuckled at the sheer subversiveness. This was better than screwing the system by not paying taxes or towing cars with an illegal truck. It was brave. As different as they were, Stump and Yo would both have enjoyed this.

"Mr. Fingerman?"

"Before the doors opened, I noticed a scuff on my shoe and bent down to clean it off. The elevator opened and a pair of black shoes stood in the open door. While I was cleaning my shoe I heard a few muffled noises I presume to be silenced gunshots and I sneezed. Then next thing I know, the black shoes were gone, I was alone in the elevator with Mr. Mastramouro, and he had a bunch of bullet holes in him."

And the crowd went crazy. Frank Fortunato and his defense team high-fived and chest bumped and winked at a few members of the jury. The audience of fans laughed and cheered. Reporters scribbled furiously.

Malcolm banged his gavel with newfound authority and threatened everyone with expulsion if they didn't shut right up.

Brad's testimony was not quite what Brittany expected to hear, and her face showed it. Now he brings up the sneeze? Where was the smooth-talking tough guy? Where was the cornball movie dialogue? WHAT HAPPENED TO THE GODDAMNED JAPANESE ACCENT? Who was this guy and why was he telling lies?

Tim shot a look back at Brittany. She shook her head, just as bewildered as he was. He turned back around to ask more questions.

"So, did you see who shot Carmine Mastramouro?"

Brad looked at Brittany and said he was sorry with his eyes.

"No. Unless you count his shoes."

Tim rubbed the highest part of his nose and decided to plug ahead.

"Okay, you saw some shoes. Can you tell us about them?"

"They were black."

"Uh-huh. That's it? They were black? Can you tell us anything else about them? Were they lace ups? Were they loafers? Were they clown shoes? What kind of shoes are we talking about?"

"They were black. Lace ups. And I'm not sure what else."

"That's what you brought us all here to listen to. You saw a pair of black shoes."

Giggles stood up, barely controlling his laughter.

"Your Honor, I move to dismiss the case. They got nothing!"

Malcolm shushed Giggles. "I don't believe Mr. Irikura is done yet. Mr. Irikura?"

"Ah, well, yeah. Okay. Think back, Mr. Fingerman. Brad, can you tell us any details about the shoes?

Brad was really sweating now. He had imagined the testimony part would be the easiest of the whole thing. Nobody was trying to kill him while he was up there, and he had decided to tell the truth. His plan was to tell exactly what he had witnessed, nothing more, and let Frank know that he hadn't actually seen anything incriminating. Why would he want to kill him if he had nothing to offer the prosecution's case? Frank would get off and Brad could leave and stop worrying about guys in overcoats with jailbroken nail guns. It was so simple it was brilliant. Except that now everyone was staring at him. And he couldn't remember anything except those dumb black shoes. Why now? Why obsess on those? How could they possibly be relevant? He had bent down to clean his shoe and sneezed and when his eyes cleared he saw those dumb shoes and their dumb laces and their dumb label.

"There was a label."

"What did it say?"

Brad had always been good under pressure. Considering the amount of pressure he was under right then, you'd think he would have been able to prove Fermat's Last Theorem. He closed his eyes and trusted his mind to come up with something worth saying out loud.

Brad had never actually thought about the shoes. He had always been focused on the sneeze, hoping to remember some lost frame of vision from when his head was shaking around. But never the shoes. And still, he had nothing.

"I'm sorry."

Tim deflated and the crowd murmured and Frank's team grinned like the bullies they were.

Giggles stood up to state the obvious.

"Pardon me, Your Honor. But this is a joke."

Speaking of pardons, do they give those to star witnesses for being an asswipe?

Pardon.

Brad then realized how beautiful a thing the subconscious mind is. Oh sure, sometimes it would land you in embarrassing situations by switching words around, words like "mother" and "girlfriend" during therapy, but it also did some heavy mental lifting when you least expected it to.

"Pardon."

Tim turned around.

"Excuse me?"

"Parda. The label on the shoes said 'Parda.'"

Tim looked over at Frank. Then back to Brad.

"Parda?"

Brad was as sure of that as anything he had been in his life. He *was* good under pressure.

The team of lawyers supporting Tim suddenly huddled and began talking amongst themselves in hushed but excited voices. They called Tim over and explained their excitement to him. Tim nodded and returned his focus to Brad.

"So, let's just go over this one more time. You were in the elevator when Carmine got shot. You bent down to clean a scuff mark off your shoe, giving you an excellent view of the murderer's black shoes. And on one of those black shoes, you saw a label that read 'Parda,' P-A-R-D-A. Do I have this correct?"

"Uh, yeah. Sorry."

"No further questions, Your Honor."

Giggles stopped laughing with Frank and his crew long enough to stand up and thank Brad for coming by. They had no questions for the witness. Frank gave a thumbs up as Brad was escorted out.

The Rest of the Trial

Brad was whisked out of the courtroom by Brittany alone, taken to his car, and released without so much as a "Thanks for ruining my life" from either one of them. His testimony had caught everyone off guard and now it was over.

Meanwhile, what neither of them realized was that the prosecution had exactly what they needed. The shoes Brad mentioned were a one-of-a-kind custom pair, cobbled by a Korean guy in Brooklyn. Prada knockoffs. *Parda* was the cobbler's little joke. He spoke perfect English and knew full well how Prada was spelled. It was also right there on the shoes Sal brought in for him to copy, but he was pissed when Frank didn't want to pay what the work was worth.

The state asked for a recess while they tracked down the cobbler, and Malcolm granted it because he goddamn felt like it.

Yes, there was more to the trial than Brad's testimony. It was a murder trial. Of course there was more to it. But, Brad was the important part. His testimony was the meat of the matter that got Frank convicted, even with the jurors he had bought off.

Naturally, Giggles objected and filed motions and all the other bullshit defense lawyers will do, but ultimately, it was no more effective than yelling at those kids to get off your lawn.

In the end, the jury took only four hours to convict Frank Fortunato of murder in the first degree.

A month later, in a quick hearing, Malcolm sentenced him to life.

ONE
YEAR
LATER

Frank "Fancypants" Fortunato

Frank was dead. Rumor has it he lasted about six weeks in prison before getting shanked with a sharpened toothbrush for substituting generic cigarettes for Marlboro Reds.

He was given a hero's funeral in Flushing and his obituary in the *Post* was glowing, although it did refer to his former occupation as "head of one of the most powerful crime families in New York."

Malcolm and Lola

Malcolm and Lola got married. And joined a swingers club. They couldn't be happier.

Brittany

Brittany was late for a production meeting. So it was odd that she kept thinking about the Bureau. Her days now were filled with worries about ratings and booking her next guest and boy was she behind on writing her book. She hardly ever thought about Project Fancypants. And she tried not to think about the time just after Frank's sentencing that Jarvis pulled her aside and showed her the rest of the data he finally retrieved from her fried computer. It showed a lot more. Not everything, but enough to realize that Frank didn't kill Carmine. It was Sal. He just couldn't let Frank do it. Seems he had also paid the cobbler for a pair of shoes just like Frank's.

Another piece of recovered video showed Frank entering the hallway, stopping, and then running off. There's no way he could have done it. Brittany watched the footage and let it soak in. Then she poured a can of Pepsi on the computer and went to return her new agent's call. Jarvis kept his mouth shut and got his promotion.

Today's episode was "Stripper Love Triangles." Not quite the hard-hitting, crime-oriented show she had imagined herself hosting. But Brittany lived in a sweet penthouse apartment, dated an underwear model, and instigating babymama fights sure as hell beat coming up with nicknames to impress Anfernee.

Brad

Brad's Crammers! campaign was by now a sensation. As predicted, college students bought them by the case, and binge drinking was all the rage. So, hurray. Presumably, the campaign won a slew of awards, but Brad couldn't have told you for sure. He never checked.

Brad was not Brad anymore. At least not the Brad we knew.

He was no longer the pretentious ad guy concerned with perfecting that onion-dip print ad or the lost soul scrambling to get ahead in the world of in-house agencies. And he certainly wasn't hiding.

Brad had become a landscaper with a thriving business in Islamorada, Florida. His advertising-trained eye for composition and color translated quite well into deciding where to put the Chinese fan palms and choosing complementary groundcover. And to top it off, there was nobody telling him the climbers weren't target-market appropriate, and no one was trying to glom on to the credit for the edgework.

It was all Brad and that felt good. There was no more magical thinking. No more wondering where the next vine would take him. The only vines left in Brad's life were the overpriced ones he planted for the retirees who hired him.

And he painted at night. So far, nothing MOMA-worthy, but it sure made him happy when he sort of got down on canvas what he saw in his head. Maybe he'd try to sell them one day. Stranger things had happened.

He and Gracie divorced without so much as a whimper. Turns out the Brad she had asked for when her husband called from the rooftop was a CrossFit trainer with whom she had recently begun a meaningless affair. So they called it quits and it was easy. Brad wanted nothing from her and she didn't want to give anything up. Win-win.

FYI, the name of Brad's business is Fingerman's Landscaping. He decided to stick with his actual name, despite what he found in Dr. Yo's trunk.

The lockbox. Brad opened it to find Yo's entire plan to disappear: a brand new passport, brilliantly faked birth certificate, an authentic-looking social security card, a fully loaded .45, a pound of rock-star weed (man, Yo loved weed), and $380,000 in twenties. Altogether, there were three lockboxes hidden in the trunk. The grand total ended up being north of two million dollars of untraceable cash.

According to the documents, Yo's new identity was named Nicholas Hamilton Steele. Nick Fucking Steele.

A lot of guys would have taken Nick Steele's identity—used that birth certificate to get a new passport and driver's license with their own picture, and enjoyed the perfect credit of a man who hadn't bought anything for the last ten years. It would have been so easy to slide right into that lifestyle, disappear into the generic landscape of America, and never look back.

But Brad didn't apply for a new passport with his own picture and he didn't get a new driver's license. He tossed them both, along with the gun, into the Atlantic on his way over the Seven Mile Bridge just below Marathon.

Make no mistake. Brad wasn't a fool. He took the money. And the weed. But not the name. After all he'd been through, it just didn't seem right.

Nick Steele wouldn't have worn a chicken suit to sneak up to the courthouse. He would have jet-packed in. Nick Steele wouldn't have told the lame, boring truth Brad told. He would have made up something cool and appropriate for Jerry Bruckheimer to option as a Tom Cruise vehicle. Nick Steele would have never started a landscaping business in the Florida Keys or used a pair of pliers to extract the last few drops of paint from a tube to finish his painting. Nick Steele just wasn't Brad Fingerman.

Fuck Nick Steele.

Acknowledgments

Thank you to everyone who supported me while I wrote this book and, more important, while I waited.

But, especially . . .
Adriann Ranta, who never stopped.
Robbie Goolrick, who I can never thank enough.
And Ben LeRoy. I just . . . I mean . . . Thank God for you.